ABOUT THE AUTHOR

Jane Peart, award-winning novelist and short story writer, grew up in Asheville, North Carolina, and was educated in New England. Although she now lives in northern California, her heart has remained in her native South—its people, its history, and its traditions. With more than twenty-five novels and dozens of short stories to her credit, Jane likes to emphasize in her writing the timeless and recurring themes of family, traditional values, and a sense of place.

Ten years in the writing, the *Brides of Montclair* series is a historical family saga of enduring beauty. In each new book, another generation comes into its own at the beautiful Montclair estate near Williamsburg, Virginia. These compelling, dramatic stories reaffirm the importance of committed love, loyalty, courage, strength of character, and abiding faith in times of triumph and tragedy, sorrow and joy.

Senator's Bride

Book Twelve
The Brides of Montclair Series

JANE PEART

ZondervanPublishingHouse
Grand Rapids, Michigan

A Division of HarperCollinsPublishers

Senator's Bride
Copyright © 1994 by Jane Peart

Requests for information should be addressed to:
Zondervan Publishing House
Grand Rapids, Michigan 49530

Library of Congress Cataloging-in-Publication Data

Peart, Jane.
    Senator's bride / Jane Peart.
        p.   cm. – (Brides of Montclair series : bk. 12)
    ISBN 0-310-67151-5 (pbk.)
    1. Family—Virginia—Williamsburg Region—History—20th cen-
tury—Fiction. I. Title. II. Series: Peart, Jane. Brides of Montclair series :
bk. 12.
    PS3566.E238S45   1994
    813'.54—dc20   94-2149
                                                                        CIP

Edited by Anne Severance
Interior design by Kim Koning
Cover design by Art Jacobs
Cover illustration by Wes Lowe, Sal Baracc and Assoc., Inc.

Printed in the United States of America

94 95 96 97 98 99 00 01 02 03 / DH / 10 9 8 7 6 5 4 3 2

Prologue

FOR NEW READERS of the family saga of the Brides of Montclair—and to refresh the memories of readers of the previous books in the series—the following summary is presented.

The members of two Mayfield families—of English and Scottish heritage and both early settlers in Virginia—have been friends and neighbors since before the American Revolution. Their lives and destinies have been interwoven through many generations. In the two books before this present one, *Mirror Bride* and *Hero's Bride,* we have now entered the twentieth century.

Several years have passed since we left Kip Montrose and the Cameron twins, Cara and Kitty (from *Hero's Bride*). All three young people were profoundly affected by the First World War in which they all played vital roles, Kip as an aviator in the volunteer Lafayette Escadrille (attached to the French army); Cara as an ambulance driver; and Kitty as a Red Cross nurse. Now all three have returned to America and are trying to find their way in the post-war world.

Emerging into adulthood are the three children of the artist Jeff Montrose (Blythe Cameron's son by her first marriage to Malcolm Montrose) and his late wife, Faith. Faith, the daughter of Garnet and Jeremy Devlin, perished tragically in the sinking of the Titanic in 1912. Their three children, Lynette, Gareth, and Bryanne, have been separated since the tragedy. Their grief-stricken artist father, Jeff, has sought solace in the art colony in Taos, New Mexico. Lynette lives at Cameron Hall; Gareth is at boarding school; and Bryanne lives with her grandmother Garnet in England.

Senator's Bride begins on the eve of 1920 and brings new people into the lives of the Montrose and Cameron families—people who will change their lives dramatically.

Brief Family Background

Jeff Montrose is Blythe Cameron's son by her first marriage.

Scott, and Cara and Kitty (the twins) are Blythe's children by her second marriage to Rod Cameron. This make's Jeff, Scott, Cara, and Kitty all half-siblings, and, therefore, Jeff's children are Scott, Cara, and Kitty's nieces and nephews.

Jonathan Montrose is Jeff's half-brother, both being sons of Malcolm Montrose, Therefore, Jonathan's children, Kip and Meredith, are cousins of Jeff's children.

Since Garnet Devlin (Cameron) was Rod Cameron's sister, she and Blythe are sisters-in-law. Since Garnet's daughter Faith married Blythe's son Jeff, they also have mutual grandchildren: Lynette, Gareth, and Bryanne.

Part I

Cameron Hall

December 1919

chapter

1

LYNETTE MONTROSE stood at her bedroom window, staring out into the wintry darkness. It was New Year's Eve and guests would soon be arriving for her Grandmother Blythe's first Open House since the war's end. At eighteen, Lynette would be participating in the festivities for the first time. She should be feeling excited and happy; instead, she was gripped by an inexplicable sense of melancholy. *What on earth is wrong with me?*

Shivering, she turned back to the room, cozy with the glow of lamplight and the warmth from coals burning in the fireplace. Her glance fell on the lovely new red velvet dress, a gift from her aunt Kitty Traherne and her first really grown-up evening gown, spread out on the bed ready to put on. Only a few days before, Lynette had been ecstatic about finding it in its gilt-bowed box under the Christmas tree. But now she felt no particular anticipation about wearing it.

Maybe she was feeling the normal let-down because the holidays were nearly over and she would soon be returning to school. Or maybe it was the familiar sadness of yet another Christmas spent apart from her father, brother, and sister that made her feel this way.

Lynette smoothed her hand over the rich fabric of the dress. How dear of Kitty to buy it for her. But then, ever since Lynette had come to live at Cameron Hall after her mother Faith's death, Kitty had spoiled her. It was almost as if Kitty was trying to make up for what she perceived to be the neglect of his parental responsibilities by Jeff Montrose, Kitty's half-brother. Of course, Lynette's father, Jeff, *had* sent her a Christmas present—some heavy silver-and-turquoise Indian jewelry from New Mexico, where he was living now. But even his selection of the gift stung a little. If he knew her better, he would have known that the bracelet and necklace were the kind she would never wear!

Lynette felt instantly guilty. She had tried not to resent her father for distancing himself from her both geographically and emotionally. Not just from her, of course, but from her brother Gareth, too, and their younger sister, Bryanne.

Maybe she shouldn't blame him. When their mother died in the aftermath of the sinking of the *Titanic,* their grief-stricken father had been inconsolable. He had left everything in the care of others—his flourishing career as an artist, his island home, Avalon, and his three children. Lynette had tried to understand, but ever since their mother's death, the little family had been adrift—Bryanne, living at Birchfields with their maternal Grandmother Garnet Devlin; Gareth at school; and she here at Cameron Hall with Grandmother Blythe. It had been nearly seven years now, and they were still apart.

For the last few years Grandmother Devlin had used the war as an excuse for not bringing Bryanne back to Virginia, thwarting all attempts to reunite the motherless children by forcing their father to accept his responsibility in making a home for the three of them.

Gareth had spent some time with their father in Taos, New Mexico, but at Grandmother Blythe's insistence, he had been sent back here to Virginia and enrolled at Briarwood Prep. At least now they could see each other on holidays and during summer vacation. But it was Bryanne who concerned Lynette most. Growing up in England, she scarcely knew her Virginia family.

Maybe it was just because she was the oldest that Lynette so deeply mourned the loss of both parents and dreamed often of a reunion with her brother and sister. Now at eighteen, she seemed more conscious than ever of the inner loneliness she tried to mask all these years.

Of course, no one knew . . . at least, no one acknowledged her loneliness. After all, why should they? No doubt, they would probably only wonder how one could feel bereft when surrounded by people who loved and cared about her. Certainly she had had everything a child could possibly want—her own room, lavish toys and games, even her own pony.

Perhaps Kitty had guessed and for that reason gave Lynette her special attention. But when the war started, Kitty had left to become a Red Cross nurse in England. Her other cousins had joined the war effort, too. Kitty's twin, Cara, had gone to France as an ambulance driver, and their brother Scott had joined the army. With everyone away and her grandmother busy with all sorts of volunteer work, Lynette's loneliness had been especially keen.

She had sometimes been able to lose herself in reading. Especially such books as *The Secret Garden* and *The Little Princess* by Frances Hodgson Burnett, in which she could identify with the abandoned young heroines, imagining that someday someone would come along and rescue *her,* ending her loneliness forever.

But the war was over now. Kitty and Scott were both back at Cameron Hall, and life here was almost the way it had always been. Why then tonight was she feeling so sad, so close to tears?

Maybe it was because of the letter from Bryanne that had come only two days ago. Although most of Brynnie's letters were filled with humorous anecdotes of teachers and fellow students, field trips, and school events, between the lines Lynette could read how much her little sister hated the strict English girls' boarding school where their other grandmother had placed her.

Thinking about it brought on a feeling of anxiety, and Lynette took the envelope out of her letterbox and opened it. In a twelve-year-old's deplorable scrawl, Bryanne had written:

Dearest Lynette,

I'm back at my dreadful old school after Christmas at Birchfields. We stayed in the estate manager's house where we lived during the war, because the big house is being completely redone—"put back the way it was," as Grandmama says, before it was turned into a hospital-convalescent home for Allied officers. As you might imagine, there were workmen all over the place—painters, plasterers, carpenters—and scaffolding and paint buckets sitting around everywhere. There wasn't much for me to do, because Grandmama was so busy telling them all what to do, then staying nearby to see that they did it to her satisfaction!

I did have my horse to ride, of course, though the stables are not restored yet. Only my dear old pony who is out to pasture nowadays and Duchess, my horse, are there. There was no one my age to go riding with, though, since most of my school chums spent the holiday in London with their parents. I'm sure everyone had a jolly time at pantomimes and parties.

11

Was Christmas lovely in Mayfield? I try and try to remember what it was like, but I can't. I'm not even sure if the memories I do have are real, or if I've imagined them from pictures in books! Do write soon and tell me all about it.

Ever, your loving sister,
Bryanne

It was clear to Lynette that, in spite of the privileged life Bryanne was living with their wealthy grandmother, her sister felt deprived and every bit as lonely as she did. So what could be done to change things? To bring them all together again?

Suddenly Lynette knew what her New Year's resolution would be, the goal she would set for herself. She must do something to heal her family's wounds, arrange a reunion for the three of them and their father. Perhaps she should talk with Gareth first. Now that the war was over, perhaps they could travel together to England and bring Bryanne back to Virginia. Then maybe her father would return from the Southwest and they could all go home to Avalon and be a family again.

Just then there was a quick tap on the door. It was Kitty's voice, asking, "Lynette, are you ready?"

"Not yet. But I will be in a few minutes." Lynette shrugged off her kimono and slipped the ball gown over her head. "Come in."

The bedroom door opened and Kitty entered. "Need any help?"

Lynette pivoted toward her, holding out the flared skirt. "Do I look all right?" Kitty drew in her breath. At eighteen, Lynette had become a real beauty. Having outgrown the coltishness of her early teens, her figure was gracefully slim, her peach-bloom skin fine-grained, her dark-lashed eyes almost violet blue.

"The dress is perfect, dear, you look lovely," Kitty assured her, knowing it was much more than the dress.

"Do I? I'm not sure about my hair though. . . ."

"Here, let me." Motioning Lynette to sit down at the dressing table, Kitty picked up the hairbrush. Freshly washed, the young woman's hair was as slippery as silk, and it took three tries to sweep it into a French twist.

"Sorry to put you to all this trouble, Kitty," Lynette sighed. "Maybe I should get my hair bobbed . . . like yours!"

"I wouldn't recommend that. Richard wants me to let mine grow again." She anchored the upswept hairdo with the last of twenty pins and a rhinestone comb. Kitty laughed. "There! It looks very soignée, if I do say so myself, like the latest Parisian style," she declared, handing Lynette a mirror. "Take a look."

Lynette turned her head to view her cousin's handiwork. "Oh, I like it! It looks so . . . sophisticated. Thanks, Kitty." She put down the mirror, stood and gave her cousin an impulsive hug. "Oh, Kitty, I missed you terribly! I'm so glad you're back!"

"I'm so glad, too, and grateful." Kitty's tone became serious. "There were times in France when I was afraid I might never *be* back. I used to dream about Christmas at Cameron Hall and wonder if I'd ever celebrate again . . . the way we used to." Quickly her smile was back. "But here I am at last! This will be Richard's *first* time with us, you know."

At the mention of Kitty's husband, Richard Traherne, Lynette winced a little. Her aunt had returned to Cameron Hall to marry a man who was a cruel casualty of the war and was confined forever to a wheelchair by a wound that had shattered his spine. Richard would never walk again. Yet they seemed happier, more in love than any couple Lynette had ever seen.

Their wedding in October had been touchingly beautiful. Everything seemed to shine with a particular brilliance—the blue sky, the sun spilling through the gilded trees that surrounded the small house in the woods called Eden Cottage, where the ceremony took place. Richard, holding himself as erect as possible in his wheelchair, his handsome face chiseled to a kind of Grecian-sculpture fineness by the suffering he had endured, its pain-etched lines giving it a strength of character more compelling than mere good looks. Kitty, as radiant as any bride could be, in her simple cream knit ensemble, her eyes meeting his unwavering-ly as they exchanged their vows. Never were the ancient promises spoken with more loving conviction: "I will love, honor, and cherish you in sickness and in health, for richer or poorer, for better or worse, until death do us part."

Listening to this pledge, Lynette had felt her throat constrict and quick tears had sprung to her eyes. In that sacred moment she had determined she would never marry until she loved with the same devotion that Kitty and Richard felt for each other.

"Can you believe that soon it will be 1920?" Kitty's question brought Lynette back to the present. "Shall we go down now and start welcoming in a brand-new year?"

Trying to shake her earlier feelings of depression, Lynette forced a smile. For Kitty's sake, for her grandmother's, too, she would try to enjoy the party, although she had never felt less like celebrating.

Decorated for Christmas, Cameron Hall sparkled. In the curve of the staircase festooned with swags of evergreen and red velvet bows, stood the ten-foot-tall cedar tree, trimmed with glittering gilt balls and other ornaments collected over the years. This year there were also frosted cookies and animal-shaped gingersnaps along with the tinseled branches. In the polished brass chandelier, crimson candles caused the crystal prisms to dance with rainbowed color.

As if following the dictates of the old-time carol, the halls of the mansion were literally "decked with holly." Every surface boasted its own special arrangement. Pinecones, spruce boughs, and red-berried pyracantha encircled pyramids of fruit. On tables at either end of the dining room, a gleaming silver punch bowl held the famous Cameron eggnog and a cut-glass one shimmered with cranberry punch.

Rugs had been rolled up in one of the parlors, and the floor waxed for dancing. A quartet stationed on a small platform in the windowed alcove were already playing danceable melodies.

Kitty went to check on Richard. Finding him comfortably settled and engaged in conversation with a family friend, she went to help her mother receive the guests who were arriving in a steady stream. This was Blythe's first large-scale party since Rod Cameron's death, and Kitty knew her widowed mother would appreciate her help.

Left alone, Lynette gazed over the crowd, hoping to spot her brother. Even though Gareth didn't like fancy parties, he had promised Grandmother he would come. Tall and attractive, with a pleasant manner and quiet sense of humor, Gareth was already the target of the hopes of many young Mayfield ladies. But he avoided most social affairs, preferring the solitary pleasures—tramping through the wooded acres of Avalon or riding his horse along its winding bridle paths. Although the house was unoccupied now, Lynette suspected that spending time there was her brother's way of holding on to all they had lost.

Lynette moved among the crowd, stopping to speak to people she knew, catching snatches of conversation, much of it a discussion of some of the political issues of the day. A recent local election had captured the attention of most of the men, and some of the ladies were

14

commenting about the much-debated amendment to the Constitution, giving women the right to vote. *How boring!* Lynette thought. At her school, the top priority among her fellow classmates was not current events but whom to invite to the next party!

Her gaze circled the room, lingering on a young man who stood talking with her uncle Scott Cameron, Kitty's brother. Recognizing who it was immediately, her pulse began to race. Frank Maynard.

Lynette had first met Frank several years ago, while attending a church in Mayfield with her grandmother and Scott. The three were leaving after the service when Scott called to someone just ahead of them. The man turned around, his face breaking into a wide smile. "Scott!"

Lynette and her grandmother paused as the two men moved to greet each other. Standing a little apart, Lynette observed the man. He was not quite as tall as Scott, trimly built, with light brown hair and neat features. It was his smile, however, and his fine gray eyes that gave him a distinctive appeal.

Scott pumped his hand. "When did you get back?"

"A few weeks ago. I'm setting up law offices in Mayfield and getting ready to move back into the old family homeplace." Then, over Scott's shoulder, Lynette's eyes met his, and suddenly she was glad she had worn her blue eyelet dress and the new straw hat trimmed with cornflowers.

"Come over and say hello to Mother, Frank," Scott was saying. "And I don't believe you've ever met my cousin, Lynette Montrose."

Lynette could not remember much about the introduction or the few pleasantries that followed. She did, however, recall Frank's firm handshake, the feel of his palm on hers through her lace mitts. Then she was in the carriage, and they were on their way home to Cameron Hall.

"You must have dinner with us sometime soon, Mr. Maynard," Blythe said graciously.

"That would be my pleasure, Mrs. Cameron."

"Let us know when you're settled, and we'll fix a date."

"I'll look forward to that, thank you." Frank's eyes again rested briefly on Lynette before he said goodbye.

The next Sunday, hoping to see Frank Maynard at church, Lynette had even rehearsed something to say to him, something he might think witty or clever. But when she had scanned the congregation for him, he was nowhere to be found. Nor did he appear the next Sunday or the one after that. Since she didn't want to appear overly interested, she had resisted the impulse to mention Frank Maynard to Scott but had listened for any information she might glean through casual conversation. However, by the time it came up, the summer was almost over and it was time for her to return to school.

Lynette had realized that it was silly to let a chance meeting make such a lasting impression. In spite of that, she had found herself fantasizing other meetings, other imaginary conversations with Frank Maynard. Of course, Frank was a much older man, probably almost as old as Scott! Somehow, that very fact had made him even more intriguing. From the little she had been able to learn, she knew that Frank, from an old Mayfield family, had served as an aide to a colonel and had been stationed in Washington, D.C., first, and then in London during the War.

When she was back at boarding school, Frank began to appear frequently in Lynette's thoughts and daydreams. At Dunbarton Academy social life was restricted. Even the monthly tea dances, attended by boys from the nearby prep school, were boring because the guests all seemed so hopelessly juvenile compared to Frank. Lynette found herself imagining unexpected meetings and romantic rendezvous with the dashing older man.

Since Frank had become almost a fantasy figure, seeing him in person now was quite a shock. As she stood there staring, he caught sight of her, smiled, and started toward her. For some reason she could not explain, her reaction was to whirl around and hurry away in the other direction. Her ridiculous behavior was impossible for even her to understand. What a fool Frank must think her!

Looking for a possible refuge where she could compose herself, Lynette glanced into the music room. There, under one of the several bunches of mistletoe tied with green and red satin ribbons, was a couple locked in an embrace, kissing under the mistletoe!

Not wishing to intrude on their privacy, Lynette backed away. As she swiveled into the hallway again, she collided with a gentleman.

Embarrassed, she moved away from the starched and pleated white-shirt front. Without lifting her eyes to see who it was, she stammered an apology. "Oh, I'm so sorry! Pardon me, I didn't see. . . ."

Strong hands steadied her. "It's all right. Got your balance now?"

The voice was familiar. Lynette raised her head and looked straight into the amused face of Frank Maynard.

"Miss Montrose! How very nice to see you!"

"How do you do, Mr. Maynard," she replied breathlessly. She made an ineffectual attempt to smooth her hair back, and as she did so, loosened the rhinestone pin, which fell to the floor with a *plink*.

Simultaneously bending to retrieve it, they bumped heads. "Excuse me," they murmured in unison. Then each reached for the comb and bumped heads again. "Sorry," both said, laughing a little.

Frank helped Lynette up. When they caught each other's eye, they couldn't contain their hilarity and, once started, they couldn't seem to stop.

Finally, weak with laughter, Lynette leaned against the wall, taking long breaths. "Oh, my goodness!" she gasped. Twisting up the straying tendrils of hair, she tried to replace the comb. "I must look a mess."

"Not at all," he insisted gallantly. "You look very charming, in fact." Frank grinned. "But you *are* out of breath. Let's go sit down somewhere for a few minutes to regain our equilibrium."

The couple who had occupied the music room came out, glanced at Lynette and Frank somewhat self-consciously, then sauntered down the hall. "Shall we?" Frank motioned to the now empty room, and Lynette nodded and followed as he led her to the cushioned window seat.

"I haven't seen you lately, Miss Montrose. At church, I mean. . . ." Frank stopped abruptly and frowned. "Uh-oh, I shouldn't have said that. I sound like one of those inquisitive old ladies who grill you if you miss one church circle meeting. I really didn't mean to check up on your church attendance."

"I know." Lynette smiled. "It's quite all right. I've been away. I go to Dunbarton Academy."

"So that's why I haven't seen you." Frank hesitated, then added, "I missed you."

"You did?" Lynette's eyes grew wide.

"Why, yes. Since I moved back to Mayfield, I looked for you with your grandmother and Scott . . . hoped to see you, in fact." He paused. "Of course, I've been so busy settling into our old house and getting my law practice established that I haven't had much time to renew old friendships or make new ones. Scott, on the other hand, has been most helpful. In fact, he's invited me to come here several times, but something has always intervened, I'm sorry to say."

"Well . . . so you're here now," Lynette said for lack of anything else to say.

Frank smiled. "Yes, and I couldn't be happier about it."

With that awkward beginning and after her initial shyness wore off, Lynette soon found that she and Frank had much more in common than she had dreamed—Viennese waltzes, Sherlock Holmes mysteries, and autumn in Virginia.

"Do you enjoy poetry, Miss Montrose?"

"Oh, please call me Lynette. And yes, I do, very much, especially Tennyson and Longfellow," she said eagerly, then wondered if he might think her taste uncritical or overly sentimental.

But Frank smiled, struck a pose, and began to recite:

> "Under the spreading chestnut tree,
> The village smithy stands.
> The smith a mighty man is he,
> With large and sinewy hands . . .
> And looks the whole world in the face,
> For he owes not any man."

His smile broadened. "I loved all Longfellow's heroic poems. In fact, I think much of my own viewpoint of life has been shaped by his writings."

"It's Tennyson for me . . . *The Idylls of the King,* in particular," Lynette rushed on, elated with Frank's revelation about himself. "That was my parents' favorite. My father is an artist and painted some of the legends . . ." She hesitated before adding shyly, "My brother and I were named for two of the characters—Gareth and Lynette."

"A charming tale . . . a lovely name," Frank said quietly.

When the sound of laughter and noisy conversation from the front of the house subsided, Lynette realized with a start that nearly three hours had passed since she and Frank had first sat down together. The next thing she knew the grandfather clock in the hallway was beginning to strike.

"It can't be midnight already!"

"But it is! Almost time for the new year . . . the beginning of a new decade."

At the first ponderous strokes, Lynette spoke in an awed whisper, "Isn't it amazing to think how many New Year's Eves this house has seen?"

"At least two hundred, I'd guess. Open houses at Cameron Hall are legendary. I don't know whether you've heard or not, but it's been told in our family that the Camerons and the Maynards have a mutual history."

"We do? Tell me about it."

Frank's gray eyes twinkled. "Well, I have it on very good authority that my grandfather was smitten with your Grandmother Garnet when she was a young girl. Of course, she wouldn't give him the time of day, so I've been told, and he nursed a broken heart for many years before he fell in love with the lady he eventually married, *my* grandmother."

"That's fascinating, Frank. I've heard that Grandmother Garnet was quite a belle in her day."

"And there's an even more recent story about the connection between our two families, though I wonder if it's judicious to spill family secrets. . . ." He hesitated, a slight frown puckering his brow.

"Oh, Frank, don't tease!" Lynette exclaimed, thoroughly curious now. "Tell me!"

"It's well-known in the Maynard family that my great-aunt, Fenelle, was once engaged to your grandfather, Rod Cameron."

Lynette shook her head in disbelief. "What happened?"

"I'm not sure. I think she broke the engagement, or maybe he fell in love with Blythe . . . but, just think, if things had worked out in either case we—you and I—would be related . . . second cousins or . . ."

"Cousins once removed?" Lynette suggested.

"Or . . ." Frank glanced up at the ribboned bunch of mistletoe suspended above their heads and lifted one eyebrow—"kissing cousins?"

They laughed a little self-consciously as the last strokes of the clock reverberated through the hallway. Shouts and blowing whistles, honking horns and the strains of "Auld Lang Syne" began echoing through the house.

"Well . . . ," Lynette ventured, "since we're *almost* cousins and it *is* an old holiday tradition . . . I . . . why not? Happy New Year, Frank!" and she leaned toward him.

He met her halfway, leaving a light kiss on her soft lips. "Happy New Year, Lynette," he said softly. "Somehow I have the feeling it's going to be a special kind of year."

When Lynette returned to Dunbarton in January, she had to pinch herself often. Had that magical New Year's Eve actually happened, or had she dreamed it all up?

19

The more she relived that evening, the more unreal it seemed. The Frank Maynard of her daydreams had paled before the reality.

He had been such a good listener, had seemed so genuinely interested in everything she had to say that Lynette had found herself expressing opinions and ideas she had never shared with anyone before, certainly not with a stranger. But Frank had not seemed like a stranger, not even from the first, and the fact that he was years older than she had not mattered.

Two weeks after she was back at school, a small package arrived for her. When she read Frank's name on the return address, she opened it excitedly. Inside was a small brown suede leather book bearing a title in faded gold letters—*Selections from Tennyson's Idylls of the King*. It was an old edition containing some black-and-white illustrations from the original engravings done by one of the pre-Raphaelite artists.

At the marker locating the story of Sir Gareth and Lady Lynette, she found a note:

> Did I mention that one of my favorite pastimes is browsing in secondhand bookstores? As luck would have it, I found this volume on one such excursion and naturally thought of you. Hope your year is going well and I look forward to seeing you again next summer.

> F.

She reread the line again: "Naturally I thought of you."

Naturally? Did he really mean that? Lynette was ecstatic. She would have loved to write reams in reply. But she knew that protocol dictated that she simply thank Frank for his thoughtfulness.

Still she was touched and thrilled by his gesture and felt even more definitely that she and Frank Maynard were soul mates. The only cloud to mar her happiness was the fear that he might consider himself too old for her. Well, time would take care of that! she thought. In the meantime, long after the "lights out" bell, she lay in bed, writing imaginary letters to him. In these letters, she poured out all her hopes and dreams, believing that if he could read them, he would understand.

Composing sentences for Frank's eyes only, Lynette began to see herself in a new light. Her goals became clearer, her determination stronger. Up until now, she had been thrust by circumstances into a position of helplessness, with no control over what happened. *Things,* she decided, *are about to change.*

By the time Lynette came home again for the summer, she found Frank among the group of young men Scott occasionally invited to Cameron Hall for a discussion of current events, particularly civic issues and community concerns. As the editor of Mayfield's only newspaper, he liked to hear a diversity of viewpoints on which to base his editorials.

These were informal gatherings. Buffet suppers were served on the side terrace on the warm summer evenings. Although Blythe acted as hostess, with Kitty and Lynette usually present to help, the women were not included in the discussions that followed.

However, the early part of the evening was strictly social. Despite Lynette's concern that Frank thought of her only as a schoolgirl, her admiration of him grew. All year at school, she had feared coming home to learn that Frank had become engaged while she was away. But she was inordinately relieved to find he was still very much a bachelor, one who was consistently attentive. But how was she to prove to him that the difference in their ages was no impossible barrier to a romantic relationship?

Part II

chapter
2

London, England
1920

SITTING IN the crowded double-decker bus swaying and rattling through the city streets, Jillian Marsh peered through a grimy window. All postwar London seemed painted in shades of gray—the shabbily dressed moving like automatons along the sidewalks, the dusty store windows displaying shopworn merchandise. The city had lost its prosperous look, its well-bred elegance. It was even hard to remember what it had been like then, when the city was lively and bustling and full of color. Where was the London of her youth, when she had returned as an eighteen-year-old debutante, fresh from a Swiss finishing school?

No one thought the war would last nearly five years. In the beginning everyone said it would be over by Christmas. At first the air was electric with excitement and gaiety. There were dozens of parties where she had danced and flirted with young men in bright regimental uniforms. Then the grim reality had set in and those same young men left for the battlefields. Many of them had died "somewhere in France." Others had come back to find their family estates depleted, the country itself bankrupt. The kingdom had paid a bitter price for its victory. Some said that price had been a whole generation of England's finest.

No one knew better than Jillian herself what a cruel mockery that war had been. Both her brothers had been killed—Jerod, at the Marne; Tony, when his ship was torpedoed. Her parents, too, were gone. Her mother had died in the dread Spanish-flu epidemic that had swept the nation in '17; her father, soon afterward, devastated by the loss of his beloved wife and sons. Their country house in Kent had been requisitioned by the government as a refuge billet. Everything and everyone . . . gone.

Jillian recalled with a little shudder how Mr. Billington, the family lawyer, had tried to explain the loss of the family fortune. She still didn't quite understand how the seemingly endless supply of funds that had assured the best schools, the riding horses, and music lessons could have disappeared. But slowly the brutal truth had to be faced and accepted. There was nothing left. Or why else would she be having to find some way to support herself?

Still, Jillian knew she was no worse off than the majority of Britons. She was young, healthy, reasonably intelligent. She'd manage. Straightening her shoulders, she sat up in the seat, opened her shabby purse and took out the folded newspaper ad, rereading it for the dozenth time:

WANTED: REFINED YOUNG LADY—
must be well-educated,
preferably fluent in French,
skilled in social graces—as companion-governess
to American matron and granddaughter, age 12.
must be free to travel.
Reply in own handwriting, stating credentials, references, to . . .

Here followed a box number, care of the *London Times*.

The ad had appeared a week ago, and Jill had responded immediately, applying in her best hand on the last bit of good stationery she owned. Within days of posting the application, she had received an answer written on heavy monogrammed vellum in a bold, angular script, and signed with a flourish—*Garnet C. Devlin*—requesting that she come to the Claridge Hotel for an interview.

Jill replaced the scrap of newsprint in the inside pocket of her handbag. She felt her stomach tighten. Nerves? Or simply hunger, since she hadn't eaten since breakfast early that morning? Probably nerves. She had never been interviewed for a position before. Never dreamed it would be necessary to seek employment. Yet here she was, on her way to meet a prospective employer!

She took out her compact, flipped open the lid, and took a quick look at herself in the mirror. Did she look like a serious candidate for the position of governess to a twelve-year-old girl? She considered her reflection doubtfully. In spite of having recently turned twenty-four, she looked awfully young. She snapped the compact shut. She'd just have to hope that her other qualifications would compensate for the lack of visible maturity.

Jill reviewed the wording of the ad. The employer was an "American matron." She'd never known any Americans except the few American army officers she had met at some of the dances. She had thought them rather arrogant, too pushy. But I can't be prejudiced, she reminded herself, realizing the truth of the old adage, "Beggars can't be choosers!"

Whatever this American woman is like, I'll take the job . . . that is, if it's offered. Besides, what choice do I have? She didn't know how to use a typewriter, and even factory workers were being laid off now that the war production had come to an end. She tapped her purse with her fingers in reflection. *Goodness knows, I have most of the qualifications I need for this job.* She was well-educated, she could read and speak some French and a little Italian, and she was certainly free to travel! Her softly curved mouth tightened in determination. *Besides, I need this job desperately. So I shall get it and start a whole new life!*

Just then the bus jolted to a stop. Seeing that she was only a few blocks from the fashionable hotel where her interview with Mrs. Devlin was to take place, she pulled the buzzer and prepared to get off.

Covering the distance to the hotel with brisk steps, Jillian entered the once-plush lobby of the Claridge, noticing that it, like every other public building in London, looked a little old and tired. Waiting for the lift that would take her up to Mrs. Devlin's third-floor suite, she checked herself in the mirrored panel between the bronze elevator doors.

Her Worth ensemble had held up surprisingly well. The fitted jacket with velvet collars and cuffs still had style, although the skirt might be a little long for the new trend. But the brown velvet hat, bought in Paris the fall before the war, looked as chic as ever. All in all, she felt satisfied that her appearance, displaying a certain flair and good taste, would meet with the approval of her prospective employer. The fact that her gloves were mended and her shoes needed new soles didn't show. At least Jill fervently hoped not!

At the third floor the operator slid back the filigreed metal door, and Jillian stepped out onto the carpeted corridor. Outside the door,

27

emblazoned with gold numerals, she took a long breath before knocking.

After a few tense moments had passed, a maid in a black uniform and frilly white apron, answered.

Jillian cleared her throat. "I'm Miss Marsh. Mrs. Devlin is expecting me."

The maid nodded. "Come this way, please. I'll tell Mrs. Devlin you're here." She ushered Jillian into a sitting room, then left.

Although elegantly decorated, the room had a cool, impersonal look, with no clue as to the personality of the woman she had come here to meet. That is, at first glance. Then Jillian noticed several photographs in ornate silver frames, resting on a table between two velvet-draped windows. Curious, she walked over to inspect them.

One was a large picture of a graceful young woman in a satin gown with a sweeping train, fashioned in the style of the last century. In her dark hair she was wearing three white plumes—the requisite for a formal Court Presentation. There were two smaller pictures—one, of a handsome little boy in a sailor suit, holding a toy sailboat; the other, of two darling little girls in ruffled frocks, ribbons in their blond and brunet curls, one several years older than the other. Was one of these children the granddaughter for whom Mrs. Devlin was hiring a governess?

Once more Jillian's gaze swept the room, taking in every detail of the lavish decor—the velvet draperies, tasseled and valanced, the folds fanned out on the flowered rug; the French furniture, arranged in conversational groupings about the room; the lamps with their elaborate crystal prisms. The quality of the furnishings was mute evidence that this was one of the most expensive of the hotel suites. Very few people could afford such luxury these days . . . except maybe rich Americans.

"Good afternoon, Miss Marsh." The woman's softly modulated voice hinted at an accent Jillian couldn't place.

She wheeled about. As a young woman, Garnet Devlin must have been stunningly attractive, Jill surmised. Though age had made faint inroads, skill and style had preserved much of the woman's youthful beauty. Elegantly coiffed silver-blonde hair set off the iridescent turquoise taffeta tea gown she was wearing, its long full sleeves trimmed with a narrow band of pale mink.

"Good afternoon," Jill replied, wondering how long the woman had been standing there. Had she seen her examining the photographs? Apparently so, for a shadow crossed Mrs. Devlin's features as she gestured to the larger photograph. "My daughter Faith, lost tragically in the sinking of the *Titanic*. A loss from which I shall never recover."

She moved regally into the room and motioned to Jill to take a seat on one of the fragile-looking Louis XIV chairs while she sat down on the other. "I've been looking forward to meeting you, Miss Marsh. I've ordered tea for us so we can have our little chat."

Jill, hands clasped tightly in her lap, was conscious of Mrs. Devlin's evaluating glance upon her. Was she measuring up or had she already failed in some way to meet the woman's expectations? Then she noticed that Mrs. Devlin was holding the letter of application in one well-manicured hand.

"I liked your reply to my ad. I could tell right away you'd be exactly right for what I have in mind."

Her remark jolted Jillian. She had heard that Americans were direct, but she had not expected so quick an acceptance. An English lady would be far more subtle, ask many more questions about a prospective employee's background. She would at least wait until tea was served to observe the applicant's manners. Jill realized that she had a lot to learn about Americans.

"You see, not only am I looking for a governess for my granddaughter Bryanne, but a companion . . . someone young and lively and pretty." She laughed gaily. "And now that I've met you, I can see you fill the bill perfectly." Mrs. Devlin seemed pleased with herself as she tapped Jill's letter with her forefinger. "I say I am looking for a companion for my granddaughter, but it is for myself, too. Someone to shop with me, play cards with, handle some light correspondence, that sort of thing. You see . . ."

Mrs. Devlin broke off as the maid entered with the tea tray and set it down in front of her. For a few minutes she busied herself pouring the amber liquid into the teacups. As her fingers moved gracefully, handling the delicate china, Jill not could not help notice the sparkle of several large diamonds. She passed a cup to Jillian along with a folded embroidered napkin, then offered her a plate of crescent-shaped sandwiches and iced petit-fours.

Feeling a fresh hunger pang, Jillian resisted the impulse to take several. Instead, she nibbled daintily on a cream cheese sandwich and took a sip of tea.

"As I was saying, Bryanne's mother, my daughter Faith, is dead, and her father . . . might as well be." Mrs. Devlin's mouth thinned in disapproval. "Nonetheless, Bryanne is my responsibility now. She is away at boarding school at present, and I'm living here temporarily. My townhouse is closed, and my country home, which was turned into a hospital during the War, is undergoing complete renovation. I'm sure you can understand why." Mrs. Devlin sighed, affecting an air of martyrdom.

"Anyway, I shall be taking Bryanne out of that institution soon," Mrs. Devlin went on. "I must confess I was extremely disappointed when I last went to visit her." Here she fixed Jillian with a baleful look. "I do hope you're not a product of an English girls' boarding school!"

"No, I attended school in Switzerland. My mother was in frail health, and my parents went there for her health and enrolled me at the Chalet École. After she recovered, I remained behind to graduate."

"I thought as much." Mrs. Devlin nodded approvingly. "Anyone can see you're a lady. Precisely what I want and need in a role model for Bryanne. Recently I went down to see her and I was shocked, I can tell you. It seems that most of what they teach the girls is to hit a ball around a field with some sort of stick . . . at least, that's all they did the afternoon I was there. And the outfits are deplorable. For the prices I pay for her school uniforms . . . well, she might as well be wearing a gunnysack!

"As for giving a young lady any sense of correct carriage or deportment . . ." Mrs. Devlin shook her head. "It was deplorable! And Bryanne has gotten *fat* when we've all been on rations! But then what can you expect from a diet of potatoes and sugary tea? No wonder she's begun to look like a little pudding! Well, something must be done about it right away." The woman set her teacup down with an emphatic click.

"She will leave at the end of the term and that is definite. I would have yanked her out right then and there, but what would I do with her here? There's nothing for a child in a hotel." Mrs. Devlin refilled Jillian's cup. "That's when I got the idea of advertising for a companion-governess, someone suitable to travel with us." She stopped abruptly and looked up. "You *are* free to travel, aren't you?"

"Yes, I am." Jillian was still stunned by the rapidity with which the interview had progressed to this point.

But Mrs. Devlin did not wait for details and pressed on. "I was

30

planning to take Bryanne home to Virginia—that's our home originally—but I've been so distressed about her. I felt I couldn't take her back there the way she is now. I mean, her relatives who haven't seen her since she was a wee thing . . . well, we have our work cut out for us, my dear." Mrs. Devlin sighed once more. "My intention is to ready Bryanne to take her place in society by the time we return to Virginia. Did I mention that the child is a Montrose?"

There was time only for a quick shake of the head before Mrs. Devlin launched into a recital of Bryanne's heritage.

"At least, on her father's side. The Montroses are one of Virginia's first families, the pioneers who went to America when it was still a British colony. But my granddaughter needs to be prepared, trained for her role. As I said, I feel you will be perfect for the job." Mrs. Devlin paused long enough to beam at Jillian.

"I should like for you to begin in three weeks. Of course, your salary will commence immediately." Then, as if in afterthought, Mrs. Devlin's smooth brow puckered in a slight frown and she asked, "You *will* accept the position, won't you, Miss Marsh? It may take six months . . . maybe even a year or more, but we shall make this an enjoyable experience. We'll travel, expose Bryanne to the art and culture of the Continent. Perhaps we'll even go to Egypt. I've always had a desire to see the Pyramids. Thus, when we eventually return to Virginia, Bryanne will be a credit to both of us."

When Mrs. Devlin paused at last, Jillian recaptured her wits. "If you please, don't you think we should discuss the matter a little further?"

"Of course! How thoughtless of me. You want to know the salary I intend to pay?" Mrs. Devlin mentioned a figure that caused Jillian's eyes to widen.

"Oh, it isn't the salary that concerns me, Mrs. Devlin. I just think perhaps I should meet your granddaughter, since I am to be her companion and you expect me to exert so much influence. Don't you think we should see if she likes me first, if we would get along?"

"*Like* you! She'll adore you, my dear. And there's no question that you will like *her*. Bryanne is a delightful child, an easygoing, merry little soul, as agreeable as the day is long! But if you really feel you must, we could arrange for you to accompany me on the next visitor's day, and you can see for yourself. Would that satisfy?"

Jillian nodded, somewhat relieved. Things had been going much too fast, and she was a bit dizzy. "I think that would be quite satisfactory, Mrs. Devlin."

"Good. Then it's settled. Is this where I may reach you in London?" The woman held up the envelope in which Jillian's letter had been posted and examined the return address. Seeing her nod, she said, "Very well, I'll write to let you know when we can drive down to Devon. And don't bother with one of those public conveyances," she added with an airy wave of her hand. "My driver will pick you up."

When Jillian stepped outside the hotel, her head was spinning with the amazing Mrs. Devlin's plans for the three of them. Apparently the woman never took no for an answer. Still not quite believing her good fortune in securing such a well-paid position with such ease, Jill walked for a while in a daze. When she finally realized she was walking in the opposite direction from the bus stop, she turned to retrace her steps, reliving the conversation with her new employer.

She had actually done it! Gotten the job! But it suddenly struck her as ironic that she should be so elated over her new position. Because her family had lived abroad for so long, Jill herself had never had a governess. But from stories told by her friends about the tricks, teasing, and other sorts of harassment inflicted upon that poor breed, Jill had concluded that in most English households, the lot of a governess, like the policeman in Gilbert and Sullivan's opera, "is not a happy one."

Of course the war had brought many changes to the old class system in England. Then, too, Mrs. Devlin was an American, and Americans *were* different. At least, Jillian thought, she was gainfully employed. Had even been paid in advance, for Mrs. Devlin had insisted on giving her a check to confirm their agreement.

Preoccupied with these thoughts, Jill didn't see her bus coming until it was at the corner. She ran to catch it, and once settled in her seat she contemplated her future. Mrs. Devlin had mentioned travel. With her money, no doubt their travel would be first class trains, hotels, and accommodations. She had also mentioned taking her granddaughter back to Virginia. Jillian had dreamed of seeing America. *Virginia,* she mused. *Now what had Uncle Greg said about one of our ancestors going to the Colonies before the American Revolution?*

Gregory Marsh, Jillian's great-uncle and her only living relative, lived alone in Kentburne, a village about thirty miles south of London. Maybe she should pay him a visit. Yes, she'd send along a note, tell him about her new job, and find out what he knew about the Marsh family history.

Getting off at her stop, Jillian spotted an old woman selling daffodils. The sight of the yellow-bonneted blooms suddenly seemed a good omen. Throwing caution to the winds, she placed a generous amount of pocket change into the gnarled chapped hand of the flower vendor.

Inhaling the fresh scent of the bright blooms and thus cheered, she walked on with a lighter step. The small bouquet would brighten her drab "bed-sitter," the bleak one-room apartment she had called home since coming back to London. Happily, she would not be living there much longer!

chapter
3

After dispatching the note to her uncle, asking if she could come down for the weekend, Jillian received an immediate reply:

> My dear girl, I am more than pleased that you want to come for a visit. Although I've just a small cot now, there's a spare room, so I hope you'll plan to spend the entire weekend. I've obtained the housekeeping services of a nice Mrs. Crombie who comes in three times a week to see to things and is an excellent cook. I think we can make you comfortable, and I am looking forward with a great deal of pleasure to seeing you.

The very next Friday Jill packed a small valise and took the bus to Paddington Station, bought her ticket to Kentburne, and found an empty second-class compartment. Having done very little traveling during the War, Jill now noticed the worn upholstery and badly chipped paint. As with all other nonessentials, apparently no maintenance had been done for the last five years.

As the train pulled slowly out of the station, Jillian gazed out the window, thinking that even the people standing on the platform looked drab and forlorn. She wondered if she would find Kentburne as dreary and hoped not, for she had such happy childhood memories of holidays spent at her grandparents' house there.

Though the village was only a short distance away, the train made numerous stops at the small towns along the way, and it was two hours before Jillian arrived. Stepping onto the platform, she glanced about her with a sinking heart. No longer was the station house surrounded by trim borders of blooming flower beds behind white-painted pickets.

With all the young men away at war, there had been no one to tend them, and only the elderly or disabled were left to manage.

Sighing, she set out on foot for her uncle's rented cottage, only a short walk from the center of the village, he had said. She had become accustomed to walking long distances in her war-time job as a messenger for the War Office. Now she often did so to save precious bus fare.

The village itself looked much the same as she remembered—a cluster of stone cottages, a greengrocers' market, a pub, a clothing store and hat shop and, at the end of the street, the gray church with its Norman tower. Just past the center of town a wooden signpost marked "Priory Lane" led into a narrow, winding road. A few yards farther on stood a quaint thatched-roof house. This must be Uncle Greg's "cot." Jillian hurried on, opening the gate and walking through a rambling garden to the red-painted door.

Uncle Greg himself answered her knock and greeted her warmly. "Jillian! Come in, come in, my dear girl. How very nice to see you!" He opened the door wider so she could step inside. "How long has it been?" Jillian opened her mouth to reply, but he answered his own question. "A year or two, I think . . . on the sad occasion of your father's funeral, wasn't it? But then we'll not dwell on sad things. The important thing is that you're here, so we'll have a spot of tea and settle down to catching up. Here, let me have your things." He took her small suitcase and set it down beside a Victorian coatrack.

"You have a job, you say?" he went on. "With an American lady?"

Jillian smiled to herself and hurried to get a word in while he helped her off with her coat. "Yes, a Mrs. Jeremy Devlin. She's in her sixties and enormously wealthy, I gather."

"Hmmm. Jeremy Devlin . . ." Her uncle repeated the name as he hung up the coat, waiting until she had unpinned her hat and handed it to him. "The name is familiar. I wonder if I may have met her at some gathering or other . . . perhaps at the Ainsleys' at a dinner party when I was home on leave from a tour of India. If I recall correctly, her husband was with a publishing firm and the lady in question was a real 'stunner' as we used to say—glorious hair, lovely figure, charming manner of speaking."

"It certainly could have been the same person, Uncle Greg. Mrs. Devlin is still a handsome lady and her accent is . . . well, I thought it strange, but it may be just a regional dialect. She's from one of the southern states, Virginia."

"Yes, now that you mention it, I'm quite sure it was the same one. Come where it's warmer, and we can talk some more," he suggested, leading Jillian into a small parlor, where a fire blazed in the cozy fireplace. There were books galore and tea already set out on a wheeled teacart. "I don't have much company nowadays," Uncle Greg said, motioning Jillian to one of the comfortable chintz-covered chairs. "Oh, the vicar comes by once a week or so. He's quite a local historian."

"That's interesting, Uncle Greg," Jill interrupted, "because that's one thing I wanted to discuss with you—our ancestors, the Marshes, that is. Mrs. Devlin intends to take her granddaughter back to Virginia and has asked me to accompany them when they go. I'm not sure, but I seem to remember that we had an ancestor who was a Colonist, didn't we?"

"Well, not in the strict sense of the word. Most of the Englishmen who went to the Colonies were second sons, you understand . . . the rule of primogeniture existed here for centuries—first-born son inherits everything. So a disinherited second or third son was often tempted to seek his fortune in the Colonies. Some of them managed to get magnificent King's Grants and became prosperous plantation owners." Uncle Greg chuckled. "Most probably the King later regretted his generosity when those same men became leaders in the Revolution!"

"Was it a second son in the Marsh family who went to America?"

Uncle Greg shook his head. "The Marshes were too wealthy, too powerful, owned too much land to leave unless . . . for some reason they had lost their fortunes or came to grief through some other such disaster." He paused, holding out a plate of poppyseed cake. "Here, Jillian, help yourself. It's one of Mrs. Crombie's prize recipes, and she'll be insulted if we don't eat every crumb."

Jill took a generous slice. "But wasn't there a great manor house on the bluffs overlooking the village? And didn't that house belong to the Marsh family at some time?"

"Yes, but it wasn't built originally for the Marsh family. It was once a monastery. You see, during his reign, Henry VIII took vengeance on the Catholic Church for blocking his marriage to Anne Boleyn. The result was the dissolution of the monasteries. Monksmoor Priory was actually taken from a prosperous order of monks and given to Basil Marsh, one of the king's loyal favorites. The Marsh family lived there for generations. Then, if memory serves, the main manor house was sold, and the Dower House was . . ." Here, Uncle Greg's demeanor changed, and a light flickered in his faded blue eyes. "Something quite remarkable has occurred to me. In the late 1880s, the Dower House was dismantled, or at least part of it, and moved, brick by brick, to the *United States!*" He inched to the edge of his chair. "I'll have to check this out with the vicar, but I do believe he told me something else about that when I first came here to live upon my retirement from the army."

"What, Uncle Greg?" Jillian asked, her own interest piqued by his excitement.

"That Dower House was inherited by a wealthy American widow who had it moved to . . . yes, I'm almost certain the vicar said it was . . . *Virginia!*"

"Fascinating," Jillian murmured. "And what about Monksmoor Priory? Whatever became of it?"

"I believe there were plans to turn it into a girls' boarding school at one time. But before that could be done, it changed hands again, and then the war came along. No doubt the old house has been abandoned, left to decay. No one can afford to live in a place like that these days. And there are no institutional funds to restore the old homes."

"Is it far from here, Uncle?" Jill asked. "Could I walk there, just to see it for myself?"

"Oh, yes, it's quite a pleasant walk in good weather. Can't say why I haven't been over there myself." Uncle Greg, stimulated by Jill's interest in one of his favorite topics, settled back in his chair. "If you like, after we've had our tea, I'll get out some of the old books and ledgers. You'll be able to see a record of births, deaths, marriages, and other transactions, such as land bought, sold, or . . ." He lowered his voice mischievously—"*stolen.* There are rogues among the aristocracy, you know, even in a family as prestigious as ours."

Jill and her uncle talked through the afternoon, poring over the old books he had brought down from the attic, their leather binding tattered, the pages yellowed and curled at the edges. While outside, the sky darkened, thunder rumbled, and the rain began to fall in torrents.

By midmorning the next day, the weather had cleared and Jillian set out for Monksmoor Priory or what might be left of it. She walked to the village, past the stone church and the vicarage and followed the narrow country road that led up the hill. At its crest, through the swirling mist, she saw the outline of a building that must be her ancestors' mansion. It had a certain lonely splendor, and Jillian halted, as much to accommodate the sudden rush of emotion she was experiencing as to catch her breath from the steep climb.

In the next few minutes, she tried to imagine what it must have been like for that young woman, Noramary Marsh, whose story Uncle Greg had related to her the evening before, to leave this place in 1745 and board a sailing vessel to travel thousands of miles across the treacherous ocean into an uncertain future. In a strange way Jill felt a bonding with this unknown ancestress. Soon she would be embarking on a new adventure, and she had no idea where it would eventually take her.

On Sunday Jill accompanied her uncle to services at the church. "You must meet the vicar, my dear. I know he'll want to show you the cemetery with some of the Marsh tombstones, but we'll have to make sure that he knows what time your train leaves," Uncle Greg warned with a twinkle in his blue eyes. "Otherwise, he'll keep you overly long, and you'll miss it."

The church was unheated, and the ancient stones seemed to have taken hostage the accumulated winters and held them in a damp chill. Jillian tucked her hands into the sleeves of her coat, feeling the penetrating cold creep all through her.

The service was mercifully short, for on this day, the vicar had chosen to use the brief form of worship. The words referring to Christ "and he had compassion on the multitude" seemed appropriate as the balding minister turned to bestow the final blessing. It seemed particularly appropriate, even prophetic, that the closing prayer was one for guidance for those facing new challenges, for travelers, for the unknown future. Jillian followed along with the other parishioners:

Direct us, O Lord, in all our doings with Thy most gracious favor and further us with Thy continual help; that in all our works begun, continued and ended in Thee, we may glorify Thy Holy Name and finally, by Thy mercy, obtain everlasting life through Jesus Christ our Lord. Amen.

After the benediction, everyone scurried to the exit doors, probably seeking home, hot tea, and a welcoming fire. But Uncle Greg put a restraining hand on Jillian's arm. "I'll have a word with one of the acolytes, and ask him to tell the vicar that we'd like to see him for a few minutes."

He approached the altar where a small, rosy-cheeked boy in starched surplice and red cassock was having difficulty extinguishing one of the tall candles and waited patiently until the task was accomplished. Jillian watched as an animated conversation ensued.

A satisfied smile on his face, Uncle Greg returned to the pew. "He'll give the vicar my message. I asked him to meet us by the gate leading to the cemetery."

Outside, the sky was overcast with a misty shower falling. In all probability, it would soon turn to rain, Jillian predicted. She shivered in her light coat.

Then almost as if summoned, the smiling vicar appeared, his black cape billowing in the sharp wind. "I understand you are interested in viewing some of the epitaphs." He shook his head regretfully as he pushed open the ornate iron gate into the graveyard. "This place was in terrible shape when I came here. I spent many hours scraping off the moss so the names could be seen. Some are very old indeed. Now, I suppose it is the Marsh family stones you want to see?"

It was with a unique thrill that Jillian followed him down the gravel path to a plot marked by several granite headstones. The vicar and Uncle Greg stood conversing in low tones as she stepped in and out between the markers until she found the ones she was looking for— *Simon Marsh, 1718–1756*, and *Leatrice Emery Marsh, 1724–1768*. This would be the older half-brother of Noramary Marsh, the young girl who had been sent to America. Apparently Simon had been buried here with his wife. Alongside these were four other markers, presumably their children—Thomas, Colin, Roger, Matthew. But where was the grave of Simon's stepmother, Noramary's mother, who had died giving birth to her?

Then she saw it, standing a little apart from the others—a stone cherub, its chin resting on one chubby hand while the other stroked the head of a lamb. Moving over quickly to the marker, Jillian read the inscription:

ELEANORA CARY MARSH
Beloved Wife of Norbert Marsh
Born 1712, Died 1732
Too beautiful, Too good, Too young, Too soon

Unexpectedly Jillian's eyes filled with tears and she blinked them away, relieved that Uncle Greg and the vicar were too engrossed in their conversation to notice.

"Well, my dear, we must be on our way if you are to have some lunch before your train leaves," Uncle Greg reminded her.

They thanked the vicar, and Jillian walked back to the cottage with her uncle without further comment, caught up in the overwhelming discovery of this link to her past. Still, it was the future that beckoned now. When she said her good-byes, promising to keep him posted, Jillian found herself looking ahead to the next bend of the road.

chapter
4

WHEN JILLIAN returned to her flat late Sunday afternoon, she found a note from Mrs. Devlin, saying that she would come for her on Wednesday for the drive down to her granddaughter's school.

"I fear we shall have to sit through some dreadful program, as it is Parents' Day, and the teachers take pride in showing off their students' talents, piano recitals and such," wrote Garnet Devlin. "But it will give you a chance to meet Bryanne, and that is our main reason for making the trip."

She ended by stating the time she would arrive, then signed her name. Mrs. Devlin's handwriting was, like her, dramatic, distinctive. Jillian smiled as she refolded the letter and put it back in the envelope.

Jill dressed carefully for the occasion. She had used some of the money Mrs. Devlin had advanced to buy a new blouse, some good gloves, and some grosgrain ribbons to refurbish her hat. This would be an important meeting, and Jillian wanted to make a good impression. She remembered enough about her own teen years to know that Bryanne Montrose would either like her or detest her on sight. Of course, it could be the other way round. There was just as likely a possibility that Bryanne would turn out to be an obnoxious brat, spoiled by a doting grandmother!

Precisely at ten, Jillian's awe-struck landlady knocked at the door of her flat, announcing in hushed tones the arrival of a chauffeur-driven limousine. Mouth agape, eyes popping, she watched as Jillian went downstairs, then out to the sleek, silver-gray Rolls, escorted by Mrs. Devlin's driver, uniformed in a matching gray.

When Jillian climbed into the back seat, she found Mrs. Devlin, exquisitely attired in a suit of Persian blue wool, the jacket fashioned as a Cossack tunic, its high-necked collar and cuffs banded in black astrakhan fur. If it hadn't been in such perfect taste, her outfit might have been considered theatrical, but it suited her. The hat was a darker blue velvet, trimmed with an ornamental silver pin and veiled over a face that, even at close range, seemed scarcely lined.

As the automobile purred down the Devon country roads, Mrs. Devlin outlined the day's plan. "I'm sorry to have to expose you to such a tedious time, but we'll take Bryanne out for tea at the inn afterward. But first I suppose we'll have to endure one of those awful games!"

Jillian's mouth twitched in an effort to suppress her smile. The look of distaste on her employer's face revealed that Mrs. Devlin did not share the British proclivity for active sports. But from Jill's own brief experience at an English girls' school, she knew that physical exercise was considered a necessary part of any young lady's complete education.

The rest of the drive, given to a discussion of the European trip that Mrs. Devlin was planning, passed quickly. Soon they were turning into the long graveled drive leading to Sylvan Court School for Girls.

In spite of Mrs. Devlin's negative comments about the day's activities, Jill was anxious to meet Bryanne Montrose. She was predisposed to like the child, to be her friend and ally, possibly even her protector, for the simple reason that having a grandmother like Garnet Devlin could not be easy!

Jillian would never forget her first glimpse of Bryanne. The young girl had come running down the stone steps from the balustraded terrace where she had evidently been watching for her grandmother's car. She came now, braids flying, hat hanging by its strings and bobbing behind, collar and tie askew, black cotton stockings sagging, but with a sweet smile on her plump face.

"Gramum! Gramum! I'm so glad to see you. I was afraid you weren't coming!"

Jillian's heart tugged at those poignant words. Had Mrs. Devlin disappointed the child before? Jillian would not have been surprised. After all, the woman had confessed to finding these visiting days trying. She glanced at the two of them—the child ready to fling herself into her grandmother's arms in a spontaneous welcome, the woman bracing herself.

Garnet put up both kid-gloved hands to straighten the brim of her hat. "Good heavens, child, do be careful! You nearly knocked me over," she admonished in the wake of her granddaughter's fierce hug. "Here now, let me have a look at you." She gave a disapproving cluck as her eyes moved critically over Bryanne's person. Then the frown disappeared, and she patted the girl's rosy cheek affectionately. "Bryanne, my dear, I want you to meet Miss Marsh, your new governess and our traveling companion."

The girl turned wide, sparkling blue eyes on Jillian. "Oh, that's really keen! I'm ever so glad to meet you. Gramum wrote me about you." She thrust out her hand and grabbed Jillian's, pumping it vigorously. "Does that mean I can leave school, Gramum? This place is such a . . . well, I'd much rather come live with you again . . . and Miss Marsh, too, of course."

"At the end of the term, my dear. That's the best I can do," Garnet said. "I'm making the arrangements now. We'll be going to the south of France when you're finished here. Now, can we take you out for tea, or do we have to . . . I mean, is there a game for us to watch or some sort of program we must . . ." She looked to Jillian for help.

"Oh, there's just to be a recitation and some of the music students will play their instruments and then we'll all sing the school song and *then* we can go," explained Bryanne breathlessly. "But first, you have to go in and speak to my dorm teacher, Gramum."

Jillian liked Bryanne immediately. Although she sensed that here was a child of enormous inner resources, there was also a vulnerability about her, an almost aching need to be accepted and loved. You could see it in her eyes, in the longing look she turned on her grandmother, yearning for her approval.

Jillian thought again of Garnet Devlin's words on the day of their first meeting: *My daughter Faith, tragically lost in the sinking of the* Titanic— *a loss from which I shall never recover.* Was Bryanne somehow expected to take the place of Mrs. Devlin's dead daughter, a daughter whom death had idealized, probably out of all proportion to reality? If so, Jill pitied the child.

After the program in the school auditorium, the three climbed into the waiting limousine, Bryanne on one of the pull-down jump seats. The child kept up a running monologue as they drove to Sylvan Arms Inn.

Mrs. Devlin lifted an elegant brow and, glancing at Jill, rolled her eyes and sighed. Jill, on the contrary, found Bryanne's enthusiasm

43

natural and appealing. It was clear that she was enjoying every minute of her holiday!

In the dining room of the inn, they were served an elaborate tea. It annoyed Jill that Garnet constantly corrected Bryanne's manners, frequently interrupting the girl's eager narration of incidents at school. Bryanne, obviously wanting to please, punctuated her recital with "Sorry, Gramum." By the end of teatime, Bryanne became noticeably subdued.

Sorry to see the girl's spirits dampened and hoping to make her feel better, Jillian complimented Bryanne on the silver heart locket she was wearing over her school uniform.

The girl brightened immediately. Pulling it forward so Jill could see, she pressed the spring and the locket flew open. "Lynette sent it to me for my birthday. See, I put her picture inside."

"She's very pretty," Jillian said, leaning over to admire the likeness. "Is Lynette a special friend?"

"Oh, no, Lynette is my sister. She's older than me."

"Older than *I*, Bryanne," Mrs. Devlin corrected automatically. Turning to Jill, she explained, "Lynette is my other granddaughter. She lives in Virginia. You would never guess these two were sisters, would you? Lynette is the image of her mother at that age."

It was at *that* moment, Jillian realized later, that she made the decision to become Bryanne Montrose's champion. When the afternoon wore to an end and the girl was returned to her school, Jill relinquished part of her heart along with the obligatory handshake.

"Well?" Mrs. Devlin turned to Jillian as they drove off. "Have you changed your mind, or do you still want to take on this job?"

While the woman's attitude strained Jillian's patience, it strengthened her resolve. Grooming Bryanne to become a debutante seemed irrelevant. More important was giving her the assurance that she was loved and accepted just as she was.

"Oh, yes, I do," Jill replied firmly. "I believe Bryanne and I will be great friends."

When Bryanne retired to her room for the night, she could hardly wait to write her sister:

Dearest Lynette,

Guess what? The most exciting thing has happened! Gramum has decided to take me out of this awful school at the end of the term! I can't tell you how glad I am. But the best part is that she has employed the most darling young woman to be my . . . well, not exactly my governess, I'm much too old for that . . . but as a sort of companion. I'm not quite sure what her title is. But anyway she'll live with us and travel with us when we go to the south of France for the summer. Gramum has rented a seaside villa there. It's not going to be entirely a holiday, she said, as I'll be studying French and botany . . . the flora and fauna of Côte d'Azur, do you suppose? Anyway, I'm delirious with happiness to be out of this prison for good!

Oh, I didn't tell you about Miss Marsh, Miss Jillian Marsh. Don't you simply love that name? Sounds like a Charlotte Brontë heroine. She's very pretty, not governessy at all. Has gobs of soft brown hair, a beautiful complexion, and the most extraordinary eyes with long dark lashes. I know we are going to get on famously. She doesn't treat me like a child at all. Uh-oh, the bell has just rung for lights out. More later.

Love,
Brynnie

chapter

5

Letters between the Cameron twins,
Kitty Traherne and Cara Brandt, 1921 to 1924

Eden Cottage
Fall, 1921

Dear Cara,

I hate letters that start out with apologies. But since I haven't written in a long time, you must be wondering what has been going on here. It has been such a busy summer. I have been helping Lynette get off to her first year at Teachers College, shopping for appropriate collegiate clothes, driving her to Fredericksburg, meeting with her prospective roommate and family, then helping both girls get their room in order, with curtains, bedspreads, and other things to make their "home away from home" cozy and comfortable for the year ahead.

I am so proud of Lynette. She has shown such maturity and responsibility. I think her decision to become a teacher was well-advised. I'm sure you agree. After our experiences during the War, you and I understand how important it is for a woman to prepare herself to be independent, to take her place in the world.

Since you and I have found our own identity, have realized some of our goals and dreams, I want this for Lynette. She has such sweetness and depth of character, in spite of her motherless childhood and with an absentee father.

Of course, I also hope that one day she will find her ideal mate, just as you and I have done. Although your happiness with Owen was sadly brief, you did know that completion that only a truly compatible relationship can bring.

And even though Richard's health remains precarious, I count each day we have together as precious. He is everything I could possibly wish for in a husband. Our life is as nearly perfect as one could imagine. The weather here is still fine—warm, sunny days and crisp nights. So in the mornings, I work in the garden and Richard directs from his wheelchair, enjoying the beauty that surrounds this enchanted place. Sometimes we even lunch out in the grape arbor. Evenings are especially lovely, sitting before our fireplace as we listen to music on the phonograph, or Richard reads me one of his latest compositions. We talk endlessly and are continually discovering new and delightful things about each other.

Oh, Cara, I feel so fortunate to have found someone like Richard who is so brilliant, so kind, so dear. He stimulates me to be more creative, to think more deeply about life. With each day that passes, I love him more and more and am so grateful to God for sparing his life, despite the cruel injury.

Well, I must not run on so, but I did want to share my life with you. It brings us closer somehow, even with your being thousands of miles across the ocean. Please write and tell me what you are doing, the people you are working with . . . everything! And don't make me wait too long to hear from you.

Ever your loving twin,
Kitty

*   *   *

Paris, France
January 1922

Dearest Kitty,

Now that Christmas is over, Paris is gray and cheerless. Outside it is drizzling—a fine, cold mist. All the beautiful snow that fell on New Year's Eve is lying in frozen, filthy clumps along the edges of the streets and sidewalks.

All the children in the orphanage have some kind of respiratory problems—from sniffles to bronchitis—and I wish I had some of your nursing skills to see us through the epidemic! However, I do the "grunt work" of keeping the nurses supplied with hot water, clean towels, and little handkerchiefs for the tiny red noses! But there is some compensation. Running up and down the steps from the basement laundry to the nursery dozens of times a day with armloads of linens is keeping me slim. What a few sets of tennis used to accomplish!

Speaking of tennis . . . those old carefree days in Mayfield seem an eon ago. I can hardly remember the life I used to live back then. Everything seems now to be divided by "before" and "after" the war. Even my life with Owen in our small parish gets dimmer with each passing day. We were so terribly young, weren't we?

Not that I would change a moment of those two years. Neither would I want to relive them. Owen taught me so much and prepared me for what I am doing now, even though he didn't realize it, of course. If he could only know how he expanded my heart, broadened my interests, my concerns for other people, the whole world! Maybe he does!

Oh, Kitty, you would love these children as I do! Lately I have been working in the nursery, where they bring the new orphans, some of them scarcely more than infants. Think of it . . . both parents dead, deprived of care, helpless to defend themselves. One baby has really crawled into my heart. She is a fragile little thing, her skin almost transparent, her eyes huge in her small pale face. Her name is Nicole, and she requires a great deal of care. It takes hours to feed her, and then she sometimes falls asleep in my arms, and I hold her . . . longer than I am supposed to. But she is so special.

Owen and I wanted lots of children. We talked about it often. I guess I'm substituting now for the life I thought I would have with Owen after the war. Owen used to quote the Bible, "Sufficient unto the day," along with a saying of his Quaker grandmother, "Be present where you are." That's what I'm trying to do. I feel this is where I'm supposed to be at this particular time. What God has for me next, I don't know.

Love always,
Cara

*   *   *

Eden Cottage
November, 1923

Dear Cara,

Richard is gone. He died peacefully in his sleep, holding my hand. I am numb, still hardly able to believe it has happened. Even though I thought I was prepared, even though I knew we were living on borrowed time, when the end finally came, it was almost impossible for me to grasp it.

He was given a military funeral with all the honors, but I felt cold and removed from it. I saw no glory in the war. I saw too many die. Such a waste. Richard, particularly, with his brilliance, his talent, his zest for life. He had so much to give, and now he is dead.

I have been going over his poems. Not to be morbid but to feel I'd not completely lost him. It is in his poetry that Richard is most himself, the Richard I knew and loved. Most of these poems are unpublished, although the few that were published received critical reviews. But he was a perfectionist, and I can see the many corrections and rewrites he did. Reading them in this form leaves me astonished and in awe. Who knows what he might have become, given his allotted fourscore and ten?

Believe me, Twin, I'm not wallowing in self-pity. I am going on with my life, grateful for having known and loved a wonderful man, knowing without doubt that he loved me, too. I am going to close the cottage. I don't think I can live here again. Not by myself and certainly not with anyone else.

Do keep me in your prayers. I see a long, lonely road ahead and I need all the love and support of my friends, family, especially yours, my dear Twin.

Always,
Kitty

*   *   *

Paris, France
April 1924

Dear Kitty,

Everything is in bloom over here now. The garden is lovely. Not, of course, to compare with the one at Cameron Hall but beautiful in its own way. I am just grateful the dreary winter is over, and the children can go outside to play.

It's amazing to me that French children play the same games we played as children, called by different names, of course. It is wonderful to watch them play, hear the chatter and laughter of the little ones who have lost so much. Of course, they don't fully realize their loss. The orphanage is all they know. It is their home. But I sometimes wonder what their fate will be when they are too old to stay here any longer. Most French families have been impoverished by the war, the husbands and fathers dead, so there haven't been many adoptions. No one can afford another mouth to feed. War is so insane. The scars never seem to heal.

As you can imagine, my days are full and busy. I did, however, have a week off and went over to see Aunt Garnet at Birchfields. Bryanne was also home for the holidays, and I met her English governess, Jillian Marsh. She has one of those peaches-and-cream complexions that American girls all envy and eyelashes one would die for! But besides all that, she is a lovely person, all warmth and charm. I tried to persuade Aunt Garnet to take Bryanne to Virginia next fall but could get no firm commitment from her. She used my bringing up the subject to launch into her usual tirade about Jeff. So it seems hopeless. The only thing I would suggest is to let Lynette come to England for a visit.

I wish you could see Nicole, my particular "pet" at the orphanage. She is so cunning, Kitty, and so bright. We are not supposed to have favorites among the children, and I try not to, but she is such a darling!

You mentioned Kip's being at loose ends. Why doesn't he get hold of himself? We've all been dealt terrible blows by the War. But at least he has a child, which is more than either of us can say. The trouble with Kip . . . no, I'm not going to get into that! I have a tendency to criticize, as Owen used to point out gently. Sometimes he would quote Scripture to me, Matthew 7:3 especially: "Why do you look at the speck in your brother's eye, but do not consider the plank in your own?" Well, I have plenty of "planks" in mine! I do love Kip—you and I have known and put up with his foibles since childhood—and I sympathize with his losing Etienette, but he has more to live for than many other survivors of that tragic time.

If you see him, give him my best anyway. I really mean that.

Love,
Cara

chapter
6

Summer 1925
Cameron Hall

THE SUMMER after her graduation from Dunbarton, Lynette's spirits had never been lower. Frustrated in her attempt to achieve her heart's goal of reuniting her brother and sister as a family, she felt miserably isolated.

Her plan to get a teaching certificate had been tacitly accepted by the family, and she enrolled at Teachers College for the fall semester. It was a long and difficult year for Lynette. Postcards and infrequent letters from Bryanne further dampened her hopes that Grandmother Devlin would ever give Brynnie the freedom to return to Virginia. Maybe not until her sister was twenty-one and could make her own decisions. Even this last letter, while heartening to learn of Brynnie's relief in leaving the girls' school, suggested that the European tour would be only another delay tactic staged by their grandmother. Who knew how long they would be traveling?

At the end of the term, Lynette went home to Mayfield, almost dreading the long summer stretching ahead. Then, quite unexpectedly, Frank Maynard entered her life again, and suddenly everything changed.

Their first encounter years before had been happenstance. Or was it? Lynette had often wondered afterward. She had nearly given up hope that anything would ever develop from her schoolgirl crush. Their

51

meetings had been few and far between, usually in some social setting crowded with other people. Then one day a few weeks after Lynette's graduation, they met by accident.

Time had hung heavy on her hands since her return. She was not interested in joining the Mayfield social scene, nor was she ready for the many church and charity activities that occupied her Grandmother Blythe.

Driving home one day after doing some errands for her grandmother, Lynette, on impulse, took the old county road instead of the newly paved one. Spotting a sign that read "ESTATE SALE AND AUCTION TODAY" at the end of a drive leading to one of the older homes, she decided to stop and investigate.

Browsing among the boxes of books spread out among clocks, dishes, and other assorted miscellany of household goods on the wide lawn, she heard someone call her name and turned to find Frank looking both surprised and pleased to see her. They talked a while, discussing the items for sale and exchanging a few pleasantries. Afterward, both armed with a varied selection of purchases—an old fan and a Dresden shepherdess for Lynette, mostly books for Frank—he walked with her to her car.

When he discovered that she had not yet eaten lunch, he asked if she would like to go with him to the small country inn nearby. Intrigued with each other, they found that their differences seemed to melt away during the lunch, which lasted nearly three hours.

After that day Frank and Lynette spent many summer afternoons together. From the first, they found each other totally compatible, the difference in age the only problem, and that only for Frank. Gradually as their feelings for each other grew, there was a blending of two devoted hearts, two searching souls; two minds, intelligent and inquisitive; two personalities, quiet and trusting.

They met often on Sunday afternoons for the band concerts in Mayfield Park, then went for a soda afterward. They attended other auctions, browsed in bookstores, went canoeing on the river. Since both loved the written word, notes flowed between them, filled with shared thoughts, quotations, poetry, all the things that meant the most to each of them. Lynette's joy was boundless in this new, unexpected happiness. Even the concern of her aborted family reunion became less worrisome.

Then one day she received a letter from Frank in which he wrote: "To tell you of my deepest feelings, I have stolen from the poet we both admire, John Keats." Then followed the borrowed lines: *"I never knew before what such a love as you have made me feel, was; I did not believe in it.* Though Keats wrote these words, I hope you will accept the sentiment as my own."

She did, with joy! Nothing seemed more natural to her now than loving Frank Maynard. Having recently discovered the poetry of Elizabeth Barrett, who wrote of her love for Robert Browning, she answered Frank's letter, enclosing a poem from *Sonnets from the Portuguese,* adding, "We are both borrowers, Frank."

By the end of the summer, they were deeply in love. Unwilling to let the world intrude on their newfound happiness, however, it was still their secret.

Marriage had not been mentioned. Frank, who was still trying to establish his law practice in Mayfield, did not yet feel financially secure enough to ask Lynette to marry him. It was at this point in their relationship that an unexpected opportunity presented itself.

While walking in the woods one brilliant fall afternoon, Frank mentioned it to Lynette. "Mr. Bryan Creighton, one of the partners in the law firm I worked for in Richmond, is urging me to run for office. State senator. How would you feel about that? Since I'm not known everywhere in the district, it would mean months of hard work. I'd have to do quite a bit of traveling, talking to folks, gaining visibility. I'd be away from Mayfield most of the time until the June election."

Lynette did her best to conceal her disappointment. "I'd miss you, Frank," she said carefully. "And I really don't know anything about politics. But I'm sure you'd be wonderful at whatever you choose to do."

Frank reached out and touched her cheek with the palm of his hand. "Ah, Lynette, every aspiring office holder should have someone like you to encourage him." He sighed. "I'm not sure it's something I really want to do, though. But my family has always been patriotic. And it seems like a good chance to do something that might make an important difference. This part of Virginia has been depressed for a long time. I'd like to help bring it back."

"And you could, Frank. I know you could," she said loyally. "Virginia needs men with ideals."

"Well, I'd like to talk to Scott about it before I decide."

Lynette nodded. "Yes, that would be a good idea. Scott is smart and he knows this area. He could help you a great deal if you decide to run."

"And if I do, and if I win . . . would you mind being a senator's wife?"

Lynette's eyes widened and brightened. "You mean . . . ?"

"Yes, my darling, I'm asking you to be my wife . . . whether or not I'm elected senator. I just wanted to be sure you didn't mind."

"Mind? Why should I mind? But do you really mean it, Frank? You don't think I'm too young?"

He laughed softly and drew her close, kissing her protesting lips. "I think you're exactly the right age." He kissed her again, a lingering kiss, and after releasing her reluctantly, he said, "Should I tell Scott about us?"

"I don't think so," she said. "Not yet. Let's keep it our secret just a little longer." The idea of sharing their bliss was frightening to Lynette. What if something should happen to change their beautiful plans?

Shaking off the thought, Lynette forced herself to think only of the moment. Suddenly another dream seemed possible. Lynette confided to Frank her hope of bringing Bryanne to America to reunite their little family. "Even though it seems almost too late for us ever to be a real family again, I do want us to get to know each other."

Frank, who was an only child and had grown up with his own brand of loneliness, was empathic. He not only promised to help Lynette accomplish her goal but suggested that Brynnie could live with them after they married.

"Of course, we'll have to wait, darling," he said gently, "until after the election. But win or lose, we will be married."

Frank's declaration of love burst upon Lynette like spring sunshine after a long, dark winter. She wanted to bask in its warmth, its promise. Frank filled all the emptiness that had existed since her mother's death.

But she was glad they were going to keep their promise to each other a secret for a while longer. In this family, any decision brought a myriad of unsolicited opinions and advice. She was particularly apprehensive of the objections her famous father or her formidable Grandmother Devlin might put up if she told them now. She could just imagine their arguments. Frank was too old for her. His law practice was not yet solid enough to ensure a secure future for her.

But if he were to become a state senator—now that would make all the difference. She relished the satisfaction she would gain in making *that* announcement. The only thing that really mattered was that Frank loved her. However long she had to wait for all her dreams to be realized to their fullest—home, husband, children, even the delayed family reunion—Lynette was willing. Frank was well worth the wait.

Part III

New York City
September 1925

chapter

7

CRYSTAL KIRK was finally ready to leave. Everything had been done. Car packed, telephone service and electricity turned off, milk and newspaper delivery temporarily discontinued, instructions left with the landlady for mail to be held.

With the long trip to Mayfield, Virginia, ahead of her, she was hoping to get an early start and avoid the heavy morning traffic. She slipped on a cinnamon suede jacket over her beige sweater and skirt and picked up her overnight bag. In the hall she stopped in front of the mirror to pull on a brown felt cloche. Suddenly she leaned forward to inspect her reflection more closely. One hand moved up uncertainly to touch her hair. Had she made a horrible mistake?

Frowning, she confronted the result of the impulsive decision to cut her waist-length hair. It had seemed a good idea at the time. Short hair would be so much easier to manage while traveling, the operator at the beauty salon had persuaded her. Why not a Dutch-bob recently made popular by the screen star, Colleen Moore?

Crystal studied herself critically. Was it really all that becoming on *her*? Unlike the glamorous brunette actress, her hair was the color of sun-ripened wheat. She had hazel eyes, a nose she had always considered too short, and a mouth that was a little too wide. This new hairstyle made her look even younger than her twenty-eight years. In fact, she looked more like Buster Brown than Colleen Moore. How had she allowed herself to be talked into such a foolish thing?

Well, it was too late to do anything about it. What did it matter, anyway? She didn't know anyone in Mayfield except the Dabneys. Besides, this was to be a period of intense work, not a holiday.

She jammed on her hat and turned away from the mirror to take a last look around her New York apartment. Unexpectedly, she felt a strange reluctance to leave. With her hand on the doorknob, she paused. Why this puzzling feeling? Had she forgotten something? Left something undone?

For months she had been planning this trip. She had received a generous advance from a prestigious travel magazine for a photography project. The assignment was a real feather in her cap as a professional photographer. Why now did she feel this hesitancy?

These four rooms had been home for the past five years. She had come here soon after Sandy's death. Her war correspondent husband had been killed just before the Armistice in 1918, leaving her a widow at twenty-two. Her gaze swept the living room, its windows overlooking Washington Square and the park, the white plastered walls hung with some of her own photographs—the New England landscapes for which she was becoming known, tastefully framed. The spare modern interior with its clean-lined furnishings suited the pared-down life she had been living, a life some might call monastic.

Partly to survive, partly to fulfill her own ambitions, Crystal had concentrated on perfecting her craft. She had worked hard, struggling to attain recognition in a field where there were still relatively few women. Focusing on her career had cut down on her social life. But since she had no plans to remarry, she had no qualms about turning down invitations to parties or dinner dates with eligible men. During the last two years, she had gradually begun to reap some success in her chosen career. Her photographs had won several awards, and a gallery was interested in sponsoring an exhibit.

Coincidentally, the idea for this project that she had sold to *Vagabond* had its inception years before when visiting her college roommate, Sue Dabney, in Virginia. On that visit she had noticed many impressive antebellum mansions that were falling apart due to abandonment and neglect.

"Most of these families date back to the War Between the States," Sue's mother had told her. "And of course nobody can maintain those huge old homes anymore. Why, some of those households required twenty house servants to keep them up. Honey! Who can afford that kind of help nowadays?"

Driving along the back roads around Mayfield, Crystal had been dismayed to see that many of the mansions were fast becoming architectural derelicts. Her artistic interest was spurred, her sensibilities aroused to think that every vestige of these plantations, once small worlds unto themselves, was rapidly vanishing. Soon there would be no trace of them, no evidence that they had ever existed, and with them a whole lifestyle—a gentler, more leisurely era—would pass from the American scene. Something should be done to save them, Crystal decided.

Now, she thought with satisfaction, *something is going to be done, and I'm going to do it!* Her idea—a picture-story on antebellum mansions in the South—had been accepted by *Vagabond* magazine. On imperishable film she would capture lasting portraits of these stately homes before they disappeared forever.

So why was she standing here, paralyzed with indecision? Her small station wagon was parked at the curb outside the apartment building. All she had to do was walk outside and be on her way.

Yet an unsettling premonition gripped her. She felt almost as if she were saying good-bye, as if this were the end of something. What nonsense! She would only be gone for a month, six weeks at the most.

Quickly she gathered up her camera bag and portable tripod, then taking a final look around, she pressed the deadbolt, went out, and closed and locked the door behind her.

Crystal drove slowly up the long, winding drive. Directly ahead stood a stately Georgian mansion, perfectly maintained, set like a jewel on a sweep of velvety green lawn. Coming to a stop in front, she gazed up at it in awe. This was certainly *not* one of the "sad old ladies" she had come to photograph. This must be exactly how it had looked when handsome carriages arrived here in colonial days, bringing elegantly dressed guests to balls and celebrations.

So complete was the illusion that Crystal would not have been surprised if the rapping of the polished brass knocker had summoned a white-wigged, liveried butler. Instead, the door was opened by a thoroughly modern young woman of about her own age, casually dressed in a kelly-green sweater and plaid skirt. Her rich copper-colored hair was bobbed, her brown eyes warm.

"Mrs. Cameron?" Crystal asked.

The young woman smiled. "No, I'm her daughter, Kitty Traherne."

The name registered immediately. This was Sue's friend, the one who had married a war veteran and was recently widowed. It was *her* small house the Dabneys had suggested that Crystal might be able to rent during her stay. They had understood that it had stood empty since her husband's death more than a year ago.

"Oh, well, let me introduce myself. I'm Crystal Kirk. I'm a houseguest of the Dabneys and . . ."

"Yes, of course, Sue phoned about you. Won't you come in?"

"Forgive me for intruding on you at a busy time," Crystal said, following the woman through a magnificent hallway and into a parlor. "Susan tells me you're leaving for Europe in a few days."

"It's quite all right, and yes, I'm going to France to visit my sister there."

They settled in two comfortable chairs flanking a marble fireplace, and Crystal got right to the point. "Well, I'm sure you have a great deal to do, so I'll be brief. You see, I'm a photographer, and I'm looking for a place to stay while I'm on assignment. Sue said you might consider renting yours."

"How long do you plan to stay in Mayfield, Miss Kirk?"

"It's *Mrs.* Kirk. I'm a widow," Crystal corrected quietly and saw a flash of sympathy in the other woman's eyes. "I expect to be here a month or six weeks. It really depends on how my search for subjects goes. It's been quite a while since I've been in this area, and I'm not sure if what I'm planning to photograph still exists. My idea is to capture on film some of the beautiful old plantation houses before it's too late . . . so many are disappearing. . . ."

Kitty nodded. "I know what you mean. Isn't it a shame? Some of them are falling to pieces, with the original owners long gone and no one else able to buy them or to maintain them without a large staff of servants."

"Not this one, though," Crystal said, glancing about the room with undisguised appreciation. "This house is wonderful!"

"Yes. Fortunately, except for a few years right after the War Between the States, it has been kept up. It is one of the few homes that has remained in the same family since it was built." She paused. "Well, it sounds as if you have an interesting few weeks planned, Mrs. Kirk. And yes, I was hoping to rent the cottage while I'm away. It would be nice to have someone in it. Would you like to see it now?"

"Oh, yes, I would!"

"Then I'll get the keys and we can walk over there. Eden Cottage is just through the woods."

She disappeared and Crystal took a moment to assess her surroundings—the creamy paneling, the polished mahogany Chippendale tables, the ornate frame displaying what must be a family portrait of earlier days hanging over the fireplace. Soon Kitty was back, a ring of keys rattling in her hand. "Come along. It's such a lovely afternoon, it will be a nice walk."

As they started down the drive, a handsome Irish setter bounded from the side of the house, his plume of a tail wagging.

"This is Tamish, my dog," Mrs. Traherne explained, bending to stroke his glossy russet coat. "He'll lead the way. He knows it well. My husband and I lived there for nearly five years, up until a few months before his death."

As they passed a well-tended garden, a tall, auburn-haired woman in a gardening smock waved a gloved hand. Returning the wave, Kitty explained, "My mother, Blythe Cameron. You'll meet her later."

They walked on in silence, then turned off a worn path leading into the woods. Tamish, like a red streak, preceded them.

"He thinks he's going home." Kitty smiled. "He was devoted to Richard, keeps thinking he'll be back. . . ." Her words ended in a long sigh, and Crystal felt her pain. Even though Sandy had been dead nearly seven years, there were still moments when she missed him terribly.

As they came upon a clearing in the woods, Mrs. Traherne pointed. "There it is. Eden Cottage."

In the distance Crystal could see a dusty-pink-brick-and-white-clapboard cottage nestled under towering trees, a flagstone path zigzagging up to the porch. The dog dashed ahead, circling the house and sniffing the corners.

"He still thinks we live here," Kitty said. "I guess he's looking for Richard." She whistled for Tamish, and he came panting up to her. Putting both hands under his muzzle, she looked down into those pleading eyes and said quietly, "Take your place, Tamish, and *stay*."

The dog turned and trotted obediently to a spot near the gate. Then with a sigh that was almost human, he flopped down and put his head between his paws.

To lighten the poignancy of the moment, Crystal gestured toward the house. "It looks charming."

"Wait until you see it inside. You'll be better able to tell if it's what you want. A few years ago I had the place rewired and installed a modern kitchen and bathroom. But until we moved in, the house had remained the same as when the last bride of Montclair lived here."

"Bride of Montclair?"

Kitty smiled. "Montclair is the Montrose family's home about half a mile through the woods from here. Eden Cottage was originally the architect's model for that house. Traditionally it became the 'honeymoon house' where the sons of the family brought their new brides to live for the first year of their marriage, or until they had families of their own and needed more space."

Kitty Traherne took the key ring out of her jacket pocket and went on talking as she looked for the right key to unlock the front door. "Although the house stands on land once owned by the Montrose family, it was deeded to me, along with three acres surrounding the cottage."

Finding the key and without further explanation, Kitty stepped up onto the porch and unlocked the door. Pushing it open, she beckoned, "Come on in."

Crystal followed Kitty slowly through the rooms of the compact, yet spacious little house. Everything—the furnishings, the exquisite appointments—was in scale and spoke of impeccable taste and loving care. "It's perfect! A dream cottage."

Watching her reaction, Kitty felt suddenly choked with emotion. She hadn't expected this.

Crystal caught the expression of grief on the other woman's face and knew how difficult it must be for her to allow another person to take possession, even temporarily, of a place that obviously still meant so much to her. "Are you *sure* you want to rent it?" she asked with concern. "Have someone else living here?"

Kitty composed herself immediately. "That's very sensitive of you. Truthfully, I wasn't sure until now. But I can see you'll love living here, so I can release it without any regrets. I couldn't . . . *wouldn't* . . . rent to just anyone though." She smiled. "Sue is the one who said you'd be right for it. She said you were an artist and would appreciate the things Richard and I chose for this house."

"Not everyone considers photography art," Crystal told her with a rueful chuckle. "I studied art and painted before I became interested in photography. But now . . . well, photography *is* art to me. It's the way I express how I feel about the world, about life, about people and places. . . ." She broke off with a shrug. "But the debate goes on—photographer or artist?"

"I understand. Labels are confining, misleading, aren't they?" Kitty asked sympathetically. "My husband was a poet. He received quite a lot of recognition in the short time he published. He was called a war poet—like Rupert Brooke or Joyce Kilmer. Had he lived, I believe he would have been much, much more." She bit her lip and turned away, but not before Crystal had seen her eyes mist.

"I'm going outside now," she told Crystal, "and leave you alone in the house for a few minutes. You need to get the feel of it, to know that it will belong to you for a time."

Crystal moved around the rooms again. As she did so, she felt a subtle warmth, a serenity steal over her, permeating her very core. The fatigue brought on by the tension of the long trip, the uncertainty of her quest, eased away. In a strange way, she felt she had truly come "home."

When she came out onto the porch, stepping into a patch of late-afternoon sunshine, she found Kitty Traherne sitting on the steps, stroking Tamish's head in her lap.

"I'd really like to take this, Mrs. Traherne," Crystal said. "That is, if you agree."

Kitty nodded. "I'm glad. I think you'll be happy here."

"I do, too. I can't explain it, but the house has such a—a welcoming feel."

"That's what Richard always said. That houses have personalities just like people and whoever lives in a house leaves an imprint. That's why, when he knew he didn't have much longer to live, he wanted to go to the hospital." She gave a wistful smile. "He didn't want the house where we had been so happy to record any suffering or sorrow or tears."

Later, driving back to the Dabneys, the keys to Eden Cottage in her purse, Crystal felt like singing. She could not remember having been this happy in a long time. She knew she was going to love living in that little house. It would be the perfect sanctuary for her, giving her the peace and privacy she needed for the work ahead of her.

Crystal also felt a renewed optimism about her project. Living in the little cottage in the woods, with years of tradition and history in its very walls, she would get a real feeling for the South she had come to photograph, to capture before it all slipped away and disappeared forever. This would be her finest work. She knew it!

chapter
8

"WHO WAS THAT I passed on the way in? The Ford station wagon with New York license plates?" asked Scott Cameron as he came in the front door.

"My new tenant," replied his sister Kitty, who was just crossing the hall into the library. She paused. "I've rented Eden Cottage."

About to hang up his jacket, Scott halted, looking surprised. "You *have?*"

"Yes. To a friend of Sue Dabney's."

"What made you decide to do that?" He was curious, knowing how much the small house meant to her. She had closed it after Richard's death, and as far as anyone knew, had never gone back.

"Come on in here and I'll tell you about it," Kitty called over her shoulder as she walked into the book-lined room where a fire had just taken flame. She stood with her back to the hearth, waiting for her older brother to join her. As he entered, Kitty was sharply reminded of their late father, Rod, whose portrait, painted at his prime, commanded a prominent place in the room. Both men had the same wavy russet hair, the same strong aquiline noses, the same truth-seeking eyes.

Without Scott's having to repeat his question, she answered him. "I thought it was a good idea. Healthy, too. Emotionally healthy, I mean," she announced firmly. "Richard would never have wanted me to keep the cottage as a kind of shrine."

"Good thinking," Scott said briskly, then more gently, "I'm proud of you, little sis."

"That house has a long history of happiness and shouldn't be closed up just as we shouldn't be closed," Kitty went on matter-of-factly. "I've come to believe we should be open to whatever life brings. I'd like to think someone else can be happy there."

It was evident to Scott that Kitty had given the matter a great deal of thought. "So who is this mysterious renter?"

"She seems to be a very interesting lady, a professional photographer."

Scott tapped his forehead with the heel of his hand in mock dismay. "Oh, no!"

"Now, wait," Kitty protested. "Let me finish. . . ."

"You forget, I run a newspaper. I've worked with photographers. I *know* their type—temperamental, ornery, hard to get along with—you name it!"

"She's not at all like that, Scott. She's very pleasant and, I might add, quite pretty."

"A *pretty* photographer?" Scott moaned. "Spare me!"

"What's going on in here?" asked an amused voice. "The way you two are going on, it sounds like old times."

Brother and sister turned toward the doorway, where Blythe Cameron stood looking from one to the other. Her smile traced tiny lines around her sensitive mouth. Although past middle age, she retained a youthful grace and her rich auburn hair was as yet untouched by silver. The gray knit dress she was wearing was brightened by a persimmon scarf, tied at an angle over one shoulder.

"'Evening, Mother." Scott went over, kissing the cheek she turned to him, while Kitty moved a cushion on the sofa to make room for Blythe to sit down beside her. "Kitty was just telling me she's rented Eden Cottage . . . and to a female photographer, of all things!" he added with an air of disbelief.

"Scott's being difficult, Mama." Kitty laughed. "But he'll change his tune when he meets her."

"Yes, I think he just might." Blythe cast a speculative glance at her son.

At thirty-seven, although attractive, intelligent, and with an ironic but not caustic sense of humor, Scott was still a bachelor. Unlike some veterans of the Great War, he had come home with a sense of purpose and determination. Within a few months he had purchased the failing *Mayfield Messenger* and had taken over the editorship of the paper. For the last few years, getting the local newspaper back on its feet had consumed all his time and effort. As far as Blythe could tell, there had been no time for romance. "That's right, Scott. Kitty tells me Mrs. Kirk is delightful. And I can vouch for her beauty."

Scott shook his head and smiled dismissively. "For how long have you rented the place, Kitty?"

"Just until I get back from France. Mrs. Kirk paid two months in advance, and I told her that if she left before then I'd refund her money."

"Well, I hope it works out . . . for your sake." Scott sounded doubtful. "That is, if she doesn't turn the bathroom into a darkroom."

"We've already covered that. She told me she intends to take all the negatives back to be developed in her studio in New York."

In spite of himself, Scott was interested. "What will she be photographing?"

"Old homes, plantations, churches, old buildings, that sort of thing. She has a contract with *Vagabond*."

"The travel magazine, eh?" Scott's tone was negative. "They tend to overplay everything. I can see the layout now. . . ." He squared his hands as if framing pictures. " 'The Picturesque Old South—Past Glories of the Fallen Confederacy' . . . et cetera, et cetera."

"Scott, you're so—so . . ."

"So *what?*" His smile broadened to a grin.

"I don't know . . . iconoclastic, maybe!"

"Not at all. I just don't like the idea of some Northern opportunist making money at the expense of a South that's digging itself out of fifty years of economic depression imposed by . . ."

"Please, Scott!" Kitty cut him off. "Save it for one of your editorials. For pity's sake, let's change the subject."

"All right, little Sis," her brother conceded with a smile. "Having the place occupied is a good thing."

"I agree, Kitty. As usual, you've made the wise and practical decision." Blythe patted her daughter's hand fondly. "Well, Scott, what's new at the *Messenger?*"

"Why does that question somehow strike me as redundant?" he teased. "What's new at a newspaper? Why, *news,* of course! Seriously, though, there's nothing new I can print yet. We don't have verification, but there's a strong rumor that Senator Wilcox is going to resign before his term is out."

Blythe looked surprised. "But why would he do that?"

Scott shrugged. "Good question."

"He's been here forever, hasn't he?" Kitty asked. "At least as long as I can remember."

"That's right. And that's part of the problem. There are a lot of people who feel he's been coasting, not really representing the area. Things have been changing, and he hasn't kept up. Talk is, he's gotten much too comfortable in the job, likes going on junkets, and spends more time on the golf course than he does in his office. More damaging is the common knowledge that he has a few cronies he favors and isn't above handing out political plums. Nobody's proved anything. At least, not yet. But even if the rumor about his resignation isn't true, he's going to have some stiff opposition when he comes up for reelection."

Scott rose from the chair he'd taken by the fire. "If you ladies will excuse me, I think I'll take a walk down to the stables and see how Sean's doing." Sean McShane was the young Irish man, son of Rod Cameron's old horse-breeding friend, who had recently been hired as the head trainer for Cameron Hall Stables. "That is, if I have time before dinner, Mother."

Blythe waved him off. "Run along, dear. And do ask Sean to join us, won't you? I don't like to think of his eating alone so much."

"I don't think Sean minds that at all." Scott grinned. "I suppose, if you'd grown up in a home with five rowdy brothers, you'd enjoy a solitary meal once in a while yourself, Mother!"

"Yes. He seems perfectly content in Dad's old apartment above the stables," Kitty added. "He has his radio and his books, and he can come and go as he pleases."

"Well, perhaps, but ask him anyway, Scott," Blythe insisted.

Scott promised to do that, and left the two women sitting by the fire. When he was gone, Blythe said to Kitty, "What a shame Scott didn't want to take over the running of the stables himself after your father died."

"But, Mama, it's working out perfectly now that Sean's here. I'm sure Daddy would be pleased with the arrangement. Dan McShane was one of his oldest, closest friends, and he loved all the boys. But Sean was his favorite, and you know he was practically born on a horse! I think it's the best thing that could have happened after Scott decided to buy the *Messenger*."

"Yes, but . . ." Blythe looked thoughtful. "Rod so hoped that his son . . ."

"I know, Mama. Daddy might have been disappointed at first, but I think he'd also be very proud of what Scott's done with the paper. It's won awards, you know, for being one of the outstanding small-town newspapers in the state." Then she added, "And I really think Sean loves it here."

"I suppose you're right, dear." She knew that it had been Rod's dream to have his son follow in his footsteps. Of course, he had first wanted Blythe's son by her first marriage to Malcolm Montrose to come in with him. But Jeff had been determined to pursue a career in art. That decision had caused a rift between the stepfather and son that had never been fully bridged. Then Rod had pinned his hopes on Scott, only to be thwarted once more. Blythe suppressed a sigh. If life had taught her anything, it was that one cannot make one's adult children's decisions for them.

"Where's Lynette?" Kitty asked, changing the subject. "I haven't seen her since early afternoon."

Kitty's question brought to Blythe's mind another troubling problem. "She went over to Avalon. Jeff and Gareth are leaving for Taos next week and she wanted to spend some time with them . . . with her brother, anyway." Blythe frowned. "I think she took some of her watercolors to show her father, but she may be too shy to do it."

"Well, no wonder!" Kitty declared in exasperation. "Jeff doesn't encourage her, Mama. Calls them 'pretty little paintings' when she wants more from him. She wants to be taken seriously, needs some constructive help. I can't understand why Jeff—" She broke off, knowing that criticism of her half-brother was a touchy subject.

Blythe had always been defensive of her firstborn. Had reason to be, since Jeff had always been self-absorbed and had become even more so since the death of his wife years ago. The explanation that he was a well-known artist preoccupied with his career was no excuse, in Kitty's mind. Other people had been hurt, she knew—his children, most especially.

As if picking up on her daughter's secret thoughts, Blythe remarked, "A letter came for Lynette today from Bryanne. And I got a postcard from her, too. Here, I'll show it to you."

"Where are they now?"

"In Italy. Venice, I think. At least that was the postmark on the card."

"Doesn't Aunt Garnet ever plan to bring Brynnie back?" Kitty's voice was edged with bitterness.

"Of course!" Blythe said generously. "She's written that she has inquired at Miss Dunbarton's about enrolling her next year."

"*Next year!*" Kitty was incredulous and started to say something more, then appeared to think better of it. She rose from the sofa and went over to the fireplace, her whole body rigid with anger. One hand on her hip, she placed the other on the mantelpiece, tapping her fingers impatiently. Then she turned around and held out her hand. "Let me see what she says." Taking the card her mother handed her, she read it, then handed it back, saying indignantly, "I think it's absolutely criminal that those three have been separated all this time! I'm sure Faith would hate it!"

Blythe threw out her hands in a helpless gesture. "There wasn't anything we could do about it, Kitty. The war, you know . . ."

"Oh, Mama, the *war* . . . it was over nearly five years ago! You know perfectly well that something could have been arranged. Bryanne is almost seventeen and hardly knows any of us . . . not even her own brother and sister!"

At the pained expression on her mother's face, Kitty was contrite. She came over and gave Blythe a hug. "I'm sorry, Mama. I know how badly you feel about it. It's Jeff and Aunt Garnet who are to blame! They resent each other so much, and Lynette and Gareth and Bryanne have been the pawns in their tug of war."

"But Jeff . . . you know, he was just devastated after Faith's death."

"Yes, but he's their *father!* He could have done something, should have tried anyway."

"Well, he *did* take Gareth with him to New Mexico. . . ."

Kitty started to say something else but knew this discussion would go nowhere and only cause her mother more distress. At that moment they heard the slam of the front door and running feet along the polished floor outside the library.

"That must be Lynette." Blythe cast a significant glance at her daughter. "Now, Kitty, don't express your feelings in front of *her*."

A moment later a tall, dark-haired young woman came into the library. "I'm home, Gram, Kitty."

"Hello, darling," Blythe welcomed her. "There's a letter on the hall table for you. From Brynnie."

"Oh, wonderful!" Her face brightened. Lynette turned and ran out of the room.

Picking up the pink envelope with its foreign stamp, she dashed upstairs to read the letter in the privacy of her own room. She would share portions of the letter with the whole family later. But sometimes

Brynnie wrote of things that should be kept just between the two of them. After all, sisters sometimes needed to confide in each other.

She settled herself on the window seat and began to read:

Dearest Lynette,

I think Grandmama really means it this time. She isn't studying travel brochures or asking fellow guests at the hotel about this tour or that cruise. I don't see how she can put it off any longer, do you? She has run out of excuses, I think.

I'm tired of being "educated, polished, cultur-ized" or whatever Grandmama thinks she has been doing with me these last few years. Of course, Jillian is a love. You'll adore her, Lynette. However, she *is* Grandmama's employee, and she must put the best face on it when Grandmama decides something. She is fluent in French and Italian and manages all the tickets, the currency exchange, and sees that our luggage gets on the right train and nothing gets lost. She is truly a marvel and stays as cool as the proverbial cucumber under the most trying circumstances.

I honestly believe Grandmama would just as soon spend the spring at Birchfields. But her conscience must be bothering her, although she keeps blaming Father for our not being together. She says if he would only "settle down and provide a home for his children" . . . but we aren't children anymore, are we? And I've come to think Father is as "settled" as he will ever be. Would you want to go to New Mexico to live? In a way that sounds rather exciting—desert sunsets, cowboys, cactus, pueblos, Indians. Gareth sends me postcards from there when he visits.

But I must end this letter. Jillian just stuck her head in the door and says we have another cathedral or museum or something to go look at. Since I have to make a report every evening at dinner on my "cultural activities" of the day, I'd best close with much, much love.

> Always, your loving sister,
> Brynnie

Lynette folded the letter and put it back in the envelope, then went over to her desk, took out stationery, filled her fountain pen, and began to write a reply. She, too, had secrets to share.

chapter

9

CRYSTAL NAVIGATED her small station wagon from the county road onto the narrow lane that led through the woods to Eden Cottage. Braking to a stop, she leaned on the steering wheel and gazed at the little house. Nothing had changed in the week she had been in the area except that now it had a waiting, expectant look.

Eager to take possession, Crystal hurried up the flagged path onto the porch, fitted the key into the lock and turned it, almost holding her breath. Stepping inside, she stood motionless for a full minute, glancing around. Sunlight poured through the windows, gilding everything in its path—the fine antique furniture, the clock on the mantel, the hearth bricks and basket of logs beside it. She noticed that even a fire was laid in the fireplace, ready for the strike of a match to bring it to glowing life on the first cool evening.

Crystal felt embraced by warmth and welcome. Kitty Traherne was right. This house was an enchanted place—built with love, lived in with love, filled with love. What a miracle she had found it . . . even for a short while.

Two days later, Crystal entertained her first guest, Sue Dabney. Although she planned to maintain a strict working schedule, it seemed only fair to return Sue's hospitality and show her appreciation for the Dabneys' tip about the cottage.

Sue was equally as enthusiastic about the charms of Eden Cottage as Crystal. "I've never been inside before," she confessed. "When Kitty and her husband lived here, no one dared come unless invited. I was never a particular friend of Kitty's even though we all grew up here in Mayfield and moved in the same social circle. I was really closer to her twin."

Crystal was puzzled. "Twin? I knew she had a sister in France, but she didn't mention that they were twins."

"Yes . . . *Cara*," Sue said. "She was always much more outgoing and lively . . . a flirt, really."

"Well, Kitty seemed awfully friendly to me."

"Oh, she is, but Cara was . . . well, you'd have to have known her. She did surprise everyone, though, when she up and married a *minister* who became an army chaplain. Sadly enough, he died in the war . . . a hero. In fact, both twins have had similar tragedies. You see, Kitty was a Red Cross nurse and married one of her patients who had been badly wounded. He was confined to a wheelchair and, when they came here to Eden Cottage, they lived a kind of . . . reclusive life. I suppose she wanted to protect him as much as possible. Anyway, they were madly in love. Maybe they just didn't need anyone else."

She thought of her own early married life with Sandy—busy with their work, get-togethers with other young journalists and newspaper people, parties, trips—never a dull moment. In retrospect, she rather envied the different kind of life together the Trahernes must have enjoyed.

Almost as an afterthought, Crystal asked, "What is Kitty's twin doing now?"

"She's working in a war orphanage, of all things!" Sue shook her head as if she still couldn't believe it. "Doesn't sound anything like the Cara I used to know!"

Crystal grew pensive. "War changes people. Especially people who have lost someone dear."

Afraid she had brought up a sensitive topic, Sue quickly changed the subject. "Well, I'm certainly glad that Kitty agreed to rent this place to you."

"I am, too. And very grateful to you and your mother for suggesting it. You must have given me a good reference." Crystal laughed as she set down the tea tray she had prepared ahead of time.

"What lovely silver and china!" Sue exclaimed, helping herself to a cucumber sandwich. "Did Kitty leave all this for you to use?"

"Yes, she did, and I must admit I'm a little uneasy about using museum-quality pieces for everyday use. But she left me the dearest note, assuring me that this was my house as long as I'm here, and these lovely things are meant to be used." Crystal glanced around her with pleasure. "It seems almost too good to be true."

"And what about your work? Have you started photographing any of the houses here in Mayfield yet?"

"Well, I'm still getting settled, but I must get started soon. Still, there's something about this place . . . I'm afraid, like the Trahernes, I could be perfectly content to curl up here and shut out the rest of the world."

Sue looked aghast and held up her hand. "That would never do! I've told everyone about you, and my friends are anxious to meet you. They'll probably have some ideas for houses they think should be included in your collection." She took another sip of tea. "I assume Montclair will be one of them."

"I haven't seen it," Crystal confessed, refilling her cup.

Sue's eyes widened. "You haven't? I'm surprised. It's not very far from here, and since the house is on a hilltop, it can easily be seen through the woods . . . that is, when the trees are bare. . . ." She paused, then lifted her eyebrows quizzically. "I guess that means you haven't met its owner, either . . . Kip Montrose?"

Crystal shook her head. "Then we'll soon take care of *that!*" Sue declared. "You're invited to a party at Montclair on Saturday night— the unofficial opening of fox hunting season."

Crystal pursed her mouth. "I'm not very keen on meeting people who go around on horseback chasing defenseless little animals."

Sue gave her a curious look. "Well, you're in Virginia, and you know the old saying: 'When in Rome, do as the Romans do.' But seriously, you'll have to come. It will give you a chance to meet some of the people whose homes you'll be photographing. Besides, Kip's the hunt master this year and can give you a personal tour of his plantation. He's one of the lucky ones. Most of the families around here lost everything they had in the war."

Crystal suppressed a smile. She knew Sue wasn't talking about the recent World War. From past experience, she knew that Southerners often referred to the War Between the States as if it were only yesterday, instead of sixty years past.

At last Sue put down her teacup and got to her feet. "I really must be going. Now, remember we'll pick you up about seven on Saturday evening. I do hope you brought something smashing to wear. I've told everyone I was bringing my career-girl friend from *New York City,* so they all expect you to be glamorous and sophisticated!"

Crystal laughed. "I hope they know you well enough to know how you exaggerate!"

After she had waved Sue off in her bright yellow roadster, Crystal returned to the shoebox of a kitchen to wash and put away the delicate Imari teacups. Catching a flash of movement outside, she looked through the window over the sink and saw a horse and rider cantering across the rustic bridge in the direction of what must be Montclair. As she watched, he disappeared through the autumn foliage. Could that be Kip Montrose? Recalling Sue's enigmatic remark about him, Crystal felt a spark of curiosity. Maybe the hunt party on Saturday evening would be enjoyable, after all. At least, she'd get to see the legendary house and meet its owner.

chapter

10

KNOWING THAT her friend Sue would insist on including her in some social activities, Crystal had brought along one evening dress—an apricot crepe de chine sheath with a dropped waist, satin sash, and short, accordion-pleated skirt. The style was flattering to her boyishly slim figure and, now that she had gotten used to it, her new haircut looked right, too.

Her hair, silky as corn tassels, swung just below her ears. For the "glamorous" touch Sue had suggested, she added a string of amber beads and matching pendant earrings.

"That should do it," she said, stepping away from the full-length mirror to get a better view of her overall appearance.

In one way she wished she had not succumbed to Sue's insistence that she attend the festive opening of the hunting season. She hadn't felt like partying much since Sandy's death. However, she had to admit to a certain curiosity about Montclair *and* its master.

Just after dusk, Sue and her escort, Reid Langley, arrived to collect her. As they approached Montclair, a large harvest moon hovered overhead, paving the drive with mellow light. The house, a rather rambling structure, was not the typical antebellum mansion Crystal had envisioned. Instead, it appeared as if the owners had added to it at random. Lights spilled out of the tall windows that ran the length of the deep front porch, and the sound of music and laughter floated on the crisp night air as they came up the steps.

Inside, the house was alive with sparkling light and color. From the hallway above, a magnificent circular stairway curved gracefully into the entrance hall. The rich hue of the crimson carpet was duplicated a thousand times over in the cut-glass prisms of a huge chandelier suspended from the center of the ceiling. On either side of the foyer, doors opened into twin parlors.

Crystal only had time for a fleeting impression of pale yellow walls and fine furnishings because Sue was speaking to her in a low tone, "All this is fairly new. People say Kip has been spending a small fortune to restore this place. When he came home from France, his father, Jonathan Montrose, turned the plantation over to him, and they—Mr. Montrose and Kip's stepmother, Phoebe—have been living in Scotland. Anyway, I don't care about the gossip . . . It looks splendid, and overseeing the restoration certainly pulled Kip out of that awful depression he was in for a while after . . ."

Whatever Sue was about to reveal was abruptly cut off by the approach of a tall, dark-haired man, who was moving toward them with athletic grace. In a formal red hunting coat, collared in black velvet, and ruffled white shirt, he looked incredibly dashing.

"Susan and Reid, good to see you," he greeted them before his gaze shifted to include Crystal.

"You're looking marvelous, Kip!" Sue said, then bringing Crystal forward, "I want you to meet my friend, Crystal Kirk. She's down from New York and is practically your neighbor now."

"Happy to meet you." Kip reached out and took Crystal's hand. "Welcome to Virginia *and* to Montclair."

Crystal found herself studying the face of her host. Beyond his obvious good looks, it was an interesting one. Although tanned and unlined, some past experience had marked it; his eyes, even now as he laughed, shining with humor, still held a certain sadness. If she were into portraiture, she would like to photograph this face.

Crystal was snapped out of her reverie by Sue's next remark. ". . . and she'll probably want to photograph Montclair as well." Belatedly, she realized Sue was telling Kip why she had come to Mayfield.

"I'm delighted to hear that you're so interested in us, Miss Kirk," he said. "The South seems to be forgotten these days by most Northerners. Even by some of our own Southern congressmen and senators. Isn't that right, Scott?" Kip asked half-jokingly as a man with thick russet hair and a well-trimmed mustache sauntered by.

At Kip's comment, he stopped. "Do you want an editorial opinion or an off-the-cuff comment?" he drawled with a wry smile.

Sue wagged her finger playfully at both men. "Now, you two, no politics tonight!" Then, turning to Crystal, she introduced the new-comer. "Scott Cameron, the editor of our local newspaper, meet my guest, Crystal Kirk."

With his serious expression and his air of quiet authority, Crystal might have guessed Scott Cameron to be a professor, but an editor came close. Still, upon closer inspection, she detected the sparkle of humor in his brown eyes.

"Scott wields unbelievable influence in this county. You've heard the expression, 'The pen is mightier than the sword,' no doubt. Well, his pen can be mighty sharp at times . . . two-edged, one might say!" Kip said with a chuckle.

"I'm impressed." Crystal smiled, holding out her hand.

"I assure you, the *Messenger* is not the *New York Times,*" he replied diffidently.

"Nonetheless, your editorials carry a great deal of weight around here," Sue insisted. "Don't let this show of modesty on Scott's part delude you, Crystal."

"Well, of course, not *all* of us agree with the stands the *Mayfield Messenger* takes," Kip threw in.

"I'm well aware of your opinions, Kip. But why don't you make them public? You know we run a full page of Letters to the Editor once a week. You can vent your spleen on whatever issue you wish."

Kip smiled benignly. "Ah well, I try not to step on too many toes. That could be dangerous."

"Freedom of speech—isn't that what democracy is all about?" Scott countered. "I thought that's what we went to war to guarantee."

"Which war are we talking about?" Kip teased.

Reid jumped into the fray. "What's the issue? States' rights or Federal intervention?"

"Uh-oh! Enough!" Sue exclaimed, putting both hands over her ears. "This is a *party,* gentlemen! And remember, we have a guest who isn't used to this kind of sparring." Sue put her hand on Kip's arm. "Why don't you show Crystal around the house? You've done wonders with it."

"And, as I'm sure everyone is saying, spending money like the proverbial drunken sailor." Kip laughed. "Small towns, Miss Kirk, have no secrets. Coming from a big city, you probably wouldn't know that. But everyone here knows what you're up to and can't resist gossiping about it."

When another couple joined their group, Kip stopped to make introductions, and the conversation shifted to the next day's hunt. A portly older man cornered Scott, and someone called to Sue. She and Reid drifted off to chat, leaving Crystal alone with her host. She wasn't sure that Sue had not contrived it.

A little embarrassed, she told him, "Please don't feel obligated to look out for me, Mr. Montrose. I'm sure you have other guests you need to see, and I'm quite used to being on my own," she assured him. "I'll just wander around, if that's all right. In fact, I'd like to take a closer look at some of these portraits."

"First, I don't feel obligated in the least, Miss Kirk. I know most of these people, have since childhood, and they're almost as much at home here at Montclair as I am." He smiled down at her. "If it's any comfort to you, I'm indebted to Sue. She told me she was bringing someone special tonight. She failed to tell me, however, that it would be someone so attractive."

Automatically Crystal put up her guard. This must be the Southern charm she had heard so much about. But with Kip Montrose, such gallantry seemed natural. There was something youthfully unaffected about him.

"Besides," he went on, "I love showing off my home, talking about its history." He gestured toward the paintings in their ornate gilt frames, hanging in pairs all around the main hall. "These are all portraits of my ancestors' brides who became mistress here. Some were done by well-known artists of the day, I'm told. Although I must admit I don't know much about art myself. As a photographer, you would recognize the names, I'm sure."

He took Crystal's arm and led her around the hall, pointing out that each of the ladies' portraits was coupled with that of a man.

"We hung them in sets although they were probably painted at different times," he explained. "The ladies' portraits were usually painted before the wedding, often given as an engagement gift to the groom-to-be. Of course, there were some exceptions—for instance, if the identity of the prospective bride changed suddenly." When Crystal lifted a quizzical brow, he explained, "A case in point was the *first* bride of Montclair, who was actually a substitute for her cousin who eloped with another man, practically on the eve of the wedding." Kip looked amused. "A novelist would never run out of plots with our family history."

80

Pausing before another pair, he remarked, "I don't even know if these would be considered good paintings, either technically or artistically. They've just always been here, part of my growing up, part of my life . . . like Montclair itself."

He halted abruptly, as if the thought had just struck him and demanded, "By the way, what did Sue mean when she said you were almost my neighbor?"

"I'm renting the little house that borders your property—Eden Cottage." Was it her imagination that at her words, Kip's intensely blue eyes darkened? "Mrs. Traherne rented it to me before she left for Europe."

"Ah, yes, of course. Kitty," Kip said, his mouth tightening. Then he shrugged off the sudden mood change. "Why don't we get some punch and find some place to sit down so we can get better acquainted. I'm very interested in hearing more about your project." He led her into the curved alcove off the large front parlor, then excused himself.

While he was gone, Crystal looked around, getting more of a perspective on the house. Sue had intimated that the mansion had been newly decorated. Looking through the archway into a large drawing room, Crystal noted the pale yellow walls, fine Victorian furniture, an ornate marble fireplace over which hung a huge, gold-framed mirror. At one end of the room, a small band was playing, providing music for some dancing couples. In the room where Kip had gone to find refreshments, she caught a glimpse of a long table spread with a yellow cloth, of masses of gold chrysanthemums, and white and yellow tapers in great silver candelabra.

Kip was soon back with two glasses. He handed her one. "Now, I want to hear all about you. So you're a photographer. That's an unusual profession for a woman, isn't it?"

"I don't know if it's as *unusual* as it is *new*," Crystal said with a smile. "I went to art school, taking all the traditional art courses. Then when I graduated, I tried painting portraits for a living. But I found portrait-painting to be limiting and confining." She made a little grimace. "With portraits, there are always the families to please—the aunts and uncles and cousins, too—and there is *always* something wrong with the mouth!"

Kip threw back his head and laughed heartily. Crystal joined in somewhat sheepishly. "I guess I didn't have the right temperament for pleasing people, particularly people with inflated egos, or an entirely distorted view of what they or their relatives really look like."

"I can see you're a woman with definite ideas, Miss Kirk." Kip's eyes twinkled with as much admiration as amusement.

"I suppose going into photography was testing an alternative. I started experimenting on my own with a small box camera at first, snapping people, places, trying different angles, various effects. I found it quite rewarding. Fun, really."

Kip arched a brow. "Fun? I never heard anyone describe their work as fun."

"If it isn't fun, why do it?" Crystal countered. "If your work doesn't give you some joy, some fulfillment, life becomes dull, colorless, bleak."

He narrowed his eyes appraisingly. "But what if one has no choice but to do what's been preordained for him . . . or her?"

"Nonsense! One always has a choice."

"Not always. Sometimes life hands you something you can't refuse."

"You can't live out other people's expectations of you. You have to be true to yourself," Crystal insisted firmly.

Kip regarded her with a curiously steady gaze. "You're an extraordinary woman." Then he broke into a sly smile. "But I think we're being much too serious on an evening like this. Come, let's go out on the veranda. It will be cooler and less crowded, and you can see the garden by moonlight."

Crystal felt a small warning sensation, light as a butterfly fluttering. His suggestions sounded too intimate, too romantic. But Kip was already on his feet, holding out his hand to her, and she took it. They went out onto the moon-shadowed porch and walked over to the balustrade. From there they could see the garden paths and flowerbeds, etched in a milky mist.

Kip was standing so near that she was suddenly more aware of him than of her surroundings. Frightened by her own feelings, she moved away. Her heart was pounding wildly, and she walked to the other end of the porch to calm herself. To her infinite relief, she heard familiar voices and turned to see Sue and Reid coming out through the French doors onto the veranda. Her moment of panic lifted. When Reid asked Crystal to dance, she accepted and went inside with him, leaving Sue with Kip.

Reid introduced her to several other young men, and the evening passed pleasantly enough as she went from partner to partner, making light conversation. But beneath her surface gaiety, Crystal knew her time with Kip Montrose had been significant. For some reason she was sure their meeting had been no casual encounter.

At the end of the evening, when she and Sue went to say their good-byes to their host, Kip held Crystal's hand a little longer than necessary. "Are you riding tomorrow, Miss Kirk?"

"With the hunt? Oh, no, I'm not an experienced rider, and I understand one must be excellent on horseback to ride with this hunt club."

"Not at all. That's a myth like so many other myths about Virginia and the South. The South is full of them, you know. We Southerners use them to hide our flaws. To protect our little world, we've concocted the grandest myth of all."

"And what is that?"

"Ah, no you don't! I won't tell. You'll have to discover the answer for yourself when you come to know us better," he said with a mischievous glint in his eye. "So won't you come tomorrow? I'll be really disappointed if you don't. Surely Sue or Reid can find you a gentle horse to ride. And you can always drop out at any point along the way if it becomes too much for you."

"I don't think so, Mr. Montrose. Perhaps another time."

"Well, at least you'll be at the hunt breakfast afterward at the Langleys', won't you?"

Just then Reid came up with their evening wraps, and without meaning to, Crystal heard herself promising Kip she would come.

chapter
11

EARLY MORNING sun barely touched the treetops around Eden Cottage. Crystal, dressed in borrowed tan jodhpurs and tweed riding jacket, stood at the kitchen window sipping a cup of coffee. She was nervously awaiting Sue and Reid's arrival with the gentle mount they had promised to bring for her. Crystal blamed herself for getting into this no-win situation. Why on earth had she agreed to ride with an established hunt club? She must have been out of her mind! She knew that most Virginians learned to ride almost before they learned to walk.

"You don't have to keep up or follow the chase, Crystal. Besides, only the die-hard hunters ride for leather," Sue had assured her over and over. "So don't pay any attention to them. Just relax, have fun, and enjoy the ride."

In spite of this advice, Crystal was nervous. It had been years since she'd been on a horse. Hopefully, it was like riding a bicycle—once you know how, you never forget. But she had no more time to worry, for at that moment, she saw Sue and Reid, mounted on their own horses, cantering into view, a gleaming chestnut horse on a lead behind them.

Trying to appear calm so as not to "spook" the horse, a mare named Astra, Crystal still had some qualms as Reid held her horse's head while she got into the saddle.

"Take it easy, Crystal," Reid said, smiling up at her as he stroked the mare's nose. "It's a great morning for a ride through the countryside. And the hunt breakfast at the Langleys' will be enjoyable. The whole thing's mostly an excuse for a party anyway."

Hoping that what he said was true and not wanting to be a poor sport, Crystal picked up the reins and, after Sue and Reid had mounted again, followed them down the path. They rode single file, trotting through the woods, then clattering over the little bridge that led to Montclair. As they rode by, Crystal turned her head to get a better look at the house.

In the early morning mist, the mansion had a kind of mystical beauty. But there was something about Montclair that Crystal could not quite define, something vaguely disturbing. It was a fleeting sensation, quickly dismissed as they turned sharply, jogging to the left, and emerged from the woods into brilliant sunshine. They rode for what seemed like miles, passing great orange pumpkins squatting in the meadows and silvery Queen Anne's lace quivering along the white board fences.

Riding into the field, near the starting point of the hunt, the three saw the other riders just ahead, some in their bright red hunting "pinks" and visored black velvet caps, members of Mayfield's elite Hunt Club. Noise and confusion were everywhere. The pack of foxhounds making a terrible racket, barking and whining as they whirled and spun, eager to hear the call that would set them off in pursuit of their prey.

Sensing Crystal's discomfort, Reid leaned forward in his saddle to reassure her. "Now don't be intimidated. Just keep your horse steady and, after the Tally-ho is blown and the others start up at a fast clip, just follow at your own pace."

"Or at my own *risk!*" Crystal added under her breath, her heart beating as fast as any frightened rabbit's *or, more to the point,* she thought, *the fox's.* But she took his advice and her mount, although excited by the presence of the other horses, seemed calm enough as Crystal guided her to the edge of the group, where she had a good view of the other riders.

Almost at once she spotted Kip Montrose. He cut a splendid figure, sitting erectly astride a superb bronze-colored horse, his aristocratic good looks enhanced by his well-fitting hunting jacket, the creamy stock at his throat. Immediately a suitable description sprang to mind— "Master of Montclair." He seemed the epitome of the romantic hero in a gothic novel.

Her gaze traveled over the other riders in the crowd. Some of the finely bred horses were skittish and pranced about restlessly, anxious to be off, their riders bending over them, talking in soothing tones. Other riders chatted nonchalantly among themselves, the buzz of conversation and laughter carrying on the clear morning air. Crystal had the sensation of being an "outsider," an observer to a scene that, while fascinating, was completely foreign to her.

All at once her attention was drawn to a young woman who was having difficulty with her horse, a magnificent animal but obviously high-strung. He was nervously sidestepping, tossing his head, yanking on the reins. The rider, displaying skillful horsemanship, swiftly brought the gelding under control. Then she moved to the end of the cluster of mounted riders, leaning forward to pat her horse's neck, murmuring endearments.

From her vantage point only a short distance away, Crystal studied the young woman. She was a strikingly pretty girl, her slim figure set off by the fitted scarlet riding coat. Her glossy dark hair was brought smoothly back under the brim of a perky black velvet derby and tied with a bow at the nape of her neck. To her surprise, Crystal noticed she was riding sidesaddle and so wore a long black skirt.

Just then Sue rode alongside Crystal. "How are you feeling?"

"Fine. Don't bother about me."

"Well, then, if you're sure. . . . They're about ready to start, but if you fall out, just meet us at the Langleys' in about two hours, all right?"

"Yes, thanks. Oh, by the way, Sue, who is that stunning young woman?" Crystal inclined her head toward the rider she'd been watching.

"Which one? Oh, that's Lynette Montrose."

"Montrose?" Crystal repeated. "Is she related to our host last night?"

"A niece." Sue gave a little laugh. "But then isn't everyone related to everyone else around here? There are Montrose and Cameron kin all over the county. Actually, Lynette is the daughter of Kip's half-uncle, Jeff Montrose. But she lives with her Grandmother Cameron, who is also Kip's *stepgrandmother*." She laughed again. "Don't ask me to explain. It's all too complicated for words. I'll try to fill you in later."

With that, Sue gave her horse a little kick with her booted heel and rode off to join the rest of the club waiting for the hunt to begin. A few minutes later an ear-splitting shrill on the shiny brass horn announced the official start of hunting season, and there was a roar of pounding hoofs as horses and riders rushed forward, the dogs in the lead, howling frantically as they ran.

Crystal held her reins taut in both hands, feeling the flanks of her horse quiver as the others thundered past. Not until the riders had cleared the first low stone wall did she loosen her grip and gradually ease her horse into a canter.

Crystal never tried to catch up with the hunt. With the sun on her back, she surrendered to the rhythmic sway of the little mare's stride and enjoyed the ride through the countryside riotous with color.

Sue had given her easy directions to the Langleys' home, a white-pillared mansion not far from the Dabneys'. As she dismounted in front of the house, a stable hand took her horse and directed her to the screened-in porch at the side of the house where breakfast was being served. Mrs. Dabney, Sue's mother, was already there, helping her long-time friend, Cornelia Langley. She took Crystal in hand at once and introduced her.

"I'm delighted to meet you," Mrs. Langley said. "Sue's told us all about you and why you've come. What an interesting project! Now, before I hear all about that, we must feed you."

She poured Crystal a cup of hot coffee. Then, heaping a plate full of delicious samples of ham, wild game, scalloped oysters, hot biscuits, jams, preserves, and jellies of every kind, Mrs. Langley led the way to a corner where an elderly lady was ensconced on a white wicker love seat.

"Here's someone you should meet, dear—Amelie Carvel. She knows all there is to know about Mayfield and the families that have lived here."

Mrs. Carvel's hair was a snowy halo about her head, paler than the pearls in her earlobes and around her neck. The laugh wrinkles around her twinkling brown eyes indicated a woman who had aged with grace and humor. Before leaving them together, Mrs. Langley told her, "Crystal's staying in Eden Cottage on the Montrose property."

"Oh, at Montclair? It was one of the first plantations around here, along with Cameron Hall, you know. I hope you plan to include both in your photographs. Especially Montclair. It's not the largest nor the most elaborate, but . . . ." And here Mrs. Carvel leaned forward as if she were about to reveal something of great importance. "Montclair has such a history . . . enough tragedy, romance, and adventure to fill twenty volumes."

Crystal leaned forward, eager to hear every word. Encouraged by her interest, Mrs. Carvel continued, "To begin with, it was originally built for one bride, but through a quirk of fate, her *cousin* became mistress there." The woman paused as if trying to collect her memories. "Of course, there are all sorts of legends about all these old houses, as you may well imagine. Rumors circulated soon became facts repeated over and over until no one doubts they're true. One such is told about Montclair in the years it stood empty after one of the Montroses lost it in a card game. Day after day, it is said, a carriage would drive up, and a lady dressed all in black, carrying a parasol of black lace, would get out and peer through the gates. Then she would finally get back in the carriage and drive away. Nobody knows who she was, but many claim to have seen her."

Even though fascinated by Mrs. Carvel's narrative, Crystal suddenly felt a tingling awareness. As if drawn by an invisible magnet, she turned to see Kip Montrose staring at her across the room.

He was standing at the end of the porch, leaning carelessly against one of the pillars, as casually at ease as he would be in his own home. He had the look of a man who not only knew he was universally welcome but belonged everywhere.

His tanned face had a ruddy cast after the brisk morning ride in wind and sun, contrasting attractively with the intense blue of his eyes and the gleaming whiteness of his teeth when he smiled. He was smiling now, a lazy assured smile, as if he knew the effect he was having on her.

Crystal caught her breath. Momentarily flustered, she turned away quickly from his knowing glance. Heart racing, she leaned toward Mrs. Carvel, trying to recover the thread of what the old lady was saying.

"You must see Marydell, my dear." Mrs. Carvel launched into a description of a plantation house that was of special historical significance but was scheduled to be torn down.

Just then a mellow male voice interrupted. "Good morning, ladies."

Knowing who it was before she looked up, Crystal's pulse quickened once more.

"As I live and breathe, it's Kip Montrose, isn't it?" Mrs. Carvel said almost coyly. "You handsome scamp! I declare, you look so much like your father, Jonathan, the dear boy. 'Course you're not a thing like him. *He* has the most impeccable manners."

There followed some Southern banter that was almost flirtatious between the octogenarian and the master of Montclair. When Mrs. Carvel's daughter-in-law came to escort her home, Kip pulled up a chair and sat down, angling it so as to cut off Crystal's view of the rest of the room. "You ride very well."

Crystal felt her cheeks grow warm. "At least I didn't fall off," she said, feeling that it was a foolish thing to have said.

Kip leaned forward. "I'm glad you came. I hoped you would." His eyes held hers. "Have you plans for later today?"

Crystal, usually so clearheaded, now felt quite dizzy. Looking into Kip's eyes, she felt as if she were drowning in a pool of cobalt blue. "Plans?" she echoed, dazed. "Well, I'm not sure. I . . ."

Something in Kip's smile signaled that he was conscious of his effect on her. "Whatever they were, cancel them," he grinned. "I'm giving you a guided tour of Montclair."

A warning bell went off somewhere in her head, but if she heard it, she ignored it. Instead, she heard herself say, "I'd like that very much."

"Good, I'll come by for you around four. We can walk from Eden Cottage. It's only a stone's throw from Montclair."

Crystal nodded mutely. Somehow she knew that if he had proposed a trip to Mars, she would have been helpless to refuse!

chapter
12

LATER THAT afternoon, Crystal was amazed to find herself undecided about what to wear. She had brought very few outfits with her, most of them suitable for tramping around the countryside, carrying her bunglesome photographic paraphernalia. Rummaging through her wardrobe, one that consisted mainly of sensible shoes, wool skirts and sweaters, and rain gear, she grew increasingly annoyed with herself. She couldn't remember ever being this concerned about looking attractive to a man. Certainly Sandy had never paid any attention to clothes, his own or anyone else's.

So why was she behaving like a silly schoolgirl getting ready for her first date? She wasn't willing to admit even to herself why it seemed important to make a good impression this afternoon. But it had occurred to her that Kip Montrose was the kind of man who would notice what a woman wore!

Thoroughly disgusted with herself after several discards, Crystal finally chose a heather-blue sweater set and gray flannel skirt. When Kip arrived, looking as splendid in a belted tweed Norfolk jacket and V-neck sweater as he did in a dinner jacket, she was satisfied that her choice was appropriately casual.

On the walk to Montclair through the woods, Crystal's first impression of Kip was confirmed. His charm was as much a part of him as his good looks and impeccable manners. He soon had Crystal talking about her work, drawing her out with his intelligent questions, and exhibiting an interest in everything she had to say.

Nearing the house, Crystal was disappointed. In full daylight, Montclair seemed to lose some of the magical splendor it had in the moonlight and early morning mist. In fact, as they reached the steps of the encircling veranda, she was shocked by the grim evidence of deterioration. A quick paint job must have covered the posts of the porch and given the front door a new coat of gloss, but a closer look revealed that the paint was already peeling.

Once inside, Crystal tried to mask her dismay. Last evening, the chief illumination had been candlelight as flattering to an old house as it was kind to aging ladies. Its glow had concealed flaws that were now visible. Crystal had visited enough old houses to recognize a multitude of seriously needed repairs. This was puzzling, particularly in view of Sue's remark about the amount of money Kip was spending on renovations.

"I haven't finished all the redecorating I plan to do," Kip explained, opening the door to the music room and then to the library, which Crystal had not seen the night before. "A house this size requires constant care, and the older it gets, the more often it needs something." He spoke as though this were an ongoing project, but what Crystal saw were signs of longtime neglect.

"Would you like to go upstairs?" he asked. "Or are you mainly interested in photographing exteriors?"

"Oh, I'd like to see everything! When I photograph a house, I prefer to go through it completely to get the feel of a place. Especially a house like this, where generations of a single family have lived."

"Well, come ahead then." He gestured to the winding staircase, and they started up.

On the second floor, corridors branched out in four directions as wings were added. There were six bedrooms, Kip told her, opening door after door for her to peer in. They came to a sunny nursery where, long ago, children had played and where a dollhouse and rocking horse still remained, as if awaiting their return. Crystal had the very real sense that she was walking back in time through the centuries, where, along these halls, in these rooms, real people had lived, slept, talked, quarreled, and loved—leaving an indelible imprint.

As they turned down the fourth corridor leading into the west wing, Kip took out a bunch of keys. "After my mother died—returning from Europe aboard the great *unsinkable* luxury ocean liner, the *Titanic*—" Kip's voice was laced with sarcasm—"my father shut off her rooms, never went in them again. I don't think he ever forgave himself for not being with her. You see, Uncle Jeremy was able to purchase only two tickets for the ship's maiden voyage, and my Uncle Jeremy gallantly allowed the two ladies—my mother and Aunt Faith—to take them. They followed on a slower vessel. The rest, as they say, is history." Kip placed a key in a lock and pushed the door open. "This was Mama's room."

Crystal felt a strange compulsion to venture in and look around. The bedroom furnishings were impressive—a mahogany sleigh bed, carved nightstands, an ornate bureau. In an alcove stood a dressing table cluttered with perfume bottles and a tarnished silver hand mirror, comb, and brush. A negligee lay as if it had just been thrown aside, its lace ruffles trailing on the flowered carpet. Adjoining the bedroom was a dressing room with an enormous French armoire. Standing at the entrance to the armoire, one of its doors swung open eerily, startling her. She suppressed a shudder. There was a hovering aura of unhappiness here in Kip's mother's rooms.

A sense of depression crept over her, then indignation at the overall shabbiness and neglect of these beautiful rooms. She had to bite her tongue not to demand an explanation of Kip, who seemed remarkably indifferent. Was he oblivious to the decay? Or preoccupied with other things?

Perhaps something had happened to the Montrose fortune . . . but even that did not explain everything. Sue had mentioned that Kip's father and stepmother were abroad, spending several months in Mrs. Montrose's native Scotland. It seemed strange that they could afford extensive travel yet let their ancestral home deteriorate like this. Did they not plan to return?

Crystal could not resist the question, "This is such a huge house. Do you live here alone?"

"No." He gave her a level look. "My little son lives here with me."

Crystal managed to conceal her shock. No one had told her Kip Montrose was married. If so, where was *Mrs.* Montrose?

"Would you like to meet him?" Kip was asking.

Recovering quickly, Crystal nodded. "I'd like to very much."

"Let's go then. He's probably either at the stables with his pal Sam, the groom, or down at the pond, playing with the ducks."

Kip shut the door, relocking it, then led the way back downstairs. They went through the center hall, straight to the back of the house, onto a porch and down some steps. Following a well-worn path, they passed a kitchen garden, heading toward a group of wooden buildings.

Again Kip made no apologies for the rundown appearance of the property.

Crystal was more and more confused. Was Kip blind? Did he care? Had the surface beauty of the house the night of the party been merely a glittering facade?

She had been to California, had visited the "movie" sets of the new film industry. It always amazed her how the filmmakers could create the illusion of medieval castles, of sumptuous sheik's tents, or a baronial manor. In the eye of a camera, the settings looked real. But they were only painted on cardboard or constructed of papier-maché. It was all make-believe. An illusion. Sham.

A cold possibility clutched Crystal. Was the man who intrigued her all surface and no substance? All charm and no character? The thought chilled her.

The delighted sound of a child's high voice calling, "Papa!" interjected itself into her thoughts, and she saw a little boy running across the grass toward them. He flung himself at Kip, wrapping his arms around his father's legs.

"This is Luc," Kip said, leaning down to tousle the dark curls. "Luc, this is Miss Kirk; she takes pictures with a camera." A pair of round brown eyes peered shyly at Crystal, a hint of a smile.

"Hungry, Luc?" Kip swung the little boy up and over his head, then set him on his shoulders. "Want to go in and see if Mattie made gingerbread today?"

"Yes! Yes!" Luc crowed happily.

Kip turned to Crystal. "You'll stay and have some with us, won't you? We'll wash it down with some fresh apple cider from our own orchards."

"How can I refuse?" She followed as Kip started jogging back up toward the house, with Luc laughing merrily as he clutched his father's hair.

At the back porch, Kip set Luc on his feet. "Run into the kitchen and ask Mattie to bring a tray into the sitting room, that's a good fella."

The little boy ran down along a breezeway and opened a door into the kitchen.

"As you could probably tell, most of the rooms are shut off. Luc and I have bedrooms upstairs, but we spend most of our time here in our bachelor quarters." Kip opened the door for Crystal. "Not exactly a formal drawing room, but we like it."

Like all the rooms at Montclair, this one was high-ceilinged, but it had a welcoming if rumpled look. The furniture, a large sofa and two deep armchairs, must have once been handsome pieces. Now they sagged, the leather shiny with wear. Discarded newspapers littered the floor, and sports magazines were piled on tables. On a thin Oriental rug, the pattern threadbare, was a half-built Lincoln log village, as well as some children's picture books scattered about.

"It has that lived-in look, wouldn't you say?" Kip chuckled. "Untouched by any interior decorator's itchy fingers." He scooped up a fluffy, tiger-striped cat who was sleeping on the sofa and dumped her unceremoniously on the window sill, where she gave a mew of protest and curled up to resume her nap. Moving a pillow, he gestured for Crystal to sit down.

Kip began gathering up sheets of newspaper, balling them up in his hands, then took them over to the fireplace where he proceeded to lay a fire. He threw on some kindling from a nearby basket, placed a gnarled log well back into the hearth, and struck a match to it. Soon, with some sputtering and snapping, the wood ignited.

"We'll have a nice fire going in a few minutes," he said, brushing his hands. "It's one of the things I like best about fall. I find there's something intimate and cozy about a fire. Seems to evoke memories and invite confidences." He came over and sat down beside Crystal. "For example, there's so much more I'd like to know about you."

"What would you like to know?" she asked. "My life's pretty much an open book. No deep, dark secrets here."

"Oh, I'm not so sure about that. Everyone has secrets of some sort, some things we wouldn't want everyone to know. At least, not at first. Take me, for instance. I would want you to get to know me and like me a great deal before you found out some of my faults and foibles, of which there are many. I'm sure there are lots of folks in Mayfield who would be happy to supply a list of them, if given a chance." His eyes, intense and searching, held hers. "You do believe me, don't you? I want us to become friends. . . ."

Before she could speak, Luc came running into the room. He was followed by a handsome black woman in a neat, flowered housedress, carrying a tray. Kip got up and took it from her, then introduced Crystal.

"Thanks, Mattie. This is Miss Kirk who's renting Eden Cottage. And this is our Mattie, without whom Luc and I couldn't begin to manage."

Mattie gave Kip a scoffing look and smiled pleasantly at Crystal. "Pleased to meet you, Miz Kirk. The gingerbread's jest out of the oven, so it's a little gooey."

"Just the way I like it." Kip rubbed his hands together in anticipation. "Mattie's the best cook in Mayfield County. Here, just sample this." He held out the plate of dark, spicy squares to Crystal while Mattie stood by for the verdict. Luc looked on with interest.

Crystal took a bite of the warm, spicy square, then closed her eyes to signal her pleasure and pronounced it "Delicious!"

Satisfied, Mattie smiled and left the room.

Kip poured them all glasses of icy sweet apple cider, the best Crystal had ever tasted. After devouring his refreshments, Luc took a place on the floor and began building with his logs, and Kip picked up their conversation.

"So, how long do you expect your project here to take?"

"It depends. I'll have to do some exploring first, scout out the houses that seem interesting. Then I always take more pictures than I'll need, though I won't know until I'm back in New York where I'll develop them. But I've brought plenty of glass plates for filming. And if I need more . . . well, I can send away to a photographic supply house in New York or Richmond."

"Do you plan to photograph Montclair?"

She nodded. "With your permission, naturally."

He gave a little bow. "I'd be honored."

Just then Luc interrupted. Holding up a toy airplane, he asked, "Papa, is this the kind you flew?"

"No, son. That's a Curtis Jenny. I flew Spads and Blériots."

Luc made a buzzing sound like an airplane engine, swooping the small model up and down in imitation of flight.

"You fly?" Crystal asked. "You're an aviator?"

"*Was.* I flew with the Lafayette Escadrille."

"In France? Before 1917?"

"Yes, we were first a mixed group of volunteers—English, Canadians, as well as Americans attached to the French Flying Corps."

"How very brave."

"Some thought it irresponsible and reckless." Kip's smile was ironic. "Fools to risk death for a cause."

"I would say idealistic and courageous."

95

"We were all pretty young. Had no real idea what we were getting into."

"My husband was a war correspondent. He didn't have to go, either, but he did."

Kip shot her a look of surprise. "So it's *Mrs.* Kirk?"

"Yes. But he was killed."

"I'm sorry. I didn't know. I was lucky. Many of my friends were killed." He frowned. Then staring into the fire, he said, "I lost my wife, too. Not in the war, although she was a French ambulance driver—a very dangerous job. Ambulances were often the target of bombs, in spite of their Red Cross markings." He grew pensive. "We met when we were both on leave in Paris. We fell in love and married. She died . . . having Luc."

He looked over at the little boy, who was happily engaged in building a hangar for eight tiny planes, unaware that he was the subject of their conversation.

"How tragic," Crystal said in a small voice.

"Yes, well . . . there were a lot of tragedies." Kip's eyes were haunted.

"Yet life *does* go on. Somehow. One can't mourn forever. It's been nearly seven years since Sandy died."

"And there's been no one since?" He was genuinely surprised.

She shook her head. "I wasn't looking for anyone. My work keeps me busy now." With this, Crystal placed her empty glass on the tray and rose. "And speaking of work, I must leave. I have to get organized for my exploring trip tomorrow."

Kip got to his feet. "I'll drive you back to the cottage."

"No, thanks just the same. In fact, I'd enjoy the walk. It's still light, and the woods are so lovely this time of day."

"I know this part of the county like the proverbial back of my hand, so if you ever need a guide, I'm at your service," he said with a mock bow.

"That's generous of you. But half the fun of this sort of thing is taking the byroads, the unexpected turns. Serendipity, you know. Happy surprises." Crystal went over to the child, where he was at play, and held out her hand. "Good-bye, Luc. I'm very happy to have met you."

"*Au revoir, mademoiselle,*" he said, spontaneously, then clapped his hand over his mouth, glancing at Kip. "I forgot, Papa."

"That's all right, son." Kip tousled his hair affectionately, then explained to Crystal. "Luc's part French. He's only been with me a little more than a year, so I have to keep reminding him that he's an American now."

Crystal smiled. "You must come see me sometime, Luc, at Eden Cottage."

"Could I see how your camera works?"

"Of course. I could even take your picture, if you like."

Luc grinned and Crystal thought what a handsome child he was, what a picture he would make. He looked much like she supposed Kip had looked as a little boy except for his eyes. Those snapping brown eyes were probably a legacy of his French mother. Still, no doubt he'd be a heartbreaker when he grew up. Just like his father.

Kip walked with Crystal to the place where the path through the woods began, then stood watching the slim figure until it disappeared through the pines. He was intrigued. He had never met a woman like Crystal Kirk—staunchly independent, a woman with a life and a career of her own. Not the kind of woman he was accustomed to, yet Kip had always been challenged by the unknown. . . .

As she walked slowly back through the woods, Crystal was thinking about Kip Montrose and his house. Both had captured her imagination. He, handsome, charming, enigmatic; his ancestral home, as mysterious as its master. That Montclair *had* to be photographed as part of her collection was a given. But it was more than a professional decision. She was drawn inexplicably to the man. . . .

But she felt a check. Kip seemed as haunted by the past as the house. It would be a mistake to become too involved. Attractive as he was, to fall in love would be disastrous.

When Eden Cottage came into view, Crystal quickened her steps. She must get back to reality, back to making plans and being sensible. She had come to Mayfield to work, and she'd better get at it.

chapter
13

THIS IS MADNESS, Crystal told herself. She was seated in Kip's roadster, the wind whipping her hair, as they rushed along the country road on yet another impromptu adventure.

That morning he had shown up at the cottage with a picnic basket in the rumble seat. In spite of all her resolutions, he had coaxed her to abandon her plans for the day. Now he looked over at her and grinned. "You'll be glad you came, I promise."

She tried to shake her head but found herself smiling back at him instead. "You're a bad influence on me, you know that, don't you?"

"All work and no play makes Jack a dull boy, and Crystal—well, you know."

"It also makes me hopelessly behind." She sighed. "I really don't know why I let you talk me into these things. I'm usually not this . . ."

"Irresponsible?" Kip shrugged nonchalantly. "People have been calling me that all my life. I disagree. I think I get a whole lot more out of life than most people."

"I wasn't going to say *irresponsible.* What I was going to say about myself was that I'm usually not this easily persuaded to do things against my better judgment. I do have a contract, a deadline to meet."

"I let you bring your camera, didn't I? In fact, I helped load all your equipment into the car."

"Yes, you did." Crystal laughed. "But you're still impossible!"

"Irresistible, don't you mean? I do hope you find me irresistible." His eyes twinkled mischievously.

Crystal threw him a disparaging look as if his arrogance was simply too much. Yet in her heart, she knew it was going to take all her willpower to resist his undeniable charm.

When they turned into the gates of Bennett's Airfield, Crystal wasn't too surprised. She knew that flying was still an ongoing interest of Kip's and that he flew regularly. Maybe he wanted to show her the plane he piloted. His real motive in bringing her here was totally unexpected.

They got out of the car, and Kip preceded her to where a small two-seater plane was parked. The mechanic who was checking the fuselage, looked up at Kip's approach and hailed him.

"Is she all set, Mike?"

"Filled up and ready to go, Kip." Glancing over his shoulder at Crystal, he jerked his head in her direction. "Got a passenger, eh?"

Kip grinned. "If she's game."

Crystal felt her whole body tense. So that's what he was up to! She returned Kip's provocative look, knowing she could not refuse the challenge. This was some kind of test, and Crystal was determined not to fail it.

Kip turned back to the mechanic. "Got an extra jacket and some goggles, Mike?"

"You bet." Mike gave him a broad wink, reached into the second cockpit and brought out a short leather jacket, a helmet, and goggles. He looked over at Crystal, raising shaggy brows.

Kip laughed. "How about it, Crystal?"

She walked toward the two men, her heart in her throat but her head held defiantly high. Mike helped her into the jacket, and she tucked her hair under the helmet and fastened it under her chin. Then adjusting her goggles, she turned for their approval. "Well?"

They exchanged a look that gave her a temporary feeling of triumph. Then they assisted her into the cockpit, and Mike showed her how to put her arms through the harness straps. "You okay?" he asked, sounding doubtful.

She nodded vigorously and smiled while clenching her teeth tightly together so they wouldn't chatter. Her heart was pumping wildly.

She saw Kip don his gear, then spring into the pilot's seat behind her, while Mike ran around to the front and spun the propeller. A deafening roar alerted her that Kip had pushed in the starter and the engine was turning. She felt the first movement as the small plane rolled into position and began bumping down the runway.

Crystal's heart throbbed. She swallowed hard, her hands clutching the rim of the panel in front of her. She felt like screaming, *Wait! Let me out of here!* But before the words could escape through her gritted teeth, she felt the lift of the plane's wheels, the swish of the wind on her face. Then they were airborne.

Gradually her tense fingers loosened their grip, and Crystal dared to turn her head to the side and look down. She had no idea how high up they were, but below them the Virginia countryside spread out like a patchwork quilt—the soft green of the meadows; the river, like a silver ribbon; the autumn foliage, brilliant gems of color in the sunlight.

Suddenly she began to feel a sensation of heightened awareness. The noisy plane vibrated beneath her, but somehow it seemed part of her now, or she part of it. There was no fear anymore, only a sense of elation like nothing she had ever experienced.

Kip shouted something, but over the din of the engine, she could not make out his words. To reassure him, she gave him a thumbs-up.

Almost too soon, Crystal felt the plane bank and turn slowly, and she realized that they were heading back to the airfield. Then, she felt the gradual descent and the faster thrust of the wind as they lost altitude. Kip was an excellent pilot, she could tell, for she barely knew when they touched down, and the landing was executed with hardly a bump. Before she knew it, they were on the ground, rolling down the field toward the hangar, where they came at last to a full stop.

Crystal's ears were still ringing when Kip jumped down and held up his arms to help her from the cockpit.

He looked a trifle sheepish. "Are you okay?"

"Fine!"

"Do you feel I played a dirty trick on you?"

"No, not exactly," she said, taking off her helmet and shaking out her hair. "But you could have asked me ahead of time."

"I guess I didn't give you enough credit. Sorry. You're a real sport, Crystal." There was a glint of admiration in the look he turned on her. Then, his hand resting on the wing tip, he stroked it unconsciously, almost affectionately. "She's a sweet little bird, isn't she?"

In a flash of insight Crystal recognized the bond between the man and the machine. Kip was among those bold, brave, even reckless explorers who had destroyed the myth that mankind is earthbound. That kind of man would never be satisfied with the ordinary. Without that thrill, that rush of adrenaline achieved in the air, life would seem dull, lacking in excitement. What could such a man possibly do with the rest of his life that would compare?

Before she thought, Crystal blurted out the question in the back of her mind: "Kip, what are you going to be when you grow up?"

The stricken expression that crossed his handsome features at her remark startled her. She had not meant to wound. Her light comment had been made in jest, but his reaction lay somewhere in between. There was something perennially boyish about Kip that was as disturbing as it was attractive.

"What's so great about being grown up!" he shrugged. An edge of bitterness crept into his voice. "Oh, I've thought of becoming a stunt pilot. There's a big demand for that sort of thing at State Fairs. Or I could do loops and long spins for the crowd at Air Shows. But there's something macabre about that. Everyone's waiting, half-hoping there's going to be a crash." Then, to Crystal's vast relief, he reverted to a bantering tone. "Then I've thought of barnstorming . . . even crop dusting." He sighed and again there was a spark of steel in his voice. "I'm a father, after all. I've got to be responsible, become a pillar of the community. Maybe I'll run for public office, who knows?"

He gazed off into the distance. "I'd like to tell people about flying. It's the wave of the future, you know. Air travel, transportation, cargo, mail distribution—all will eventually be accepted as safe, economical, practical. People have the mistaken notion that aviation is a kind of circus performance, a hobby, a plaything for men who haven't grown up. . . ." He halted, then looked at her, a whimsical grin on his face. "Well, who am I trying to convince? You *did* enjoy it, didn't you? Come on, let's have our picnic."

"Just a minute. First, I want a picture."

"Of me? A memento of the day?" Kip put his hand melodramatically over his heart. "I didn't think you cared."

"I know a good shot when I see it," Crystal replied coolly. "Stand over there next to the plane," she directed with authority. "Rest your elbow on the edge of the cockpit . . . that's good . . . now turn your head a little to the left and lift your chin. That's right. Look up. . . ." She found him in the viewer, centered it. The sun slanted at just the right angle, accenting Kip's strong features, his eyes squinted slightly as he gazed into the sky.

Crystal caught her breath. The expression on Kip's face was that of a man looking at his beloved.

"All right?" There was a trace of impatience in his tone. "Did you get it?"

"Wait, please. I want to get a second . . . just to be sure." She slid another plate into her camera, pressed the bulb, knowing this one was perfect.

Afterward they lunched on the contents of the basket Mattie had packed for them—sandwiches of thin sliced Virginia ham on home-made bread, savory pickles, deviled eggs, containers of chicken salad, a thermos of delicious lemonade, and another of coffee.

"Oh, Kip Montrose, you're ruining me!" moaned Crystal as she munched on an oatmeal and raisin cookie. "What am I doing here, having a leisurely picnic when I should be working?"

"Haven't you ever heard the saying, '*Carpe diem*'—'Seize the day'? Why don't you just relax and enjoy all this?" Kip's sweeping gesture encompassed the cloudless sky, the fragrant meadow. The only sounds were the distant hum of bees buzzing in the clusters of wild purple asters and Queen Anne's lace.

Crystal sighed. "I suppose it's because I come from a long line of Yankee Puritan ancestors. The work ethic is strong in me. I can't change."

"You will, when you've been here a while longer."

Kip's words struck Crystal sharply. His smile was complacent, confident. She felt the tug of his charm. It frightened her because there was truth in what he said. She had *already* begun to change.

When Kip dropped Crystal off at the cottage, she steadfastly refused his invitation to dinner and took stock of her situation.

The work-filled agenda she had mapped out for herself was fast going by the wayside. In spite of her best intentions, Kip Montrose kept invading her time . . . and her thoughts. He had made a habit of dropping by Eden Cottage just as Crystal was getting ready for the day's outing, armed with her list of stops at the sites of various buildings that had been suggested as "musts" for her photographic project.

Crystal was honest enough to admit she had not put up much resistance to all these diversions. The fact was that she had fallen under his spell, so much so that it was easy to neglect her original objectives.

But from now on, she resolved, things were going to be different. They had to be. Or else she would lose sight of what she had come to

Virginia to do in the first place. Tomorrow she would get up early and be on her way, long before Kip could get another brainstorm and kidnap her for one of his adventures.

chapter

14

CRYSTAL SET HER ALARM and was up at sunrise. Today her plan was to photograph the little church at the Crossroads.

She loaded her camera equipment into the back of the station wagon, packed a sandwich and thermos of coffee, and set off. Resolutely she turned her head as she went past the house on the hill, hardening her heart against the thought of Kip's disappointment when he learned she had gone off without him. Her work *had* to come first, Crystal reminded herself firmly.

Her mind, however, could not be so easily distracted. From the first, Montclair had held a strange fascination for her, later bolstered by Mrs. Carvel's dramatic stories. But Crystal realized it was more than that. Avoiding Kip today did not solve her dilemma. Kip Montrose was disturbing not only her present work but her future plans.

Unconsciously, she shook her head to clear it as she drove along the country road, flanked by fields thick with goldenrod and lined with trees splashed bright with fall color. Everything was achingly beautiful. Or was it that everything just seemed more beautiful when you were in love? In love? The possibility that she was falling in love with Kip Montrose was very real.

She must get hold of herself! She was letting her emotions run away with her. Besides, Kip was wrong for her. And she was wrong for him. After Sandy's death, Crystal had never expected to love again, had never planned to remarry . . . certainly not someone like Kip Montrose. She should head off the inevitable end to which their relationship was moving. But how?

The trouble was, since coming to Virginia, seeing Montclair, meeting

Kip and Luc, Crystal had become aware of a gnawing void within her. A longing for love and family and roots.

Brought up by aloof New England grandparents after the deaths of her own mother and father in quick succession, Crystal had missed a real home. There had been boarding schools, lonely holidays in the austere Boston house, then college. It was with the Dabneys that she had first glimpsed a warm, fun-loving, affectionate family life. But she certainly did not know how to create one.

Her marriage to Sandy had been a relationship of friendship, youthful passion, mutual acceptance. Since Sandy had been an orphan, too, they had relied on each other for the kind of caring and support most people expect from their family. For this reason, his death had been doubly devastating.

A quick picture of her husband flashed before her eyes—as different from Kip Montrose as it was possible to be. Sandy had been homely, freckled, with a shock of tousled carrot-red hair that would never stay slicked down. He had been careless in dress and careless with money. But he had a cheerful nature, an irrepressible sense of humor, and undaunted optimism. And Crystal had loved him dearly.

But Kip . . . there was no way to explain her feelings for Kip. They were as inexplicable as they were impossible. Foolishly she had let her emotions persuade her that there could be compromise, that Montclair could become a home again. . . .

Sternly Crystal reined in her wandering thoughts. What was she thinking of? There was no way their distinctly different kinds of lifestyles could merge. She did not belong in Virginia. Nor at Montclair as its mistress. What did she know about managing a great house, entertaining, doing any of the things that would be expected of her as Kip's wife?

Most of all, there was Luc, that dear little boy. Could she be the kind of stepmother he needed, dedicated as she was to her career? And what of her photography? Would she be able to pursue her profession if . . . ? She did not even finish the thought, for she knew the answer.

Over the past five years, she had become independent, ambitious, focused. No matter what, she couldn't forget the struggle she had made to get where she was. To become sidetracked now would be a terrible mistake. That's what she had to remember.

She was relieved at that moment to see the weathered frame building of the little church come in sight, and she pulled off the road onto the overgrown strip of grass in front. The church itself was surrounded by a rustic fence where she supposed buggy horses had been hitched during the service.

A kind of autumn haze hovered over the valley, touching the old boards and giving them a sheen that might be hard to capture with a camera. She'd better get busy.

Getting out of the car, she took a long breath, savoring the faint smell of burning leaves in the air, then walked around, studying the angles, the direction of the light, trying to decide where to set up her tripod. The longer she stood quite still, studying the exterior of the church, the less troubled she felt. It was as if she were being enveloped in a kind of embracing peace.

She knew that the little church was no longer used. It had long since lost its pastor and its congregation who had moved closer to town no doubt, to a bigger, newer building. For some reason, though, Crystal felt compelled to mount the rickety wooden steps and try the double doors. Oddly enough, one side opened on rusty hinges and, after a moment's hesitation, she stepped inside.

When her eyes became accustomed to the shadowy interior, she looked around. Inside was perfect simplicity. There were twelve pews on either side of a narrow aisle leading up to an altar rail formed of a series of crosses. Six narrow windows lined the walls on two sides. Standing at the door, Crystal heard the skittering of mice, the creaking of the floor boards.

She slipped into one of the back pews and sat there for a moment, letting the stillness settle over her. After a while, she folded her arms on the back of the pew in front and rested her forehead on them.

Crystal's Christian teaching had been sketchy. Her grandparents had attended a cold, formal church in Boston, where she had been sent to Sunday school. There she had learned the Ten Commandments by rote, but could remember very little else about it. However, there had always been a deep yearning within her for some kind of spirituality, a seeking for something to believe in, something greater than herself.

She had been told that her ability to see beauty—the exquisite delicacy of a flower, the pattern of sunlight on grass, the slant of light on an old building—and to replicate it for the enjoyment of others through her camera was a kind of "gift." Somehow Crystal sensed that this was much more than a talent. It was something akin to creation. It was her Creator allowing her to see things in a certain way.

Suddenly she was humbly grateful. No matter her turmoil at present, her dilemma as to what to do about her relationship with Kip Montrose, Crystal was quite sure that if "His eye is on the sparrow," in the words of the old spiritual, then He knew all about her, too.

Why should she be discouraged? Or her heart feel lonely? She had been given a gift to use, and she would use it. Crystal's lips moved in a spontaneous prayer of gratitude: "Thank You, God, thank You! Show me what to do, what *You* want me to do, then show me how to do it."

The phrase "Flee for your life" flashed through Crystal's mind, startling her with its intensity. It was not the kind of thing she would say to herself, not her words at all.

She remained there for a few more minutes. Then she quietly left the church, calmed and fortified and with a new sense of direction.

That afternoon her work went well. Better than it had at any time since coming to Virginia. As she packed up her things to make the drive back to Eden Cottage, Crystal knew that this day at the Crossroads had been significant, both professionally and personally. She knew at last what she must do.

Kip read the note from Crystal, folded it, and put it in his jacket pocket. He did not understand. He had thought they were reaching a point in their relationship when it would be natural to talk about a future together.

But she had written that something urgent had come up and she had to return to New York immediately. What would have called her away so abruptly?

She was different, there was no question about that. He had sensed a resistance in her that he had rarely encountered in women. Perhaps that had made her even more intriguing. But he had felt sure that, given time, he could overcome any reticence she might be feeling. He had even allowed himself to imagine that together they might create a real home for Luc. Now he felt a crushing disappointment.

After reading Luc his bedtime story and tucking him in, Kip walked to the far end of the lawn. With the trees almost bare now, he could see Eden Cottage in the distance. No lights shone from its windows. Crystal had really gone then.

Suddenly a brisk wind came up, and Kip felt chilled. Pocketing his hands in his jacket, he turned and walked back toward the house. With

chapter
15

CRYSTAL WAS GLAD to be back in New York. Glad to be back in her apartment, with its clean, open space, its minimal furnishings, its white painted walls. Her senses had become satiated with old houses, antiques, velvet draperies, Aubusson rugs, and heavily framed family portraits. *This* was her world, her life. Here she could recover her real self—that self that had almost been eclipsed by the seductive appeal, the slow enchantment, the obsession with the past.

Work was what she needed. Keeping busy would help erase those entrapping daydreams of Kip and a life that could never be. Grateful for the pressing deadline to submit the first prints of the pictures she'd taken in Virginia, Crystal began a daily schedule that often left her exhausted by the end of the day.

She had taken more than a hundred pictures. All these had to be developed and critically viewed. Then decisions must be made as to which of them would require reprinting, which discarded, and which chosen for the exhibit.

After a breakfast of black coffee and toast, Crystal donned her brown denim smock and went into her darkroom. First, she mixed the developing powder with water and filled the tanks. Then, selecting the plates she would work with that day, she began the concentrated task of developing the negatives. There was always an anticipatory excitement as she waited out the ten to fifteen minutes required for the film to develop. After that, she washed off the negatives under running water and immersed them in a second tank, this time in a mixture of fixative powder and water. Again came a waiting period to remove every vestige of the silver not used on the plates. Then the plates were removed, washed, and hung in the drying racks.

When completely dry, they were carefully placed on sheets of sensitized paper to print. Next, she viewed the prints, shining an artificial light behind them onto the paper. This was the crucial time of decision. Crystal often found herself holding her breath at this point. Was the print up to the quality she wanted? Should it be darker, lighter? Should she repeat the whole process? This decision, she knew, marked the dividing line between the amateur and the professional photographer. Which prints would hold up to the critics' scrutiny when they were exhibited?

Crystal's heart was in the work she had done during those golden days in Virginia. She had known instinctively that everything she did there was touched by a quality of excellence she had never achieved before. Enmeshed in the history of each house she photographed and the people who had lived there—their joys, sorrows, tragedies, triumphs—she had sometimes felt herself almost stepping back into another century.

It had been a dangerous journey into the past. She had been spellbound, almost convinced she could stay there forever. Repeatedly she had reminded herself of the lesson learned that day at the little church at the Crossroads. Even the name seemed significant. She *had* been at a crossroads that day, and she had been given clear direction. It had been the right one, she was sure of it.

Still, Crystal wondered how Kip had reacted to the note she had left, her abrupt departure? Although he might have perceived it as harsh, a clean break was the only way. She would not allow herself any regrets.

If there were second thoughts, Crystal had only to remember the day at the airfield, when she had taken Kip's picture standing beside his plane, seen that expression on his face. . . .

She had left the photographing of Montclair for last. When she asked herself why she had kept putting it off, she had been honest enough to admit that it was because she was afraid. But of what? Of the mansion . . . or its master?

Knowing that without it, her collection would not be complete, she had firmly put aside her fears and sent Kip away, in spite of his insistence that he could be helpful, telling him he would only be in the way. It was true. But not the whole truth. Being around him was distracting, and by that time she was finding it harder and harder not to betray her feelings.

He had left reluctantly, driving his roadster down the driveway with one last cavalier wave of his hand and a shouted, "You'll be sorry!"

Smiling at his nonsense, Crystal had gone about getting ready for the shoot, arranging her tripod, looking through the viewer, studying the way the light fell through the trees. She had wished for color film that day, for Montclair had never looked so lovely with the variety of trees in their fall colors—golden maples, deep crimson dogwoods, splashes of bright red and yellow against the dark evergreens.

All the while she was setting up, she had felt a nervous tingle of excitement. That wasn't unusual in itself. But this time, just as she was about to put the dark drop cloth over her head and insert the glass plate, Crystal was seized with an overwhelming sadness.

Suddenly there was the impression of a faded debutante in tattered finery, left alone after the ball was long over and the music echoed through the empty rooms. The house as it was now was only a shell of what it had once been. Crystal began to tremble. She could almost hear the music of a waltz, see the couples—beautiful women in hooped ball gowns and handsome men in Confederate gray or black evening clothes, tails flying as they circled the ballroom—a vision of all the gaiety, the love, the laughter that had made it a real home.

If only someone cared enough, really cared, Montclair could again be a home. But who could make that happen? *Not me,* she thought. *I can't make Kip's dreams come true.*

So she had run away.

The sound of the timer went off, jolting Crystal from her melancholy thoughts. Slowly, carefully, she lifted the prints up to the light and held her breath. These were the pictures she had taken of Montclair that day.

She examined them closely. They were good but not the best of the lot. Certainly not good enough to include in the collection. Crystal backed away and let out her breath. Satisfied that she had made a professional decision not colored by sentiment, a new strength surged through her.

Montclair had been a beautiful dream, but it was not for her.

Crystal waited until all the pictures for her exhibit were submitted and approved before she at last developed those she had taken of Kip at the airfield. She knew why she had delayed, debating whether or not to simply destroy the plates, thus putting Kip Montrose out of her mind and heart forever. But professional curiosity won over her indecision. When she saw them, she was immediately transported back to the beautiful, carefree day and the reason she had fled.

In fact, looking at the pictures affected her so deeply that Crystal was tempted to tear them up and toss the scraps in the wastebasket. But they were too good to destroy.

Instead, she put them in a manila envelope and addressed it to "Kendall Montrose, Montclair, Mayfield, Virginia."

As soon as she mailed them, Crystal had felt sending them was a mistake. How big a mistake she was yet to discover.

Then one afternoon, while taking a break from her day's work and making herself a pot of tea in the kitchen, the bell buzzed from down in the entrance hall of the building, signaling a caller. Who could *that* be? Purposely, she hadn't told any of her friends she was back in New York because she felt she needed uninterrupted time to work. Truthfully, she needed time to recover from her near-fatal decision about Kip Montrose.

She went into the living room and pressed the release that unlocked the door to the stairway leading to her second-floor apartment. Within minutes there was a knock at the door. When she opened it, there stood Kip.

The shock of seeing him left Crystal speechless.

"Surprise!" He smiled and walked in, placing both hands on her shoulders. Shaking his head sadly, he looked down into her face. "Crystal, Crystal, why did you run away?" Before she could answer, he was kissing her full on the mouth.

Totally dazed, she returned his kiss, then stepped back gasping. "What are you doing in New York?"

"I've been in Massachusetts, visiting my sister, Meredith Sousa. We had some family business to attend to there. Now I'm on my way back to Virginia, but I can only stay for a day. Don't want to be away from Luc too long," he explained. "I couldn't leave without seeing you. Besides, I need to know what happened." He paused, frowning. "What *did* happen, Crystal? I was stunned to get your note and find you'd already left. Why did you leave like that? It didn't make sense. . . ."

"It makes a lot of sense," Crystal replied, keeping her voice even. "My life is here, my work is here. I'd already stayed too long in Virginia."

"But I thought we were . . . good . . . together. We were getting along famously. You were having a good time, weren't you?"

"I thought it best to leave," she said simply. "Things were getting . . . well . . . complicated, and I . . ."

"You mean you were afraid I was falling in love with you?"

She turned away, unwilling to meet his eyes.

"Or was it that you thought you might be falling in love with me?"

Crystal threw out her hands in a helpless gesture. "Oh, Kip, it's not that simple. I wish it were."

"I'm a pretty simple guy, Crystal. Maybe if you'd try to explain, I'll do my best to understand."

After that, nothing was real. Time seemed suspended for the rest of that gray winter day. Outside, a chill drizzle fell over the city, but the two were unaware of the weather while they talked endlessly.

At length Kip said very seriously, "I want you to know, Crystal, that your coming to Virginia when you did and being *you*—with the kind of values and discipline you have, the dedication to your chosen work—has had a powerful effect on me. You may not believe this, but after you left, I took a good look at myself, and I've come to the conclusion—well, I plan to make some changes."

The old teasing quality crept back into his voice. "You might not be able to see the changes yet, but they're real. You see, for a long time I've been floundering. Bringing Luc to live with me has had a stabilizing effect, too. I love that little fellow more than my life . . . and up until now I've let Mattie take over most of his care. But no more. I want to be a real father to him, want him to be proud of me. So . . . I've made some decisions. I just hope *you'll* consider being part of them."

"What kind of decisions?" she asked warily.

"Becoming a responsible citizen, maybe running for public office." He stopped abruptly and grinned at her. "I'll go over all this at dinner. I'm starved and I can never think well on an empty stomach. Where can I take you for dinner? Or . . ." He cast her a quizzical look—"do you cook?"

She tossed a sofa pillow at him and said with mock indignation. "Yes, of course I cook. But it would be wasted on your Southern palate. I'll take you where the food is good but plain."

They went to one of those restaurants in Greenwich Village, known by word of mouth to "insiders." The dark wood paneling was relieved by ornately carved shelves bearing brightly painted designs, and there

113

were red-checkered cloths on tables centered with candles. They were served a hearty meal of pot roast and potato pancakes, followed by a rich apple dessert in pastry shells, consumed to the music of a trio of ruddy-faced musicians playing folk music and polkas.

It was late when they got back to her apartment, and Kip phoned for a taxi to take him to the Manhattan hotel where he was staying. When he hung up, he turned to Crystal. "I hope you can put everything aside tomorrow and spend the day with me."

She started to protest a busy schedule, but in the end she agreed. When his taxi arrived, her gave her a quick kiss and was gone.

After he left, Crystal was shaken. She hadn't meant for any of this to happen. Kip had walked back into her life out of the blue. No, that wasn't quite true. She suspected that the pictures she had sent him had fanned the spark between them. Well, it was too late now. Maybe Kip's coming here had to be. Maybe she had to face her feelings and decide what to do about them, once and for all.

Crystal did not sleep well that night, and in the morning, she was just as indecisive as she had been the evening before. She felt keyed up, confused, and Kip's arrival at midmorning didn't help.

"What would you like to do today?" she asked, pouring him a cup of coffee and wishing her brain were clearer, her resolution to resist his charm firmer.

He grinned. "Play tourist. Take a Staten Island ferry and see the Statue of Liberty."

The day was crisp and bright, the sea air tangy as the little boat moved out of the crowded harbor. But when the world-famous statue came into view, Crystal and Kip were oblivious to the magnificent bronze symbol, they were too much aware of each other.

Standing on deck and leaning against the rail, Kip gazed down at her. "My real reason for coming to New York was to ask you to marry me," he confessed. "I know you care for me . . . you just won't admit it. And I'm mad about you . . . you're the most interesting, the most intriguing woman I've ever met . . . though I still can't figure you out." He scratched his head, then grew serious again. "I want you to be part of my life . . . part of *our* lives—Luc's and mine. Please say you'll come to Virginia and marry me."

Crystal could only stare at him. "You refuse to understand, don't you,

Kip? My work is here in New York. I can't just drop everything I've worked so hard to accomplish."

"Who says you'd have to do that? You can photograph in Virginia as well as here, can't you? What's the problem?"

Crystal shook her head. "Kip, you're absolutely impossible! I get other assignments. I travel," she spelled out, as if to a very small child. "That's how I came to Virginia in the first place, remember? My next idea could take me anywhere in the world."

"But I admire your work. I wouldn't stand in your way, Crystal."

"You wouldn't mean to, Kip. But it just wouldn't work. I . . ."

He cut off the rest of her sentence with a kiss.

"Kip!" Crystal remonstrated, looking around her self-consciously. He opened his mouth to say something, but guessing what it might be, she interrupted, "Don't say it, Kip. Please don't."

"Why, Crystal? What are you afraid of?"

They argued all the way back, Kip at his most persuasive, and Crystal protesting every argument he advanced. In the city they caught a Fifth Avenue bus. Kip's arm went around her, and she didn't move away but leaned against him. They passed Central Park and, noticing the still-colorful trees, Crystal pointed, commenting on their beauty.

Kip only smiled. "But they don't really compare to Virginia in the fall, do they?"

Getting off the bus at the next stop, they walked hand-in-hand, window shopping, talking and laughing as if they had all the time in the world. But as they neared Crystal's apartment, they fell silent. The time was short now. They both knew it, began to feel the tension mount. Then it was time for Kip to take a taxi back to his hotel and on to Pennsylvania Station to catch his train.

He stood and shrugged into his overcoat, saying glumly, "I hate to leave you with nothing settled between us."

"But it *is* settled, Kip."

"Then I don't like the way it's settled. When is your exhibit in Richmond?"

"It's set for April."

"Promise me you'll come to Mayfield then, after the exhibit? Give us another chance?"

Crystal hesitated, and that moment of hesitation was her undoing. Kip took full advantage of it and kissed her, preventing any further argument. The kiss was long and deep, heady with possibilities. Breathlessly she pulled away.

"Then you will come!" Kip said triumphantly.

Realizing it was pointless to deny what her heart was demanding, Crystal sighed and nodded.

Kip smiled, saying softly, "Until spring, darling."

"Until spring," she agreed.

He kissed her again; then he was gone.

Part IV
Mayfield, Virginia
March 1926

chapter

16

In the editor's office of the *Mayfield Messenger*, Scott Cameron impatiently moved a pile of papers to the other side of his cluttered roll-top desk and swung around in his swivel chair toward the window overlooking the Square. From there he could see the Confederate War Monument—a bronze cannon with its pyramid of balls and a plaque underneath, listing the gallant Mayfield County men who had lost their lives in the Cause that had also been lost.

The octagon-shaped fountain sparkled benignly in the early morning sunshine. Several elderly men sat on the surrounding benches while fat pigeons waddled by in their daily pursuit of spilled popcorn and crumbs. It was the picture of small-town serenity. But Scott knew better. Appearances were deceptive. Behind the postcard impression of this sleepy little Southern community, old wounds that had never healed throbbed beneath scar tissue.

Scott's gaze traveled to a large sign towering over a vacant lot just down the street. In large red modern letters, it read: "Woodridge Construction Company—Part of Mayfield's Past Building Mayfield's Future." A good slogan, Scott had to admit. Ironically, it was currently the source of heated debate. People on either side of the issue were vehement in their opinions. The city council itself was divided as to whether Woodridge should be given more permits to tear down some of the town's historic old buildings and build new ones.

A case in point had been the new *Messenger* building itself. Construction on it had begun before Scott came home from Army duty in France. Its architecture, replacing the old dark red structure built in 1850, had created a furor, many of the town folks complaining that it looked like a granite corrugated box! Some of them had hated to see the historic building go. During the War Between the States, people had gathered outside, waiting for the casualty lists to be posted. The paper's morgue held copies of the issues announcing the births, deaths, and weddings of the residents of Mayfield for generations back, and everyone had some sentimental reason for not wanting the old place torn down.

Of course, Scott had to admit that this building was much sounder, especially the composing room where the paper was turned out twice a week. In the old building, the floors had been so warped and slanted the Linotype operators had been forced to block their chairs so as not to slide away from their machines. So most everyone who worked at the *Messenger* had to concede, however reluctantly, that a new building was necessary. Woodridge had made the lowest bid and was awarded the contract. *Curious coincidence,* Scott rubbed his chin thoughtfully, *that so many contracts for new buildings in Mayfield have gone to Woodridge in the past few years.*

Strangely enough, Hal Woodridge had dropped by to see him late the afternoon before. "No special reason," he had said. But the conversation had turned quickly to politics, to the vacant seat in the state senate left by Senator Wilcox's retirement.

"Who do you think would make a good replacement, Scott?"

Scott had shaken his head doubtfully. He wasn't going to be tricked into naming someone that Hal might take as an endorsement before all the players were on the field. "Too soon to tell. I'm sure there will be plenty of candidates before it's all over."

"Well, let's hope it's someone who's looking ahead, wants to put Mayfield on the map, not one of these old fuddy-duddies who's afraid of progress."

In other words, thought Scott, *not someone from the Historical Society or the Heritage Preservationist Club who wants to keep Mayfield just as it was before the war*—meaning, of course, the War Between the States.

Scott had been noncommittal with Hal, and the man had soon left. But this early "fishing expedition" had given Scott pause. Whoever was elected to the office, the *Messenger* ought to have some input. He'd have to talk to some people he respected, get their ideas of who would best represent the area in the state capital.

Scott leaned back in his chair, stretched his arms up and clasped his hands behind his neck. He stared out at the familiar scene on the

Square. He loved this town. The thought of coming back home, being part of all this place represented, had kept him going on many a day during the war.

Of course, when he did return, he had found many changes—changes he hadn't expected, some he didn't like. To play some part in just how Mayfield developed had been his main motive in buying the nearly bankrupt newspaper, building back its circulation, its impact on the community. When fellows like Hal Woodridge started showing interest in who got elected to the State senate, Scott felt real uncomfortable. What did the man hope to gain?

Before he bought the paper, Scott had given some consideration himself to running for public office. He had thought of the city council. But he had found himself too busy trying to bring the ailing newspaper back to life to become involved in local politics. Still, the thought had lingered in the recesses of his mind. Particularly whenever he heard rumors of graft, or corruption in high office, or a politician taking advantage of the position in which the people had placed him.

Scott believed passionately in the principles of Thomas Jefferson. He loved his country and what it stood for—democracy. "To make the world safe for democracy." Isn't that what they had all fought for? Not only during the American Revolution, but in the more recent conflict of 1918?

Naturally, if he ran for office, he'd have to give up the paper. Scott sighed deeply and whirled around again to face his desk. Maybe it was better to try to shape public opinion by finding a good candidate and backing him. Maybe the pen *was* mightier than the sword. Well, he'd have to give it some more thought.

A glance at the wall clock told him it was time to go home. He was reaching for his coat jacket when he remembered something else. Today was the day Aunt Garnet was supposed to arrive, bringing with her his young cousin, Bryanne, and her English governess. Scott wasn't much in the mood for entertaining his feisty aunt and her companion. He could barely remember Bryanne. Hadn't seen her since she was practically a baby. Ah, well, there was no way to avoid it.

He got to his feet and, taking a last look at the jumble on his desk, he went out of the office and closed the door firmly behind him.

chapter

17

Cameron Hall
Spring 1926

Because of some mix-up in their reservation, the little party arriving from England reached Mayfield a day later than expected. Lynette had waited at the train station for hours, until the last train from Richmond had come and gone. Upon her arrival back at Cameron Hall, she had learned by telegram that Garnet, Bryanne, and Jillian had been unavoidably detained. With no information as to what time they would arrive, there was no one to meet them the next day.

Garnet hastily commandeered the only available taxicab, and they bundled into it, with much complaining over the amount of luggage by the one crusty, old porter.

"I'd forgotten how provincial Mayfield is!" declared Garnet when at last they were settled in the dusty interior.

But nothing could dampen Bryanne's high spirits. She was finally coming home, her *real* home. The minute they left the Mayfield station, her excitement rose, mounting steadily as they drove along country roads. But she didn't remember anything. Surely *something* should look familiar. All she had to go on was the descriptions in Lynette's letters. So her heart was pumping wildly by the time they passed through the gates, over which an arched iron sign spelled out in scrolled letters "Cameron Hall," and rattled up in front of the house.

At the sound of the ancient vehicle sputtering to a stop, Lynette and

Blythe rushed out the front door onto the terrace, just in time to see Garnet overseeing the unloading of their bags, while Bryanne stood shyly looking up at the house.

From poring over their photographs, Bryanne knew at once that the tall, auburn-haired lady was her father's mother—her Grandmother Blythe—and the young woman was Lynette. Although Bryanne recognized her sister on sight, she'd had no idea how lovely she was in person. She looked so cool and fresh in a light blue flowered dress. Bryanne became self-consciously aware of her own rumpled linen traveling suit. It had been terribly hot in Washington, D. C., even in early April, when they got on the train to Richmond. Accustomed to the more temperate English climate, she had found the warm Virginia weather dreadfully uncomfortable. Now Bryanne touched her hair, feeling the stickiness under the clustered curls at the nape of her neck, and attempted to straighten her limp straw hat.

But her appearance didn't seem to bother Lynette, who was flying down the terrace steps, calling, "Brynnie! Brynnie! I'm so glad to see you!"

At Lynette's exuberant greeting, Garnet turned to see her sister-in-law approaching. "Oh, Blythe, you'll never believe what we've been through! What a time we've had—" She broke off, gesturing impatiently to the mound of luggage being unloaded. "And then the train was late leaving Richmond. Some dignitary was expected . . . a senator, I think . . . and they were holding a private car for him. Such a fuss!"

"Well, you're here now, Garnet, and soon we'll have you all settled, and you can rest," Blythe said soothingly. "Just leave your luggage, and I'll have Jason come and bring it into the house." There was a slight stiffness between the two women in this first meeting after so many years.

Then Garnet took Jillian's arm and brought her forward. "Blythe, I'd like you to meet my companion and Bryanne's governess, Jillian Marsh. And, of course, this is our Bryanne."

At that, Blythe put out her hand. "Welcome, Miss Marsh," she said, then turned a radiant smile on Bryanne, who was still chatting excitedly with Lynette. "Oh, my dear, it's so good to see you! I've waited so long for this day." Putting both hands on Bryanne's face, she kissed her on both cheeks. "Lynette, isn't it wonderful to have your little sister here?"

"Oh, yes! It *is* wonderful, Brynnie! A prayer answered!"

"For pity's sake, can't you girls please do your catching up in the house? I'm perishing in this heat," Garnet declared, running her finger along the inside of her lace collar. "I do hope you have something cool to offer us, Blythe. I'm longing for some good old Southern *iced* tea!"

"Of course, come along inside," Blythe said, somewhat flustered that Garnet had managed to make her feel remiss as a hostess. "If you'd rather go right up to your room so you can relax in private, Garnet, I can have a tray sent up."

"Yes, that might be reviving. It has been a very exhausting trip." Garnet started up the stairs, then stopped, as if remembering that this was not *her* home any longer. She turned around with an inquiring look.

Blythe anticipated her unspoken question. "Your old room, Garnet. It's been prepared for you."

"Thank you," Garnet replied with dignity and proceeded up the stairs.

Blythe turned to the other travelers. "Would you like to go up now, too? Miss Marsh, you have the guest room across the hall from the one Bryanne will share with Lynette. She'll show you the way."

"Yes, that would be lovely, Mrs. Cameron. Actually, I *would* like to freshen up and change," Jillian said. "And I'm sure the girls have lots to say to each other and would enjoy a little time alone together."

Charmed by the young woman's sensitivity, Blythe readily agreed. "I'll have some refreshments sent up in a few minutes. You can rest as long as you like. Dinner won't be until seven when my son Scott gets home from his office. Then we can have a *real* reunion."

They left Jillian at the door of her bedroom, and Lynette, still holding Bryanne's hand, led her across the hall and opened a door. "And this is *our* room!" she announced with pleasure. "You can't imagine how many times I've longed to have you here sharing it with me. When Grandmother did it over, I insisted she get *two* beds. I just knew one day you would be here, and it would be like the old days—when we were little girls at Avalon. You do remember Avalon, our *real* home, don't you?"

Bryanne, standing in the center of the room, was suddenly stricken. Sadly she shook her head. "I'm afraid not. I guess I've forgotten almost everything about living in Virginia."

Lynette's face mirrored her sister's distress, and she went to her and hugged her reassuringly. "Don't feel bad, Brynnie. It was silly of me to think you would. After all, you were only four when Mama took you with her to England that spring. But don't worry. I'll tell you everything you want to know. And we'll go over to the island as soon as possible. Right now it's closed, because Daddy and Gareth are still in New Mexico. But now that *you're* here, they'll come back and we can all be together again. Like a real family."

Bryanne glanced around the room. It was a lovely, feminine room and she saw that Lynette must have added several thoughtful touches to welcome her. There was a small heart-shaped pillow with her name embroidered on it, prominently displayed on one of the two brass beds. On the dressing table were two of everything—two bottles of cologne, two boxes of dusting powder, two toilette sets of brush, comb, and hand mirror.

"Do you want to unpack first?" Lynette asked. "Or shall we just talk?"

A little dazed, Bryanne just nodded.

"Then let's sit over here, and I'll try to tell you all the things I remember about *us*." Tugging her gently by the hand, Lynette led her to the window seat, and they sat down, facing each other. "Well, we did almost everything together even though I was three years older. Mama . . . you *do* remember our mother, don't you, Brynnie?" Lynette looked anxious.

"Yes, but only vaguely. I don't even know whether it's because Grandmother has so many pictures of her, or if I really remember her," Bryanne replied. "She was very beautiful, wasn't she . . . and Grandmother says you look very much like she did."

"A little maybe . . . my coloring," Lynette said quickly and went on. "She was so sweet, Brynnie, always laughing and playing with us. We used to have tea parties out in the garden, and Mama would come. . . ."

As her sister talked, telling her wonderful stories of their childhood, nudging the memories that had been locked away for so many years, Bryanne actually began to recall the scenes, the games, the happy times Lynette was recounting.

Little by little, she felt a spreading warmth, a gradual easing of a tension she had not even been conscious of, a filling of a deep emptiness. Her sister's voice was low and comforting. Something gentle and tender was happening to her, as if loving arms were being wrapped around her, embracing her, soothing that small hurting spot in her heart she hadn't even known was there . . . until now. The healing had begun.

JILLIAN WOULD never forget her first impression of Cameron Hall. They had arrived just as the sun's last brilliant rays turned the tall windows across the front to flaming jewels. Set as it was on park-like lawns surrounded by oaks and beech trees, the splendid house had a kind of majestic dignity. It seemed a house worthy of awe and respect. It was exactly the kind of house, given her own privileged background, that under other circumstances, might have been her birthright.

But Jillian wasn't coming to Cameron Hall as a guest, she reminded herself, but as an employee. She didn't know how she would be regarded by Bryanne's other grandmother, Blythe Cameron. But on the train from Richmond, Mrs. Devlin had given her a capsule version of the situation.

"Since this is your first trip to America, Jillian, you should be aware of the differences in our two cultures. Americans tend to be quite casual about everything—manners, etiquette, protocol. Things that are important to Britishers don't seem to matter at all in the States. And the South is a case unto itself." Mrs. Devlin had laughed a little. "I don't really suppose there's any way to prepare you for Virginia or Virginians! Goodness knows, I spent half my life in England, trying to explain myself, and it was no use."

She had shaken her head, twisting the pearls at her neck with one graceful hand, looking out the window of the train somewhat pensively. "Cameron Hall, where we'll be staying, was my childhood home. My father's ancestor built it, and the Cameron family has lived there for generations. My sister-in-law, Blythe, my brother Rod's widow, is mistress there now, of course, and things will probably be quite different from what I remember. Blythe originally comes from *California*. . . ."

From the inflection in Mrs. Devlin's voice, *that state might have been the Australian outback,* Jillian thought with amusement. But she wasn't through.

"My nephew Scott will inherit it eventually. Of course, Blythe is still young enough to marry again . . . who knows? Or Scott . . ." She gave a small indifferent shrug. "But we shall see. I really don't know what to expect anymore. It's been years since I've been here, since before the war. As you know, my brother died when we were in Switzerland two years ago, and there was no way I could have left to come for his funeral . . . and no real reason to come after that."

Since, in England, the position of a governess was ambiguous, sometimes considered only a little above a servant, Jill had been uncertain how she might be received in the Cameron household. But the warm welcome given her had dispelled any of her apprehensions. They could not have been more gracious.

Now Jillian looked with pleasure around the bedroom to which she had been shown by Bryanne's sister. From the next room, she could hear the low murmur of their voices. Since she had had no sisters of her own, Jillian had often envied friends who did. She had imagined how comforting and enjoyable it must be to have a companion with whom to share one's life, and she hoped these two, who had been separated for so long, might now be able to bridge the gap quickly and become close.

Jillian took off her hat and the jacket to her suit, and untied the bow at the neck of her blouse. Glancing into the pink-tiled bathroom, she decided she would take a long soak and wash her hair.

As she lay in the tub, relishing quantities of scented bath salts she had poured in from the glass container on the shelf, Jillian rested her head and let her thoughts ramble.

Her thoughts, however, instead of being peaceful ones, were vaguely unsettling. Suddenly she was aware of the luxury surrounding her, simultaneously remembering the spirit-deadening poverty she had endured before Mrs. Devlin had hired her. It would be disastrous to become attached to this kind of life, she warned herself. Jillian knew the plans Mrs. Devlin had for Bryanne, the reason she had brought her granddaughter back to Virginia. For the past two years, the older woman had been polishing her, exposing her to the cultural "finer things" of life—the symphony and the ballet, the riding and dance lessons, the trips to museums and galleries all over Europe. All this to prepare Bryanne for the life that was to be her legacy from the past.

Mrs. Devlin had been very open about all this with Jillian. In fact, Jillian was a willing accomplice from the start. There was only one other step—a year of finishing school, followed by her debut. If the result of all this proved to be the brilliant marriage Mrs. Devlin had envisioned for her granddaughter, where would that leave Jillian?

At this thought, she sat up in a cloud of suds. When Bryanne married, what then? No bride, no matter how affectionately bonded, took her governess with her into marriage. What then, indeed?

She smiled ironically. She should forget any notion of continuing this lavish lifestyle. All this could disappear as quickly as the soap bubble that burst on the surface of her bath, as quickly as Cinderella's coach-and-four had vanished at the stroke of midnight. And there was no Prince Charming to rescue her and take her to the castle to live.

The water having grown cold, Jillian got out of the tub, wrapped herself in one of the large Turkish towels, and rubbed herself briskly. If . . . or rather *when* that happened, her own future loomed precariously. Should she return to England, or stay in America and look for another position? Well, as Uncle Greg always said, she'd cross that bridge when she came to it.

She put on a robe, then stretched out on the flowered chintz chaise lounge and picked up one of the glossy fashion magazines on the table beside her. As she thumbed through it idly, her head began to nod and she drifted off to sleep.

When she opened her eyes again, the house was quiet, so devoid of sound there might have been a moat about the place. A glance at the porcelain clock on the mantelpiece above the white marble fireplace told her it was nearly six-thirty. She'd better get dressed right away. She wouldn't want to be late to dinner on her first night at Cameron Hall!

Scott came in the front door and closed it quietly. He stood in the entrance hall for a moment, listening for some sign of activity. Hearing none, he concluded that everyone must be resting. It had been a hectic day.

Crossing the hall toward the library, something caught his eye, and he glanced in through the open doors of the drawing room and saw a young woman standing in the curve of the piano. She turned at his approach. Seeing her, he moved as if in a dream and paused again at the threshold, momentarily unable to speak.

She was in every way the personification of the picture he had carried for years in his imagination, the ideal woman he would one day possess. Her soft brown hair was a cloud about her face, her complexion like lustrous pink pearls, her eyes so clear and blue they took his breath away. The phrase about eyes being "the windows of the soul" came effortlessly to mind. She was wearing a white ruffled blouse and a slim gray taffeta skirt that barely reached ankles as slender and dainty as a thoroughbred's.

"Hello!" he said. "I'm Scott Cameron."

"I'm happy to meet you, Mr. Cameron. I'm Jillian Marsh, your cousin Bryanne's governess."

Recovering from his initial reaction and regaining his usual poise, Scott said smoothly, "Of course. I must apologize, Miss Marsh. I'd forgotten Aunt Garnet was scheduled to arrive today. I hope you had a pleasant trip."

She had time only for a polite reply before they were joined by Mrs. Cameron. Watching their affectionate exchange and his gentle manner toward his mother, Jillian was impressed. Contrary to everything Mrs. Devlin had led her to expect from American men, Scott Cameron measured up in every way to any of the young Englishmen she had known—products of Eton or Harrow or Oxford.

Remembering her own fantasizing earlier this evening, Jillian felt an inner amusement. This was the heir apparent to the "castle" in which she was luxuriating. Even if he could be categorized as "Prince Charming"—and he was good-looking enough to be—he surely already had his "princess" picked out, with a half-dozen others waiting in the wings!

chapter
19

A FEW DAYS after their arrival, Bryanne, Lynette and Jillian went horseback riding early one morning. It was still quite cool, and dew glistened on the grass as they set out. They had gone only a short distance down the drive, headed for the nearby woods, when a horseman trotted toward them along the bridle path.

"Oh, it's Sean! I didn't know he was back!" Lynette exclaimed with a lilt in her voice. She drew her horse to the side, explaining as he approached, "Sean manages our stables and is just back from a buying trip to Kentucky. He's always looking for new stock to add to Cameron Hill Farms." She raised her hand in greeting. "Good morning, Sean!"

"And a good mawrnin' to you!" he called back, coming alongside her horse.

Lynette turned in her saddle. "I'd like you to meet my sister Bryanne, Sean, and Miss Marsh, her companion. They've just come from England. And this is Sean McShane."

Sean pulled off his tweed cap, revealing thick blond hair that glinted in the pale sunshine. "I'm that pleased to meet you both." Looking directly at Bryanne, he added, "I know Lynette's been longin' for you to come."

At his greeting, Bryanne could feel a sudden rush of warmth in her cheeks. While he and Lynette carried on a brief exchange about his Kentucky trip, he sat relaxed in the saddle, giving Bryanne time to observe him.

She watched the way he gentled his horse as they talked, his hands strong and firm. His face had a ruddy glow, and he had quite the nicest smile she had ever seen. Under a creamy cable-knit sweater, his shoulders were broad, and from the length of his brown-breeched legs and the height of his boots, she guessed he must be very tall.

"Want to ride along with us?" Lynette asked him.

"Another day maybe. I've been out since dawn. It was good to get back on Shannon after ten days away, but I need to rub him down. Enjoy your ride now." His gaze moved to Bryanne again and he smiled at her and tipped his cap. Turning his horse, he rode off in the direction of the stables.

"He's such a nice person," Lynette said, gazing after him as he cantered down the path.

Something in Lynette's voice made Bryanne wonder if there might be more than friendship between her sister and Sean McShane. And almost immediately there followed a little twinge of disappointment.

As they entered the woods, she fell a little behind Lynette and Jillian. If what she thought she had noticed was true, who could blame Sean? What young man wouldn't be attracted to her sister?

Even this early in the day, Lynette was perfection. Her long dark hair swept back, tied with a red bow, fell in waves nearly to her waist. She had on a red turtleneck sweater under a beige and red checked jacket. She was so slender and graceful, yet a competent horsewoman.

Besides her beauty, Lynette had so many other attractive qualities that endeared her to others—a genuinely sweet nature, a pleasant personality, a delightful sense of fun. Bryanne had not laughed so much in ages. Who could resist Lynette? Sean McShane would be a fool *not* to love her!

Even so, some small wistful wish crept into Bryanne's heart. *Why couldn't it be me?*

In the weeks that followed, Bryanne's attraction to Sean McShane increased rather than diminished, even though she tried to tell herself that caring for him was an exercise in futility. He was always friendly and certainly seemed comfortable enough with the rest of the family on the rare evenings he joined them at the house for dinner.

But she hardly ever had a chance to talk to him alone. For the three of them—Lynette, Jillian, and Bryanne—did everything together. Riding became an almost daily ritual, and Sean often saddled up and rode along with them.

However, as the days went on and she observed them together, Bryanne began to wonder if her first impression might have been wrong. Maybe they were simply good friends completely at ease with each other. But what did *she* know about romance? Bryanne knew only what she had read in romantic novels and how much reality was in them? Still, she longed for the chance to get to know the handsome young Irishman better. But they never had a chance to be alone.

chapter
20

WITH THE ARRIVAL of Aunt Garnet and her entourage, and his subsequent uncharacteristic daze over the lovely English lady, Scott had almost forgotten about Hal Woodridge's visit to his office at the *Messenger*. However, he was sharply reminded two weeks later when he went to the Mayfield Inn for lunch.

As he entered the Grill Room, he spotted Kip Montrose and Woodridge, sitting at a corner table, deeply engrossed in conversation. So intent were they on their discussion that they failed to see Scott pass, and they soon left without noticing him at another table. *Curious,* Scott thought. *Wonder what that was all about?*

The following week Frank Maynard, whose family were longtime friends of the Camerons, called him with an invitation to meet for lunch.

Scott arrived at the inn fifteen minutes early, in time to see the lobby thronged with ladies in flowered hats and pastel dresses, and realized that Frank had inadvertently chosen a day when the Mayfield Ladies' Heritage Society was having its monthly luncheon meeting. Hoping to avoid being cornered by their assertive secretary and coerced into giving them some space on the Local Events page, he ducked behind one of the pillars until he could signal a waiter to be seated.

Shortly afterward, Frank Maynard entered the Inn and crossed the lobby with quick purposeful strides. Pausing at the archway into the Dundee Room, he surveyed the room, and seeing Scott at a far table, he raised his hand in greeting and started toward him.

Less than twenty minutes into lunch, Frank told Scott the reason for this get-together. He was giving serious consideration to running for the senate seat vacated by Senator Wilcox. "I'd like you to support me, Scott . . . and, of course, the paper's endorsement would be a big help."

Frank Maynard had a good face, Scott mused—strong features, serious expression, keen, intelligent eyes. The man's integrity was unquestioned. The Maynard name was one of the oldest and most respected in the county. A lawyer, Frank had been a junior partner in a prestigious Richmond law firm until a few years ago when he returned to Mayfield and moved into his old home. The house had long stood empty, had been scheduled for demolition with some others to make way for a proposed new highway through that part of town, which so far had not received federal funding and was being fought by Mayfield's "old guard." Frank had evidently paid up the delinquent taxes, moved in, and started restoring his old family home. Then he had opened his own small law office in one of the older buildings across the Square from the *Mayfield Messenger*.

"Why don't we go over to your office after we finish?" Scott suggested. "We can talk privately. I don't think it's such a good idea to discuss it here." He smiled and inclined his head toward the table of ladies nearby. "You never know who could be listening and might be tempted to carry a tale you might not be ready to tell."

"Fine," Frank agreed.

Personally, Scott liked Frank and thought he would make a viable candidate. But he'd like to ask some probing questions, take a reading, decide for himself if he could conscientiously endorse him.

Back in Frank's office, which had a comforting old-fashioned shabbiness about it, they continued their conversation, more freely now that there was no danger of being overheard.

"I don't know if you ever met my grandfather, Scott," Frank began, and his clear gray eyes grew thoughtful. "But although he died when I was only eleven, I remember him very well. I lived with him and my grandmother for a year once when my mother was ill. He was a quiet man, silver-haired, dignified. I didn't find out until after his death that he had played a very important and very dangerous role in the War Between the States. One that rarely received any glory, even if it was successful. And if it failed . . . it meant death by a firing squad. . . ."

There was a long pause while Frank collected his memories. "You see, he was a Confederate spy. Infiltrated some of the highest echelons of the Union Army. Sent valuable information to Lee on several strategic occasions. I learned all this from some of his friends who attended his funeral, one without military honors, by the way, because of course he had worn the Yankee uniform. But he was a man of great honor." Frank gazed out the window, squinting into the light.

"He lived his beliefs, was true to his convictions. I remember his telling me about honor, even as a little boy. That honor takes a lifetime to acquire and only an instant to lose. That we should cherish it."

Frank pulled out a watch from his vest pocket and held it for a moment, looking down at it. Then he opened the palm of his hand and showed it to Scott. It was a beautiful watch with a smooth gold case, an open white face with black Roman numerals, and thin elegant hands pointing to the time.

"He left me this, and every time I look at it, I am reminded of what he told me about honor. It's given me a talisman to live by, Scott. Honor, as I see it, is mainly honesty with oneself and others. But it is also courage, tolerance, and the right kind of humility and pride."

Their conversation continued for another quarter hour. Then Scott stood, and the two men shook hands. When he crossed the Square to his office at the *Messenger,* Scott knew he had his candidate.

That night the light in the editor's office burned late. Scott was writing his endorsement editorial which would appear in next Thursday's edition.

But before the paper came out with Frank's announcement, Kip Montrose staged a rally out at Bennett's Airfield, declaring *his* candidacy for the empty senate seat.

Within days, posters of Kip, wearing a leather helmet, goggles pushed up on his forehead, flying jacket slung carelessly over one shoulder, elbow propped near the cockpit of his plane, were plastered all over town. His campaign literature, Scott could see, was slick and professional, and his political brochures, banded in red, white, and blue, were strongly patriotic. "A man who fought bravely for his country will fight vigorously for his county in time of peace," and "Valiant in Wartime, Vision in Peacetime. Mayfield Needs Kip Montrose." Whoever dreamed up the rhetoric was not half bad, Scott thought. But somehow he suspected Woodridge's money was behind it, and that left a bad taste in his mouth. Chances were good that Woodridge was using Kip for his own ends . . . whatever they were.

The literature might influence some voters, but it didn't change Scott's mind. The *Messenger* would still endorse Frank Maynard.

Writing didn't come easy to him, perhaps because he admired good writing so much and was always striving for eloquence. Laboring long and hard over this particular piece, he was particularly pleased with the endorsement editorial.

He had begun by using a quotation he had found that seemed to incorporate the highest ideals of public service:

> Give us men a time like this demands!
> Strong minds, great hearts, true faith, and ready hands;
> Men whom the lust of office does not kill;
> Men whom the spoils of office cannot buy;
> Men who possess opinions and a will;
> Men who have honor; men who will not lie.
> —Josiah Gilbert Holland

Scott believed Frank would represent the district well, and his endorsement had been strong, but not sentimental. Convinced of the man's character and integrity, Scott was able to write persuasively. So with some regret that his endorsement would mean disappointing a lifelong friend like Kip Montrose, but with no misgivings about his choice of a candidate for the race, Scott sent his copy down to the composing room to go into the next edition as it went to press.

Scott's endorsement of Frank Maynard came out in banner headlines on the editorial page of the *Mayfield Messenger*. The ink was barely dry on the paper when through the open transom of his office, Scott heard a commotion. Then above the ruckus, he recognized Kip's voice in the outer office.

"I want to see your editor!"

A moment later the door was flung open, and an irate Kip burst in with Scott's frightened secretary trailing behind. "I'm sorry, Mr. Cameron, he insisted. . . ," she murmured.

"It's all right, Miss Stanton. Come in, Kip. I've been expecting you."

Kip covered the distance to Scott's desk in two long strides, held up a copy of yesterday's *Messenger,* and shook it. "What does this mean, Scott? I thought we were friends!"

"We are, Kip . . . always have been . . . and I hope we always will be," Scott replied calmly.

"Then why are you backing Frank?"

"Sit down, Kip. Let's talk about this."

"Not until I get some answers. Why aren't you supporting *me?*"

"Because I honestly think Frank is the man for the job."

Kip's expression hardened, and his eyes were ice blue steel. "Well, I've heard that if you go into politics, you soon find out who your friends are. But I didn't realize you also find out who your *enemies* are."

"Now, come on, Kip. I'm not your enemy," Scott said in a reasonable tone of voice.

"I think Someone said it hundreds of years ago, and it's still true today: 'He who is not with me is against me.'" Kip shook his head. "You must know how influential the *Messenger* is—how many people vote according to this paper's endorsement. Never mind judging for themselves. I never thought you'd turn against me, Scott. I guess I was wrong."

With that, he flung down the paper on Scott's desk and stormed out.

Scott sighed, swung his chair around, and stared out the window. He could see some of Kip's red, white, and blue banners flapping in the breeze in front of his campaign headquarters.

He was sorry it had to come to this. But in a contest this heated, what could he expect? A man had to be true to his convictions. Wasn't an editor's job to study the issues and present them as clearly and concisely as possible to his readers? Frank Maynard was the man for the senate job.

Still, Scott hated for an old friendship to end in hostility and animosity. Yet somebody had to win, and he was going to bend every effort to see that it was Frank. If that meant Kip lost and, in the losing, their friendship suffered . . . well, so be it.

Jillian found dinner at Cameron Hall surprisingly informal. Unlike the eight-course affairs served at English country manor homes. Although served with elegance on fine china and crystal, it was far less stuffy than some Jillian had endured during weekend parties at English country estates. There were no tedious courses, just plain, delicious food. Although Jillian observed a tiny bit of tension between the two grandmothers, she was gratified to see that Lynette and Bryanne were chatting and relating to each other as well as any pair of sisters she'd ever known. On the whole, talk flowed pleasantly, most of it concerning local people and events, centering on a local election that was soon to take place.

"I declare! Frank Maynard running for state senator!" Mrs. Devlin exclaimed when she heard the news. "It hardly seems possible that Francis Maynard has a grandson old enough to run for public office! Francis was one of my most ardent beaus!" she explained to the table at large, giving her head a flirtatious little toss. "My, how he did court me and how very naughty I was to him. Hiding when I saw him ride up the drive, making up names to scribble on my dance card so he wouldn't ask for a dance I wanted to save for someone else!" Garnet smiled a reminiscent little smile. "But I changed my tune during the war. Francis turned out to be a fine young man. Very brave, very gallant. So, tell me, what is his grandson like?"

"Very likable. But more important, honest, hard-working, intelligent. I think he'd make a worthy representative for this area."

"Of course, we have rather a conflict," Blythe said slowly. "You should know, Garnet, that Kip Montrose is running against him. It's caused quite a rift between our families, as you might imagine, since Scott and the paper are supporting Frank."

Garnet put down her fork and stared at Scott. "Whyever *not* support Kip? You've always been friends, haven't you? From childhood, I mean!"

"That's true, Aunt Garnet," Scott admitted. "But I'd already decided to support Frank, promised him I would, and that he would get the paper's endorsement *before* I learned Kip was running. I couldn't go back on my word to Frank." He regarded her steadily. "Besides, I believe that Frank Maynard is the better man for the job."

"Ah, well . . ." Garnet lifted her shoulders. "A man's word is his bond, I suppose. Too bad."

"Yes, we feel terrible that Kip took it so badly. The twins, too, were always very close to him. . . ." Blythe's voice trailed away, and Jillian wondered what she was leaving unsaid.

Scott, however, would not leave the subject. "To be quite blunt, Aunt Garnet, the only reason Kip is in the race is because he can find nothing else to do with his life. He brought his little son over here last year, but even that has not satisfied. He's not interested in farming or horses, he's tenanted out most of his land . . . and I don't think he *really* has any interest in politics. Flying is the only thing that's caught his attention for any length of time. And that seems to be more a hobby than a career." Scott hesitated, rearranging the silver at his plate before continuing. "Although, he's *using* it for all it's worth as a campaign strategy rather than confronting some of the real issues."

"Oh, dear, let's do change the subject, Scott," urged Blythe gently. "I know all this is of burning interest to you, but . . ."

"I'm sorry, Mother," Scott apologized.

"But I find it fascinating!" declared Garnet ignoring Blythe's plea. "Women getting the vote was never even thought of in my day. Well, it's high time!" she had declared vigorously. "Although, I must admit, I don't agree with some of the radical acts of the Suffragettes in England. . . ." She clucked in dismay. "Hurling rocks into the windows of the houses of members of Parliament, chaining themselves to lampposts . . . or what one poor woman did—throwing herself in front of the King's horse on Derby Day at Ascot . . . *really!* But why *shouldn't* women have the vote?" Here she tilted her head coquettishly, addressing Scott. "Women, when properly informed, are every bit as intelligent as men! And, I'd be willing to wager, even *more* capable and practical in many cases!"

Scott looked amused. "You're probably right, Aunt Garnet." Then turning to his mother, asked, "Just one more thing. Could we possibly have the election night party here? As you know, Frank doesn't have any family hereabouts anymore. And he's worked so hard, put so much into this campaign. I'd like to have some sort of celebration, win or lose, if that's all right with you."

"Yes, of course, dear. It's your home, too, Scott. You really didn't need to ask."

Only Bryanne noticed the flush that suffused Lynette's face and the secret smile tugging at the corners of her mouth. What, she wondered, had made her sister so happy?

chapter
21

WHETHER AS the result of a letter from Blythe containing a pointed request rather than a suggestion, or the fact that his mother's firm "summons" coincided conveniently with the dates of a one-man exhibit of his paintings arranged by his agent at a prestigious art gallery in Washington, D. C., Geoffrey Montrose arrived in Mayfield without previous notice the first week in May.

He came dutifully to dinner at Cameron Hall two nights in a row, was charmingly attentive to both his daughters, respectful if cool to Garnet, affectionate to Blythe, then announced that he had to go up to Washington for a day or two to consult with the gallery about the hanging of his paintings. From Washington, he sent word that some business matters in New York required his personal attention, and he would be back in Mayfield the following week.

Lynette did not seem too perturbed by this news. But Bryanne was terribly disappointed. She had hoped desperately for a chance to be with her father, to get to know him, to catch up on all the years apart. She rode over to Avalon, moped around Gareth as he worked in his garden, but could not articulate her feelings. He, on other hand, seemed completely at ease with his father's decision and made no comment Bryanne could seize upon as an opening to talk about it.

Then at the beginning of the second week, Bryanne burst into their joint sitting room. "Jillian, guess what? My father's back in town . . . at Avalon . . . and he's coming to take me out to lunch at the Mayfield Inn!"

"Oh, that's lovely, Brynnie." Jillian got up from the desk where she'd been writing a letter to Uncle Greg. "Well, we'll certainly have to see that you're all dolled up for the occasion, won't we?"

"What should I wear?" Bryanne brushed her hair back from her forehead and yanked open the closet door, then stood, hands on hips, surveying its contents with a worried frown on her face.

"Why not the pretty dress your grandmother brought you from Richmond?" suggested Jillian.

"Of course! That would be just the thing!"

The new dress was white muslin, its bodice tucked and inserted with lace, as fresh and crisp-looking as white daisies. Jillian brushed Bryanne's hair, taming its curly length into a neat cluster at the nape of her neck and tying it with a broad blue grosgrain ribbon. And when Jeff arrived, she was waiting for him in the downstairs hall, her smile radiant. Maybe Lynette was used to being identified as the daughter of the famous painter, Geoffrey Montrose, but Bryanne wasn't. At least, not yet. She loved the little stir that rippled through the dining room at the Mayfield Inn when they entered, the greeting given him by the deferential maître d' as he showed them to a window table. She heard the whispers: "My dear, that's Geoffrey Montrose, you know, the painter!" and "He's won all sorts of awards, internationally acclaimed, winner of the Waverly Galleries American Artists' prize." She listened and loved it all. This was *her* father they were talking about!

He was so handsome, like pictures of the romantic poet Byron she had seen—thick dark hair lightly threaded with silver, curling a little long on his neck, the flowing tie and coffee-colored velvet jacket.

They were seated, and gradually the murmurs died down. But Bryanne was still aware of the curious, if surreptitious, glances sent their way, as her father consulted with the waiter before ordering. She gazed at him in adoring admiration as he discussed the various specialties, decided, then handing the menu back with a flourish, added, "And the same for the young lady." Imagine! He assumed she had the same sophisticated tastes as he.

But her happy smile faded almost immediately when Jeff said, "What a nice farewell party this has turned out to be."

Farewell? The word echoed bleakly in her brain. "You're going away . . . again?" The disappointment in her voice could not be disguised.

"Well, you know Taos has been my winter home for several years now."

"But that was before *I* came. I mean, before all of us—Gareth,

Lynette, and I—were together . . . our family," she finished weakly, trying not to sound resentful but knowing that she did.

"I don't think you understand, my dear. This time of year in New Mexico, the light is magnificent, and I can paint outdoors. I can . . ." Jeff halted, his frown deepening as he regarded his daughter. Then with slight irritation in his voice: "You'll be fine here. You have your horse and your companion, Miss Marsh, and two doting grandmamas hovering over you." His smile replaced the frown as his tone became teasing.

Bryanne swallowed hard. The light-hearted remarks fell on reluctant ears. She didn't want to be coaxed out of her feeling that he was deserting her, as if her being here hadn't made any difference. The old sense of abandonment threatened to overwhelm her, and she felt a stinging sensation behind her eyes.

She blinked and stared at him. "When are you going?"

"Soon. Next week probably."

"I suppose you'll be taking Gareth." She struggled over the lump rising in her throat. She would lose them both, just when she was getting used to having them in her life.

To her surprise, Jeff shook his head. "No, your brother doesn't want to go this year."

Bryanne's heart lifted a little. At least Gareth, whom she had come to adore, would still be here.

Her appetite gone, Bryanne picked at the crabmeat souffle, and even the fresh strawberry mousse, when it came, failed to tempt her. Her father maintained his cheerful attitude to which Bryanne did her best to respond with as much zest as she could muster.

"Your Grandmother Devlin tells me she has enrolled you at Miss Dunbarton's for next year. That should be nice, my dear. Horseback riding and archery and plenty of social and educational opportunities, I understand."

"Yes, I suppose so," she answered politely, but all the while she was thinking, *Why don't you invite me to come to New Mexico with you? That would be educational and much pleasanter than a young ladies' finishing school. I could ride horses and cook for you and keep you company . . . oh, please, Father, please!* But, of course, she didn't ask, and Jeff never thought to offer such a plan.

One look at Bryanne's face, and Jillian knew that the luncheon with her father had been a disaster. She waited for Brynnie to speak.

"He's going away again."

"Oh, darling, I'm so sorry." Jillian watched as the young face crumpled and the tears began to spill. She held out her arms, and Bryanne went into them, shaking with sobs. Jillian held her, making small comforting sounds, patting her back soothingly. But she was seething inside! *How could he? How could he just go off and leave this precious person, so loving and eager and begging to be cherished?* Was Jeff Montrose so completely self-centered that he couldn't see his daughter's need?

Just then there was a gentle tap at the bedroom door, and it inched open. Lynette's worried face peeked around the edge. "I heard Brynnie crying and I . . . what happened?"

Jillian motioned for her to come in, and Bryanne turned in Jillian's arms, her eyes red. "Oh, Lynette!" she wailed, and the sobbing began afresh. "He's going away again . . . I just met him and he's leaving."

Tears glistened in Lynette's eyes and she nodded. "I know, I know, Brynnie," she whispered, a sob in her voice. "Oh, honey, I know how it hurts." The tears spilled over and ran down her cheeks. "The only thing I can tell you, the only thing that works is . . ." And here Jillian heard the usually soft voice harden—"I just don't count on him, Brynnie. Just don't expect anything." Her voice broke. "But we have each other, Brynnie. And from now on, you can count on *me*."

Jillian felt her own throat swell with emotion. Quietly she got to her feet and tiptoed out of the room, leaving Lynette and Bryanne to comfort each other.

Jeff Montrose's departure had many repercussions. Not the least of them was that of his mother, Blythe.

Coming upstairs one evening, Kitty was surprised to see her mother's bedroom door ajar. Blythe had excused herself right after dinner, saying she thought she would retire early, and left as the others were setting up the board to play Parcheesi. "I didn't think you'd still be awake, Mama."

Blythe was seated at her dressing table. Her hair, still a rich auburn, fell in rippling waves over the shoulders of her creamy lace negligee. Looking into the mirror she saw Kitty's reflection and, laying down the silver-crested brush, turned to face her. "Come in, darling. I wanted to talk to you. I've been thinking for some time that I'd like to go to

England for a while. Actually since right after your father died, but there was always something to prevent it." She paused. "You can take charge here, can't you? See to Lynette? And there's Jillian to help with Bryanne. And of course, Garnet . . ." Blythe's voice trailed off weakly. Neither of them really believed Garnet would be of much help in keeping things running smoothly at Cameron Hall.

"Of course, Mama, I'd do whatever I can. Maybe a trip would be a nice change for you. But why not go to Paris and see Cara first? I know she'd love that."

"Oh, I don't know, Kitty." Blythe looked pensive. "Cara is so busy with her work at the orphanage, she hardly has time to write, much less play tourist guide. . . ." She hesitated. "I do want to see her, of course. But it's England I've been longing to visit."

"Why England, Mama?"

"I suppose because I was happy there once. . . ." Her eyes took on a dreamy expression.

"Whatever you think is best, Mama. I'll be glad to help out while you're away . . . but I don't think you should depend too much on Aunt Garnet. She's been acting moody lately. You know she was furious that Jeff went off again, feels he deserted Gareth in particular, and that she'll have to take care of him. She told me just the other day that if she didn't see to it, he'd even go without meals!"

"I suppose she's right." Blythe sighed. She was weary of trying to find excuses for Jeff. He was her son, but he was a grown man now. And there was nothing she could do about the way he chose to live his life. If only Faith had lived. . . .

"When are you thinking of going, Mama?"

"Oh, I don't know. Maybe I should wait until this campaign is over. . . . Scott needs me here. I just wanted you to know what I've been thinking."

"Well, don't worry, I'll be here." Kitty came over to kiss her mother's cheek. "You have seemed tired lately. Now get to bed and try to get a good night's rest."

Blythe patted the hand her daughter placed on her shoulder. "Thank you, darling. I knew I could count on you to understand."

Kitty left the room, and was closing her mother's door softly behind her when she saw Garnet standing at the top of the stairway. Her aunt's face was set, the mouth fixed in a tight line, her eyes flashing fire. In a split second, Kitty realized her aunt must have come upstairs and overheard their conversation through the open door.

"Why, Auntie, I didn't see you," she said, groping for something to say.

There was an expression of outrage on Garnet's face and her mouth twisted with scorn. "Life used to be so agreeably simple. People knew their responsibilities and did their duty, whether or not it was *convenient*. Something that seems to have escaped your *brother* entirely." Garnet's voice was cold and unfeeling as it always was when she spoke of Jeff.

Kitty regarded her aunt with a mingling of pity and irritation. She loved her, but she also knew that the resentment the woman harbored toward her son-in-law was embittering her. Even though she partially agreed with Garnet's estimation of Jeff, she tried now to defuse her anger. "Well, artists are different, Aunt Garnet. They don't seem to see things quite as black and white as some of us do. Maybe Jeff feels that Gareth, Lynette, and Bryanne are grown-ups now. Besides, they do have lots of people around them who care. . . ."

"Oh, Kitty, don't! I'm not a fool. I've known Jeff for years. He's a Peter Pan, has never grown up. Has never been allowed to," she said bitterly. With this, she turned and started down the hallway toward her room.

Kitty hurried after her. "Wait, Aunt Garnet!"

"I'm going to bed, Kitty."

"But it's early. Why don't you come back downstairs and finish the game with us?"

"No, Kitty." Her tone brooked no argument.

Kitty sighed. "Well then, rest well. I hope you feel better in the morning." She leaned over to kiss her aunt, but Garnet averted her head. Kitty drew back, feeling the chill. What had happened to change her aunt's feelings, to put such a barrier between them? But then, of course, she knew . . . it was her defense of Jeff.

chapter
22

W<small>ITH ONLY</small> six weeks before the election, the senatorial race heated up considerably. Everyone at Cameron Hall had become involved. Talk at the dinner table nearly always revolved around the political scene. Both Kitty and Lynette joined in the discussions enthusiastically, as did even Jillian, who wasn't an American citizen and wouldn't be able to vote. But that hadn't discouraged her from going with Kitty and Blythe to help out at campaign headquarters—answering the phone, stuffing envelopes, mailing brochures, passing out campaign materials.

Not being old enough to vote, Bryanne was left more and more on her own. She missed the morning horseback rides Lynette and Jill were now too busy to take with her. She tried hard not to resent all the time her sister was spending on Frank Maynard's campaign. Still, there was one consolation. It would all be over the third Tuesday in June!

In the meantime, Bryanne had started taking long afternoon horseback rides alone through the woods between Cameron Hall and Montclair. One of her favorite places was the trail leading to Aunt Kitty's little house, Eden Cottage. There in the clearing, Bryanne would dismount, tether her horse nearby, and walk through the garden with its flagstone path, sit in the grape arbor, or even peek through the windows.

It was such a sweet little house, maybe like Snow White's cottage in her favorite childhood fairy-tale. It was closed up now. Kitty never went there herself. Perhaps it made her too sad to recall the days she had spent there with her husband. Someone should live there and be happy!

Bryanne had always dreamed of having a house of her own. One Christmas, when she was given a dollhouse, complete with a family of miniature dolls, she had spent hours playing with them, carrying on conversations, giving birthday parties for the "children," creating an imaginary world where everyone was safe and happy.

She had long since stopped playing with dolls. But the dream had lodged in her heart. What Bryanne wanted more than anything else would be to one day have a little house where she and a husband and children could live "happily ever after." She certainly did *not* want the social life her Grandmother Devlin was planning for her. But would she ever find someone who would love her for herself, just as she was, and want to live the kind of life she wanted?

Returning from her ride a little after five o'clock one afternoon, Bryanne saw cars parked in front of the house. Scott was probably having another one of those political meetings. Her cousin was spending as much time in the behind-the-scenes strategy sessions for Frank Maynard's campaign as he was in the editor's office of the *Messenger*.

Bryanne couldn't understand how Lynette could endure sitting in on all those boring discussions. The fact was, though, that her sister actually seemed to enjoy them, always taking great pains with her hair and dress when Scott announced one, and going down early to be sure the refreshment trays were set up in the library where the men gathered.

Well, thank goodness, no one expected *her* to make an appearance. Often these meetings went on indefinitely. On these nights, a cold supper was set out, buffet style, so everyone could help themselves. Since no one would be looking for her until after the meeting, Bryanne rode around the back and down to the stables. Maybe she'd have a chance to talk to Sean, if he wasn't too busy.

In the cobbled courtyard, she looked around, hoping Sean had seen her ride in and would come out to say hello. But no one seemed to be around, not even the little stable boy who helped out. Disappointed, Bryanne proceeded to take off Star's saddle and bridle, lead her into her stall, rub her down, and give her a bucket of oats. Then she went into the tack room to put away her gear, lingering there for a few minutes to see if Sean might show up and talk to her a little.

Not being able to think of any other excuse to delay, she walked back into the stable and stopped at one of the stalls where Lady, one of Scott's foxhounds, was nestled in a basket with her four new pups. They were still too young to be handled, so Bryanne satisfied herself by leaning over the lower half of the wooden door to watch the fat brown-

and-white spotted bodies tumbling over each other in their haste to nuzzle their mother.

Bryanne was so totally absorbed that she didn't realize her wish had been granted until a voice spoke behind her, with its familiar lilting accent. "Good afternoon, Miss Bryanne."

She whirled about, heart thumping, to see Sean entering the stable, leading Nightingale. The late afternoon sun outlined his tall figure and burnished his hair, turning it to pure gold. At the sight of him, Bryanne felt absurdly happy.

"That's a fine litter she's got, isn't it?" he asked, stepping up beside her.

"Oh, yes, they're darling!" she replied, hating that her voice sounded all squeaky.

"Have you been ridin'?"

"Yes." She felt as if the breath were being squeezed from her body and there was none left to say more.

"You've already tended to Star then?"

"Yes."

"Good girl." He nodded, and she felt pleased by the approval in his eyes.

"I guess Cato was gone. I sent him home early. Didn't see you ride in, or I'd have come up. A dandy day for a ride, wasn't it?" he said as he drew near and stood stroking the horse's velvety nose. "I've been down in the far pasture, putting this lady through her paces. I'm riding her at the show next month, you know."

"No, I didn't know."

"Ah, well, things have been in a bit of a turmoil up at the house, I imagine. With the election comin' up, and all. A local horse show isn't that much of an event with Mr. Scott, I don't think, not like it was with your grandfather, I'm thinkin'."

"You *knew* my grandfather?"

"Yes, and a grand man he was, too. He came over at least once a year to visit our farm, you know. I've known him ever since I was a small boy." Sean fished in his pocket and brought out some lumps of sugar for Nightingale, patting her neck affectionately. "She's a foal of one of my Dad's mares . . . good bloodline. She'll make a champion, I'm shure of it . . ." He paused for a moment—"though I may not be here to see it."

148

At his words, Bryanne felt something cold clutch her heart. "What do you mean?"

"Well, my contract with Mr. Scott was only for a year, and it's almost up."

"Aren't you going to stay?" she asked in a small voice.

"It's not been discussed actually. He's so busy with Mr. Maynard's campaign that he's hardly here long enough to talk."

"I know." Bryanne felt a sinking sensation in the pit of her stomach. If Sean was not going to be here . . .

"I guess we'll just have to wait and see." He shrugged. "Well, I can't keep this lady waiting for her well-earned rubdown and dinner." He started to turn the horse around to lead her back to the stall when he halted and gave Bryanne a searching look. "Have you never been to Ireland yourself then?"

"No, I haven't."

"I thought maybe, livin' in England and bein' so close and all, you might have."

Feeling somehow guilty that she had not, Bryanne shook her head sheepishly and Sean grinned. "*You'd* love Ireland!"

"I'm sure I would." She smiled, feeling as delighted as if he had just paid her the highest compliment.

"Well, I'm off now. I'll see you later," he said, giving her a little wave. Then suddenly he turned back again. "Will you be ridin' again in the mawrnin' then?"

"Yes, probably, unless there's some reason I shouldn't."

"I just wondered . . . because I'm takin' Nightingale out early and thought you might ride along. She seems to do better when she has a little competition."

Bryanne was amazed at the singing happiness of her heart at such a simple request and eagerly agreed to be at the stables by seven.

On the way back to the house, her step was lighter. Since coming to Virginia, she had often felt awkward, out of place, but never with Sean. He was so natural, so easy to talk to, and seemed able to draw her out without appearing to pry. Maybe it was because he recognized in her a mutual love for horses, the countryside, the out of doors—all the things he loved. Or maybe, because he simply accepted her.

This was a new experience for Bryanne. Grandmother Devlin always found things to correct about her posture, her dress, her speech. Jillian, because she was paid to do so, supported Grandmother's campaign to improve her granddaughter. Of course, the governess did so with great tact and gentleness. Even so, Bryanne felt that she fell short of *everyone's* expectations. Too bad she couldn't be a poised, pretty, socially acceptable granddaughter like Lynette!

Of course, Lynette was perfect . . . at least in Bryanne's eyes. She wished to be more like her. But that was impossible. She knew she was a disappointment to Grandmother and one of Jillian's few failures. Grandmother had even stopped talking about Bryanne's making her debut at Cameron Hall. Probably afraid she would be a wallflower at her own coming-out party!

When she had almost reached the house, Bryanne saw her sister standing on the terrace and stopped to gaze at her. Lynette's floppy-brimmed straw hat shadowed her face but provided a charming background for her cameo profile. She was wearing a voile print with tiny blue flowers, and she had on white pumps with small bows at the toes. Bryanne watched as Lynette moved to the edge of the terrace. There was an air of expectancy about her. Then Bryanne saw Frank Maynard sprint up the stone steps, two at a time. A minute later, they were locked in an embrace.

Bryanne gasped and stepped behind a large boxwood, out of sight. Lynette and Frank Maynard were in love! How had they kept their secret all this time, through the long campaign? Not by one look or one gesture would anyone have guessed! Or was it only she who hadn't noticed?

Bryanne turned and went quietly around to the back of the house and up to her room by the back stairway. It was there an hour later that Lynette waltzed through the door with a radiant smile. "Oh, Brynnie, the most wonderful thing has happened! Frank and I are engaged! Look!"

She held out her left hand for Bryanne to see. On the third finger of her left hand glistened a circle of emeralds alternating with pearls. "It was his grandmother's. Isn't it lovely? But you're not to tell anyone, not a single soul. I won't be able to wear it except here in our room. Frank and I are keeping our engagement a secret until after the election. But I couldn't keep it any longer from *you!*"

chapter
23

THE NEXT few weeks were the happiest Bryanne had known since coming to Virginia. Taken into Lynette's confidence, she felt closer than ever to her beloved sister. Entrusted with such a romantic secret fueled her own feelings for Sean McShane. Was this what love felt like? She wanted to ask Lynette some more about how it was for her and Frank.

But now that the campaign was entering the final weeks, the pace had become frenetic. Cameron Hall buzzed with activity. Scott, Kitty, and Lynette were constantly on the go. Even Grandmother Blythe was busy working for Frank, giving "coffees" to ladies she knew who never before had voted in an election, attending rallies, and manning the headquarters when everyone else was occupied elsewhere. The only one not caught up in the preelection excitement, Bryanne was left on her own.

Her leisurely pace felt rather strange at first. In England, especially when they were at the London town house, her days were so tightly scheduled that she never had a minute to call her own. There were music lessons and elocution lessons, dancing class, and French to refine her accent, drilling in verbs and conversation. When they were abroad, it was hardly a vacation. Grandmother always prepared a complete agenda of historic sites, museums, and galleries she must visit when they were in Venice, Florence, Rome, and other great cities of the world.

Wearily Bryanne had come to realize that Garnet's demands on her were unsatiable. No matter how well she did, there was always one more goal for her to reach. It was like teaching a horse to jump, Bryanne decided, raising the pole higher and higher.

She had hoped that when they came to Virginia, things might

change. Quite inadvertently they had. It was Grandmother Devlin again. The woman managed to create a crisis wherever she went. She plunged into every situation, full sail ahead, leaving chaos in her wake. Now, distracted from her focus on Bryanne, she had shifted her primary concern to Gareth. With Bryanne's brother as the target of her concern, she was more and more vocal in her criticism of his father, Jeff. At least, Bryanne thought with an unconscious sigh of relief, Grandmother had moved to Avalon for the present, and so Brynnie herself was not under constant surveillance.

Bryanne was enjoying her "freedom." Her daily contact with Sean was the source of much of her newfound happiness. Every morning she met him at the stable where he had saddled her horse, Star, and was waiting at the mounting block for her. Then they would set out together, ostensibly to give Nightingale the exercise she needed prior to her test at the horse show next month. But sometimes they stopped by the creek that ran between the Montrose and Cameron properties and let the horses rest for a while. Those were the times Bryanne most looked forward to, treasured afterward.

There were wonderful talks, touching on all sorts of subjects. Talks that revealed just how much they had in common. One discovery she had made—that Sean liked poetry—came one day while pausing at Eden Cottage.

Inspired by the charming woodland scene, he had recited softly:

> E'er I descend to the grave
> May I a small house and large garden have!
> And a few friends and many books, both true,
> Both wise and both delightful, too!

Looking at him in surprise, Bryanne had blurted out before she thought, "A horse trainer who quotes poetry!"

Manly as he was, Sean did not seem in the least embarrassed to admit it. "It's said that every Irishman has poetry in his soul." He smiled. "Don't you like poetry?"

"Yes, very much. That is, I like it so much better now that I'm not required to memorize it . . . like I did when I was in boarding school in England."

He chuckled empathically. "I know what you mean. I hated the confinement of a classroom, too. Had much rather be out ridin' my horse. I was Shakespeare's lad, I'm afraid. You know:

And then the whining school-boy, with his satchel,
And shining morning face, creeping like snail
Unwillingly to school.

"However," he confessed with a grin, "I'd often take my book of Yeats in my saddlebag to read with my lunch on the moor."

"Irish poets only?"

"No, not exclusively. I like your Walt Whitman, his strong, vital verse. And, of course, Tennyson. What's not to like about Tennyson?"

Bryanne felt a little lift of her heart. "Oh, yes! *The Idylls of the King* . . . I didn't have to be forced to learn those lines!"

"Romantic poetry at his best," commented Sean, allowing his eyes to rest on Bryanne for a moment.

For a moment she found it hard to breathe, then directed his attention to Eden Cottage. "That's Aunt Kitty's house, you know."

"Yes. I've wondered why she doesn't live there."

"Maybe because she was so happy there with her husband, and when he died . . ."

"She seems happy enough now."

"Well, she's busy anyway. Working for Frank Maynard in the election. Everyone is."

"And what about you?" He studied the fresh face turned toward him. "You're not interested in politics?"

"Not really, I'm afraid. I'm not old enough to vote."

"You're . . . ?"

"I'll be eighteen in August."

"Then you're the same age as my brother Michael," Sean said, taking a few steps toward the lovely little garden. "I didn't think it was possible, but I miss that fella . . . and the younger ones, too."

"So you miss your home . . . miss Ireland?" she asked, with a little prickle of apprehension.

"Oh, shure I do. But I like Virginia more and more. And this is a foine opportunity for a lad. It's not as if my dad were left in a lurch by not havin' me at home. Mike is more than capable of doin' what I did, and there's two more after him, ready to step into our shoes."

Bryanne's throat felt tight. Why was Sean telling her all this? Then she remembered what he had said about his contract. Was he trying to tell her that he was anxious to return to Ireland, to his family? What if there were some Irish colleen waiting for him?

153

As if reading her thought, Sean said, "I'm planning to go home for a few weeks at the end of summer, visit my folks, and then if Mr. Cameron wants be back, well, then, I'll come."

Bryanne tried to think of something to say to assure him that Scott was certain to want him back, but before she could say anything, Sean asked, "And will you be going back to England yourself?"

"It's been decided I'm to attend a school here next fall and—"

"It's been decided, has it?" He didn't let her finish but gazed at her with a hint of a smile. "You don't decide for yourself then?" He raised his eyebrows. "I thought American girls made up their own minds."

There didn't seem to be anything to say to that.

"I was only teasing," he said as if he realized he had discomfited her. "My black Irish humor. Growing up as I did in a big family, we're all great for giving each other a hard time. Don't pay me any mind." He smiled, and there was something in the smile and in Sean's eyes that made Bryanne feel foolishly happy. You only teased someone you liked or apologized to someone you cared about if you felt you might have hurt their feelings.

"It's all right. I understand."

Sean turned to look at Eden Cottage again. "Now, if I had a small home of my own like this one, I'd be more than content to stay."

"It is a sweet little house. I've become fond of it too."

After a moment, Sean said softly in that voice with its lilt she found so endearing, "You know, there's more to that poem I quoted, another verse besides. It goes:

> And since Love ne'er will from me flee,
> A Mistress moderately fair,
> And good as guardian-angels are,
> Only beloved and loving me.

That's what makes life truly fine. A man and a woman who love one another and are happy together in their home. That's the way my parents are. I wish you knew them."

"I do too," Bryanne said in a whisper.

"Someday you will," Sean said quietly. Without another word they walked back to where their horses were tethered, and Sean helped her up into her saddle, and they rode back toward Cameron Hall.

After that afternoon at Eden Cottage, their relationship underwent a subtle change. Without anything being arranged, Sean had Bryanne's horse saddled and ready, and they rode together every day. For Bryanne the feeling growing between them was too precious to examine, too new to explore too closely for fear it would vanish. She had never expected anything like Sean to happen to her.

Sean had so much that she didn't have, that she envied: a real family, a home he loved, brothers and sisters he was close to, a direction to his life, goals he wanted to achieve. He was strong, manly, yet sensitive. He had cared enough to share some with her. Things she was sure he didn't share with others. That must mean he trusted her. Was it possible Sean loved her?

Bryanne did not have long to wonder. Only a week after that day in the woods, they met in the ornate Victorian gazebo at the end of the garden between the house and the stables, and Sean told her so. She had cried, and he had laughingly dried her tears. "That was supposed to make you happy!" he had teased.

"It does, it did, I *am*." she protested through her tears, and they had kissed. For the first time in her life Bryanne felt she was loved, accepted, and understood in a way no one else had ever done.

Cherishing her secret, Bryanne could not help think what the family would say if they knew. How would the grandmothers accept it? She was sure Grandmother Blythe would be pleased. But Grandmother Devlin? Bryanne felt a bit guilty admitting that Garnet was somewhat of a snob. There were the "right" people, as far as she was concerned, and they were mostly *Virginians!* and then there were "others." Bryanne wasn't sure in what category Grandmother Devlin might place Sean.

What if Sean asked her to marry? Would they live in Ireland?

Her head whirled with all the possibilities.

Unknown to Bryanne, her rendezvous with Sean had been observed. Jillian had been in the library at the French windows enjoying its view of velvety green lawns, clipped boxwood hedges, sweeping down to the garden centered by the gazebo. Actually, she had been romantically day-dreaming, thinking what a perfect place the latticed gazebo, with its trailing wisteria vines providing privacy, would be for a lovers' tryst.

Then as she stood there she saw two figures emerge, Bryanne and Sean McShane. Deep in conversation, they stopped for a moment.

Then Sean leaned down and kissed Bryanne's cheek, and hand-in-hand they strolled toward the stables. Jillian drew in a startled breath.

She could only imagine what Mrs. Devlin would say if she suspected anything like this was going on. She would probably blame Jillian for not being aware of it and not nipping such an "unsuitable" romance in the bud.

Of course, Mrs. Devlin had been preoccupied with other things since her return to Mayfield, mainly the plight of her grandson Gareth. But if she knew about *this* . . . Just then the sound of the door opening made her turn. Scott was standing at the entrance to the library. Smiling, he asked, "Am I disturbing you?"

"Not at all," she replied quickly, hoping her inner confusion was not evident.

"I've been wanting to talk to you," Scott said, coming in and closing the door. "But there's been so much else going on—"

Jillian stiffened. *Here it comes,* she thought, unconsciously bracing herself for the inevitable message she had been more or less expecting. *Since Bryanne will be going away to school in the fall, your services will no longer be needed.*

Scott's first words were almost verbatim what she had anticipated. "I'm sure you're aware that my mother and Aunt Garnet have been discussing Bryanne's future. As her companion these past years, whatever is eventually decided will affect you."

"Yes, of course, I understand that." Jillian willed her voice not to shake.

"We all feel you have done a marvelous job, provided her with the affection and companionship she needed." He paused. "But you've become so much more than that. Certainly to Bryanne and—to all of us—the whole family."

"That's very kind of you to say."

"Not kind at all, just true." Scott cleared his throat, then asked, "Have you been happy here in Virginia?"

"Oh, yes, quite, in fact, very happy," she replied.

"Would you consider staying on then? I mean, even if Bryanne goes away?"

"I don't think I know what you mean. . . ." Scott was looking at her in a way she found curious and a little unsettling.

"Or maybe I'm assuming too much. Maybe you've already made plans, perhaps you're anxious to go back to England?" His voice held some other unspoken question. But Jillian was uncertain what it was or what she should answer. She didn't want him to feel sorry for her. Or to think that any decisions about Bryanne would leave her adrift, without plans.

"Oh, no, it's not that," she said.

"I wouldn't want to pressure you or anything. But I wanted to—had to—find out how you felt about it all—I mean, America, about Virginia, actually, about *us*."

Scott, usually so articulate, confident, was floundering suddenly, and it surprised Jillian. There was something in the way he was looking at her that made her heart rush foolishly. Then he moved toward her, holding out both hands. For one crazy moment she thought he might take her in his arms. But just then the sound of raised voices coming from the hall reached them. Scott lifted his head, turned to listen. He frowned.

"Uh-oh, Mama and Aunt Garnet."

Garnet's voice, cold with anger, could be clearly heard.

"Well, Blythe, you're running away again, I understand. That seems to be a habit of yours when you can't cope with things. Your *son* seems to have inherited the same trait. Never mind what chaos is left behind or who gets hurt."

"That's not fair, Garnet." Blythe's tone was grieved, then rose defensively. "Jeff's art, his work, is his priority—it has been for years."

"As *my* daughter discovered to her sorrow—"

"You know that's not true, Garnet. Faith loved Jeff. They were very, very happy. I'm sure Faith never regretted her marriage."

"You don't think that *your* running off to England is exactly the same as Jeff's going to New Mexico?" Garnet accused. "I see no difference. I think you both are shirking your responsibilities here." Her voice turned sarcastic. "I suppose while you're away, the rest of us are supposed to do your duty for you both."

"Garnet! Gareth, Lynette, and even Bryanne are no longer children. They don't need grandmothers hovering over them! Besides both Jillian and Kitty will be here, and Scott."

"Scott! A *bachelor!* What does *he* know about keeping an eye on impulsive young people!" Garnet's tone implied her disdain for Scott's abilities to manage things.

Scott's eyebrows shot up. He glanced at Jillian, saying, "I better go out there and see if I can negotiate a truce." He walked purposefully to the door, with his hand on the knob, turned and gave her a conspiratorial wink, then went out into the hall.

There he found his mother looking distraught. Garnet's luggage was piled high at the front door. At the sight of Scott, Garnet announced: "I'm moving over to Avalon, Scott. Someone has to take care of Gareth." She threw Blythe an indignant look.

"If that's what you feel you should do, Aunt Garnet," Scott said calmly. "I'll be glad to take you over there myself."

Garnet looked a little startled to have her ultimatum accepted so readily.

chapter

24

Avalon

Spring 1926

SURROUNDED BY MOUNTAINS of monogrammed luggage, Garnet looked about her with dismay and gave a small involuntary shiver. She had never understood why her daughter had been so enamored of this house, brought stone by stone from England and reconstructed on this isolated island in Virginia.

After their elopement Faith had moved here with Jeff. Grudgingly, Garnet had to admit that the place *did* have a certain austere beauty. The exterior, built of timber and plaster, was typical of the best of the Tudor period, with its beautifully carved oriel windows and richly ornamented gables over leaded casements. The original was the Dower House belonging to an aristocratic English family whose line could be traced back to the royal Plantagenets.

Probably Faith, poor darling, had tried to share her husband's enthusiasm for the place. Jeff, the son of the late Malcolm Montrose and her old nemesis, Blythe Cameron, had grown up here with his widowed mother before her marriage to Garnet's brother Rod. Thinking now of her sister-in-law, Garnet's lips thinned.

Well, she wouldn't waste a minute worrying about their latest little altercation. There was too much to be done here. She must set things straight, get Gareth organized.

Gareth. She turned her attention to the young man standing opposite her, at the moment looking rather bewildered. He was tall and thin, his weight having not quite caught up to his height. His dark hair was shaggy, needing a good trim. He was wearing stained corduroys, a worn jacket, heavy boots. But for all his indifference to appearance, there was something extraordinarily disarming about him. Something that reminded Garnet of Jonathan. Jonathan—whom she loved like a son, the son she had never had, Malcolm and Rose's son, the son she might have had with Malcolm . . . if things had been different. . . .

Sharply Garnet pulled her thoughts from the never-to-be-recaptured past. Gareth was waiting for an answer. "Where do you want me to take your bags, Grandmother?"

Her heart melted. What a dear boy he was! There would be plenty of time later to deal with his careless dress. Right now, it was important to establish a rapport with him, show him that she was here to stay and take charge. "I suppose there's a guest room?"

Gareth's brow furrowed. "I don't think so. Father never had overnight guests, and he hasn't entertained at all since Mother . . ."

Garnet checked her comments on the lack of accommodations and the necessity of always being prepared for unexpected visits. Why, at Cameron Hall or even Montclair, for that matter, visitors were expected to stay anywhere from a fortnight to a month at a time. In the olden days, when travel was more difficult, some guests stayed for up to a year!

She sighed. "Well, ring for the maid. I'll need her to put fresh linens on the bed in whatever room is available and to air it out thoroughly for now. I'll make my own selection when I have a chance to look through the house."

"But, Grandmother," Gareth said, "I don't think you understand. There *is* no maid. Father dismissed the staff before he left for New Mexico."

Garnet stared at her grandson in utter disbelief. "I don't believe it! How could he have been so irresponsible? What on earth did he expect you to do?"

"Fend for myself, I suppose. What I've always done, Grandmother . . . at least, for the last couple of years."

"Fend for yourself?" she repeated, still in a state of shock. "A young man on his own? Whatever could your father be thinking?" Unconsciously, she began to pace, her mind whirling. "Well, we shall have to do something about this at once. But until then . . ." She paused and faced Gareth, saying briskly, "First things first. I'm starved. I left Cameron Hall before dinner. And since there's no cook, I suppose we must find something to eat. Where's the kitchen?"

The rest of the house might be medieval in feel, but the kitchen had been completely renovated and modernized before Faith left on her ill-fated journey to England in the spring of 1912. It was well-lighted, well-equipped, with plenty of counters, a coal stove, and a large icebox. Garnet removed her hat and gloves and, finding a large chef's apron hanging on a hook, tied it over her fashionable ensemble and began opening cabinets and inspecting the shelves.

Gareth stood, almost at attention, as if awaiting orders. As Garnet alternately hummed and talked to herself, he shifted from one foot to the other.

Finally he suggested, "There are plenty of vegetables, Grandmother. I put in a large garden in the spring, and we can have almost anything you want for a salad or stew, or whatever you'd like."

Garnet, who had not been in a kitchen or used a stove or stirred a pudding in more than thirty years, halted in her search and surveyed her grandson with new interest. "That was very enterprising of you, Gareth. I'm glad to see you don't wander around with your head in the clouds . . . like your artist father." Hands on hips, she regarded him for a moment, considering. "You've eggs, too, I imagine. Yes, well, good. We'll have an omelet and a nice salad. That will do for this evening. Tomorrow's another thing entirely. I may have to see about hiring some help."

Thus passed Garnet's first evening at Avalon, a not altogether unpleasant experience for either of them.

The next morning when she came down to the kitchen, Garnet found the coffee already brewed. Gareth poured her a cup and greeted her cheerfully.

Pleasantly surprised that her grandson was continuing to demonstrate his resourcefulness, Garnet could not resist broaching the subject of his future. "What are your plans, dear? I mean, after the summer?" she asked, taking a sip of the very good coffee. "I can't understand why you didn't want to go to college. Or even come to England and attend Oxford. I would have been more than happy to have you make Birchfields your home if that had been your decision. You could have come there for holidays and such."

"This may sound strange to you, Grandmother," Gareth said, "but I hated the idea of four more years of school. I like being outdoors. Maybe it was growing up here at Avalon, with all this freedom, or being with my father in New Mexico. I love gardening, Grandmother. And I like working with my hands . . . love the smell of the earth . . . enjoy sawing wood and stacking it. I can't explain it. I just like it, that's all."

There was a stubborn jut to his chin that stabbed Garnet. It was Faith all over again, she realized with a start. She was reminded of her daughter's arguments with her about attending debutante parties, trying to persuade her to like what she herself had loved as a girl. How trivial such things seemed now. Why on earth had she made such a fuss over them?

But it was futile to spend time in regretting the past. There was the present to think about. Her grandson Gareth. She must help him map out his future. But this time she would be more careful. She would not be dogmatic or dictatorial but tactful and persuasive. After all, a *man* had to *do* something, *be* somebody.

So the days passed. Garnet settled in, if only temporarily. Privately she fretted over the lack of communication between Jeff and his son. Gareth seemed perfectly content with the situation and eventually with the idea of his grandmother's staying on at Avalon.

Garnet took upon herself the task of hiring a couple to clean, cook, and maintain the large house. Meanwhile Gareth spent his days as he had for the past year when he had chosen to stay here rather than accompany his father to Taos for the winter. He worked in the garden, built and repaired fences, and rode his horse through the acres of woodland on the island.

Almost a week after moving to Avalon, Garnet braced herself for a visit to the master wing once occupied by Jeff and Faith. It was a suite of rooms comprised of a bedroom, sitting room, boudoir, and dressing room. As Garnet walked through the door, she had the sensation of stepping back in time. The suite was decorated in a style reminiscent of medieval paintings—rich velvet bed draperies, elaborate tapestries, heavy carved thirteenth-century furniture.

She hesitated before she could bring herself to open the door into the adjoining sitting room that had belonged to her daughter. Here Faith had spent hours working on her tapestry designs and reading to her children. Through the diamond-paned windows, Garnet could see an enclosed garden where fruit trees, espaliered against a stone wall, were in full bloom.

Faith's tapestry frame, a partially finished piece stretched upon it, had been placed in an alcove near the windows. Garnet moved slowly across the room and stood behind the frame. She studied the design being worked. Taking shape was a border of intricately petaled roses in varying shades of red—delicate pinks to deep mauves—interwoven with ivy leaves. On a table to the right was a basket of bright-colored yarns. Propped against a vase that held a few dried brown roses that must have been Faith's models, was a card on which was printed a poem—probably the verse Faith was going to work into her tapestry.

Too vain to wear glasses even though it was now difficult for her to see to read, Garnet lifted the lorgnette she wore on a silver chain around her neck and leaned closer to read the verse:

> My life is but a weaving
> Between my Lord and me;
> I may not choose the colors
> He worketh steadily;
> Sometimes He weaveth sorrow—
> And I in foolish pride,
> Forget He sees the upper,
> And I the underside.

Faith had begun to copy the poem onto her design. A needle was poised in the tapestry cloth as if Faith had been taking a stitch when called away for some reason, intent on returning to finish it.

Tears blurred the lettering, and Garnet swallowed over the painful lump in her throat. Feeling once again the keen loss that had not diminished in nearly fourteen years, she turned away quickly and walked out of the room, closing the door behind her.

Struggling to control her emotions, Garnet went outside. She stood for a moment, taking deep breaths, hoping that the sunshine and balmy breeze would help her regain her equilibrium.

Walking around the side of the house, she came upon an addition that had been built when Jeff and Faith moved here to live. It was Jeff's studio. She could tell from the windows facing north and the slanted skylight built to catch the late-afternoon sun.

Garnet had never been inside Jeff's studio, had never seen his work except in galleries. Curious, she approached the room. Ivy grew thickly on either side of the front door, and a rambling rosebush clambered over as if attempting to conceal it from passersby. Pushing the vines aside, Garnet tried the door handle, expecting it to be locked. To her surprise, it moved easily and, with a slight pressure, yielded to her touch.

One would think that Jeff would have locked up before he left, she mused. Maybe he had taken all his paintings with him. Or perhaps all of them were placed in galleries somewhere. On the other hand, since Jeff was in Taos doing a whole new set of paintings, it was more likely that he had stored his canvases here.

Cautiously Garnet entered. Light streaming into the high-ceilinged room revealed that it was amazingly neat and orderly. Garnet had always assumed that artists' studios were cluttered and untidy, but this one was organized and workmanlike. A large easel, draped with a dun-colored linen cloth, occupied the center of the room. Beside it on a square table were containers of brushes of all sizes, bottles of turpentine, varnish, and a palette encrusted with dried paint, as if it had only just been laid aside.

Looking around, Garnet recognized this as the studio of a true professional, a man passionate about his work. Canvases of all sizes and shapes were turned to the wall all around the room. Along the back wall was a storage area with a length of wooden upright shelves in which unframed canvases could be kept.

Suddenly aware of the cold, Garnet shivered. There was a wood stove in one corner, probably to provide heat when Jeff was working in here. But since the studio had been unused for months, a damp chill permeated the place.

Rubbing her arms briskly to warm herself, Garnet walked over to the concealed canvas on the easel. This must be something Jeff had been working on and had not had time to complete before he left. Reaching out with one hand, she gently tugged away the drape.

Upon seeing the painting, Garnet let out a sigh that was almost a sob and stepped back as if struck. Although she knew that Jeff had often used Faith as his model, seeing that beloved face so accurately reproduced was a shock. Garnet had not seen her daughter since that morning in Southampton when she had kissed her and sent her off with a "Bon voyage!" to board the ill-fated *Titanic*.

The emotional impact of seeing this lifelike portrait of her cherished daughter was intense. Then, slowly, she began to take in details of the painting.

Jeff had become known for his allegorical paintings as well as those with a religious theme. Even in its incomplete state, the portrait was proof that Jeff was a master of his craft. Garnet's eyes moved over the picture, she could see that this work was to be a depiction of the New Testament incident known as "The Woman at the Well."

The background was as yet unfinished, but it was the face that caught and held one's rapt attention. The woman's expression was that of a person who has just been given the most wonderful gift imaginable. The eyes were shining; the skin, glowing; the mouth, full and sensuous, smiling, lips parted as though praises were rising from a heart overflowing with happiness.

"Oh, my darling child!" The words broke from Garnet's lips, more a cry of pain than exclamation. In all the years since she had first heard the news of the disaster, her grief had not abated. It came flooding forth now in heartrending sobs. Putting her head in both hands, she wept brokenly, her shoulders shaking.

Finally, after a period of time she could not have measured, the tears stopped. She dug in her pocket for a handkerchief to wipe her eyes and look once more at the beautifully rendered work. It was Faith, but it was a transcendent Faith.

Garnet drew up the high, wooden artist's stool in front of the easel and sat down, staring at the painting. She was unaware of time's passing. The questions she had never dared to ask for fear of hearing the answer, came now.

"Why, God? Why my *Faith*? She was so young, so happy, so loving and beloved, with so much to live for? I don't understand. I'm angry that You took her!"

Gradually her rebellious spirit calmed. It was as if from somewhere deep within her, she was given answers and, with them, peace. *Why* not *Faith?* she seemed to hear. *She never lost her delight with life . . . with the beauty of things, her spirit filled with wonderment and her virtue as radiant as a star. In the memory of those who loved her, she will always be young and fair.*

Garnet did not know the source of this reassurance, had never been a reader of poetry or the Bible, had never appreciated fine music, yet the words flowing through her heart and mind that afternoon were like a divine melody.

She thought now of the epitaph that Jeremy had chosen for their daughter's memorial stone before he himself died two weeks later. A literary man, he had taken some selections from a favorite passage in Thackeray's *The Newcomes*: "If love lives through all life and survives through all sorrows, surely it is immortal. Though we who remain are separated, if we love still those we love, can we altogether lose those we love?"

How wise, Garnet thought with new appreciation for her husband. She wished she had shown him more respect and gratitude while he was alive.

But this was not the time for remorse. Much as she had resisted coming to Avalon, she would not have missed this afternoon, with all its bittersweet truth.

With growing clarity, Garnet now began to realize that she was on the way to becoming an embittered old woman, filled with resentment, old hurts, imagined slights, and offenses where none were intended. Trying to run other people's lives, being indignant when they shunned her advice.

Life was too short for all this, she decided. Her own life—the nearly seventy years of it—had passed with frightening speed, but she had been left here when others much younger were already gone. Perhaps there was some purpose in it.

She must make the most of what time was left to her. Do better, be kinder, more forgiving, more understanding, more accepting of the differences in people, the changes in the times. . . .

Garnet was not sure how long she remained in Jeff's studio. It seemed a very long time, yet when she came out again, the sun had barely moved through the trees, and the birds were flocking around the birdbath in the garden.

That evening, when Gareth came in, she made no comment on his tousled hair, his disheveled clothing. She did not even urge him to wash up and change his shirt. She only told him when supper was ready, a rich Brunswick stew that she had made because it was cook's night off. To her surprise, he came to the table with his curly hair plastered down and with a fresh shirt on.

But it was he who was surprised when Garnet announced, "I've decided to make plans to leave in a few weeks. My house in England has been completely restored, and I'm anxious to get back. The gardens will be in bloom." She took a spoonful of the stew. "My gardens at Birchfields are quite beautiful. You really should come visit me there."

Gareth smiled, the same smile that had reminded Garnet so sweetly of Jonathan. "I'd like to do that, Grandmother. I really would."

chapter

25

PATCHES OF pink dogwood scattered among the evergreens were breathtaking along the country roads leading into Mayfield. Crystal gripped the steering wheel tensely, trying not to succumb to the fairyland beauty. She was here against her better judgment. All the way down from Richmond, she had been tempted to turn back. But she had promised Kip she would come. So, in spite of everything her innate good sense warned her might happen, she was keeping her promise.

The exhibit had gone well. Gallery owners showing her photographs were pleased. Thirty had sold at the Opening, with orders placed for others. "Last Look," as the exhibit had been entitled, had been an unqualified success.

Still fighting the impulse to turn around and flee to New York, Crystal squared her shoulders and pressed on. A promise was a promise. Besides, she was already on the outskirts of town, only miles now from Montclair and Kip.

Kip! There he was! A picture of Kip, larger than life, stared down at her from a billboard. Startled, she pulled over to the side of the road to get a better look.

She drew in her breath sharply. It was a blown-up print of the photograph she had taken of him on that October day at the airfield. Underneath, she read the slogan: "KIP MONTROSE, WAR ACE, OUR CHOICE. Montrose fought for peace. Now he fights for progress. Kip's the kind of hero we need!"

Still shaken, she started the car again and drove into town. Along the way she passed still more signs, bold and colorful: "OVER THERE, A HERO! OVER HERE, A LEADER! VOTE KIP MONTROSE." There were other signs, too, smaller, less flamboyant, announcing the candidacy of Frank Maynard. That must be Kip's opponent? What was he? And what was he like? Kip would be a hard act to follow.

Somehow, even with the numerous billboards declaring his involvement in the race, Crystal hadn't received the impression that Kip was serious about the campaign. It seemed more like a pleasant pastime for him, another lark. Still, she had to admit there was much more at stake when she caught sight of a red, white, and blue banner draped across a store front on which foot-high letters spelled out: "KIP MONTROSE CAMPAIGN HEADQUARTERS."

She shifted gears and sped by. Unconsciously following the memory of the turn that took her out onto the broad road leading into the countryside, she passed the Dabneys' white-pillared mansion and went straight by the gates of Cameron Hall, heading intuitively for the private road that led to Eden Cottage.

Abruptly she braked and pulled to a stop. Through the wooded glen she could see the house. The windows were shuttered, the place had a closed look. And there on the sloping hillside stood Montclair, the house that so held her in thrall.

A sigh escaped her. *Why did I come back? I should have listened, should have obeyed.*

Since that singular experience in the little church at the Crossroads, Crystal had bought herself a Bible and had begun to read it. Much was puzzling to her, but some parts spoke to her heart, particularly the psalms and proverbs. Now, with her thoughts in turmoil, she took a deep breath and tried to recall a particular verse that seemed meaningful: "Trust in the Lord and lean not on your own understanding."

Slowly she recalled that day at the airfield, the day she had taken Kip's picture, the very one he was now using in his campaign. Vividly she recalled that flash of insight that had come to her so clearly . . . that the glory lavished upon flyers during the war had spoiled him for ordinary things. Kip craved continual adulation, excitement, challenge, the "roar of the crowd." Coming back home after such a heady experience had been a letdown for him. And when she had asked him facetiously what he was going to be when he grew up, he had quipped, "Maybe I'll run for public office."

Poor Kip, she thought sadly. *He'll never change. His head is literally in the clouds.* Whoever shared his life had better be prepared to pick up the pieces when the balloon burst.

169

Well, that was not for her. For the second time, Crystal sighed and said out loud, "I should have listened, Lord, believed what You were trying to tell me when I was here before. . . ."

Minutes passed. It was quiet out here in the shadowed woods. Gradually peace stole over Crystal. She turned on the ignition, swung her station wagon around, and started back into town.

She couldn't leave without seeing Kip. And since it was too late to drive back to Richmond tonight, she'd take a room at the Mayfield Inn and call him in the morning. She needed time to think things through before she saw him.

Crystal's resolve faltered when she heard his enthusiastic greeting over the phone. Luckily for her, he had a campaign commitment, so they arranged to meet in the coffee shop the next morning. She had chosen that public place, knowing that she would need all the support she could get to withstand Kip's persuasive charm, to stand firmly.

And at the sight of Kip, Crystal felt a quick surge of joy she could not completely conceal. He stood for a moment at the entrance, looking for her and giving her a chance to observe him. He was so handsome, so confident and charming. He seemed charged with a new vitality, perhaps fueled by the challenge of the campaign.

Seeing her, he strode over to the booth where she waited. Sliding into the seat across the table, he reached over and took her hands. "I'm so glad you've come, Crystal! So glad you're here . . . and just in time."

She tugged gently to disengage her hands. "No, Kip. It's not what you think. I'm not staying. I've checked out of the hotel and will be leaving as soon as we're finished."

He looked stricken. "What do you mean—leaving? I want to take you to the headquarters, show you off. . . ."

"Kip, just listen," she begged. Crystal chose her words carefully, hoping that the note of insecurity in her voice would not betray her fear that he would somehow talk her into staying. She repeated all her carefully rehearsed arguments, adding to them the fact that she was not cut out to be a politician's wife. She was an artist, a professional who must pursue her own goals. He would have to understand and accept that.

If she didn't know better, Crystal might have detected a pleading tone. "I wish you wouldn't say that. Wish you didn't believe that," Kip said earnestly. "It's only going to be for a few months, and then it will be over and we can go on with our lives . . . our life together."

"But what if you win, Kip, what then?"

"I intend to win, of course, but that shouldn't interfere. . . ."

"Oh, Kip, be reasonable. It could never work," she argued, then took on a teasing tone. "Besides, I've already got my next assignment. Soon I'll be off to England to photograph cottages and castles."

He glanced at his watch impatiently, then said, "I've got to go. The meeting is scheduled at ten. But please, Crystal, don't make this some kind of ultimatum. Can't you at least wait until I'm through there, so we can talk some more. I know I can convince you if you'll give me another chance."

The fact that she knew that to be a real possibility gave strength to her closing argument. "No, Kip, don't even try. Let's just part friends. I do wish you well. If winning is what you really want, then I hope you will. Can't you wish me well, too?"

He frowned, drawing his dark brows together. "I think you're making a terrible mistake. . . ."

It was hopeless to make him understand. The mistake had already been made—coming back at all. But it would be an even greater mistake to stay longer.

chapter

26

STANDING IN FRONT of the bureau mirror in his starched evening shirt and white satin vest, Kip struggled with his bow tie. Couldn't seem to get it right. He tugged at it and started over. Why were his fingers all thumbs tonight? He was nervous, blast it! He wasn't used to feeling that uneasiness in the pit of his stomach. Why should he, anyway? Wasn't the campaign going well? His volunteers at headquarters told him it was, and Hal Woodridge kept clapping him on the back and telling him he was doing "a terrific job."

But Kip wasn't all that sure. He didn't like this feeling of uncertainty. He wished the whole thing were over and done with. What he disliked most about it was that it had alienated him from his old friends. One of his oldest, in fact—Scott Cameron. But doggone it! Hadn't Scott turned his back on him? Kip could have used the endorsement of the *Messenger*. Not having it put a question mark in the minds of a lot of folks about his qualifications for the office of senator. Most people in Mayfield trusted that paper, believed every word they read in it.

Not that Scott hadn't been fair. Kip had to give him that. His old friend had covered all his rallies, meetings, speeches to the service clubs, even the one to the Ladies' Historical Preservation Club and Fuchsia Fanciers!

Kip gave his tie a final yank. Tonight was an important meeting at the Mayfield Club. Woodridge had lined up some of the biggest names in the construction business to attend the dinner, where Kip would be the featured speaker. Hal had promised that these men would contribute heavily to the campaign if he made a good impression. They could sure use the money. Advertising and other campaign expenditures came high.

Kip reached for his gold cuff links and began to insert one in the French cuff of his sleeve when a tap came at his bedroom door. It startled him, and with his nerves already shot, the cuff link slipped out of his fingers and onto the floor. He swore under his breath as the tap came again, followed by Mattie's anxious voice. "Mr. Kip, sir, kin I come in?"

"Sure, Mattie, what is it?"

"It's Luc, Mr. Kip. He doan want to eat his supper. He jest lyin' on his bed. I think he comin' down with somethin'. Doan know jest what, but it ain't like him to be thisaway."

Frowning, Kip turned to face her. She looked worried, and it wasn't like Mattie to worry unnecessarily. Especially about Luc. She had raised eight children of her own and knew all about children's ailments. "What seems to be the matter?"

"Well, he complainin' about bein' sleepy, Mr. Kip. And he mighty flushed and hot-feelin'."

Kip's frown deepened. This recital of symptoms didn't seem all that serious. "Well, I'll look in on him before I leave. You know he spent hours yesterday on Jester, practicing his jumps. Probably just wore himself out. I'm sure all he needs is a good night's sleep. Go ahead and put him to bed." The black woman turned to leave, and Kip called after her, "Thanks, Mattie."

A few minutes later, on his way out, Kip entered Luc's darkened bedroom. Leaning over the little boy, he placed a hand on his forehead. He *did* feel awfully hot. The child moved restlessly, but he seemed to be sleeping, so Kip merely tucked the blankets more securely around him and left the room.

As he was going down the stairs, he passed Mattie coming up with a tray. On it was a glass and a bottle of some kind of tonic.

"If he wakes up, I'm goin' to give him a little of this," she told him.

Kip felt a small pang of guilt in relinquishing the responsibility for his child to his hired housekeeper while he attended a festive occasion. Well, it certainly wasn't anything he was looking forward to all that much, not like a party, exactly. This was, as Hal had pointed out, an important fund-raiser—the last big thrust before the election in three weeks. It was something he couldn't pass up. Besides, he'd always heard that children could run a fever one day and the next be as good as new. He was sure that Luc would be fine in the morning.

Kitty stirred as the bright arc of an automobile's headlights flashed into the windows of her bedroom and swept across the walls. Next came the skittering sound of pebbles thrown against the screen. Fully awake now, she sat up, hearing someone call her name.

Recognizing the voice coming from the terrace just below, she flung off the covers and ran barefooted to the window, leaned on the sill, and looked down.

Standing on the driveway below was Kip, dressed in evening clothes. But his tuxedo collar was loosened and his tie was askew. Was this some kind of prank? Was Kip up to his old stunts? At first she even suspected he might have had too much to drink and in that disoriented state had decided to make a midnight call on a whim.

She was about to reprimand him when he saw her and called in an urgent whisper, "Kitty! I need you! Luc is really sick, and I can't get hold of Doc Madison. He's on a delivery case somewhere in the county. Can you come? I don't know what to do. . . ."

There was a desperation in his tone that at once dispelled any notion that this was one of Kip's practical jokes. "I'll be right there."

Moving quietly so as not to awaken Lynette and Bryanne in the adjoining room, Kitty made a wild grab for her clothes. She dressed quickly, then carrying her shoes, she went down the stairs in her stocking feet. She would not take time to leave a note but would call from Montclair in the morning to let her mother know the situation.

Breaking all speed limits, they covered the few miles from Cameron Hall to Montclair in record time. Kip was hunched forward, clutching the steering wheel as if by the very thrust of his body he could make the car go faster. Kitty clung to the door handle, biting her lip and praying. She had no idea what she would find at Montclair. But Kip, usually so cool-headed, seemed almost frenzied. With a squeal of wheels, they swerved around the last curve and into the gates leading up to Montclair. With a neck-whipping jolt, Kip slammed to a stop in front of the house, scattering gravel as he braked.

After one look at Luc, Kitty's heart sank. Even before taking his temperature, her hand on his brow told her it was dangerously high. Gently she removed the covers and ran her practiced hands over his small body. With alarm, she noted that the joints of his knees, ankles, and elbows were burning hot and swollen.

Her throat went dry with panic. She had to swallow hard before she found her voice. "I'm not a doctor. We'll have to wait for Dr. Madison to make the diagnosis. But until he gets here, we'll make Luc as comfortable as possible and try to get his fever down." To Mattie, she added, "I'll need some compresses. Old sheets cut into squares and folded will do. And, Kip, start boiling some water."

If this was the dread disease that Kitty feared, she would start the only treatment thought to be effective in preventing paralysis and permanent crippling—alternate cold and hot compresses on the swelling joints.

The days had no meaning. One ended, another began, and Kip barely stirred from his son's bedside. Dr. Madison had confirmed Kitty's private diagnosis of Luc's illness. It was every parent's nightmare, one for which no preventive or cure had yet been discovered. With no weapon to fight it, the medical profession was helpless against this scourge of childhood that often took its victims within a few hours after it struck, or left them hopelessly crippled for the rest of their lives.

Kitty and Mattie, by turns, entered and left the silent sickroom on those beautiful early summer days—the kind of days when Luc should have been out in the fragrant meadows, riding Jester, running, playing. Each time the adults looked at the fevered child or turned his hot, little body, the terrible thought that he might never again do any of these things came like a blow to their hearts.

Mattie, with her deep faith, prayed audibly as she bathed Luc's burning skin or applied the compresses to his swollen joints. "Oh, sweet Jesus, have mercy! Lord, you heal the sick, please touch this little chile . . . and we'll give you all the glory! Hallelujah!" Sometimes she would hum softly under her breath, singing the words of praise and pleading, "Turn your eyes upon Jesus, look full in his wonderful face. . . ."

Sitting on the other side of Luc's bed, Kitty tried to catch Kip's eye to offer what little consolation she could. But his eyes, red-rimmed and puffy from lack of sleep, were fastened on his son. Kip's face was haggard and gaunt, with several days' stubble of beard and etched with deep lines. By day, his usually ruddy complexion was pale; by lamplight, it had a ghastly cast.

When she gently urged him to rest, he merely shook his head. His chin rested on hands that were clasped tightly as if in an attitude of prayer, and Kitty wondered if he *were* praying. She hoped so.

She was convinced that nothing but prayer could save Luc now, for although she was doing everything she knew to do medically, nothing seemed to be working. In cases like this, there was little that doctors could do to make a difference.

During the war, Kitty had seen men die, but she had never seen a child die. Now, with the possibility of *this* child's dying, Kitty's heart sank. What would Kip do if that happened? In the past ten years, he had lost his mother, his wife, and many comrades-in-arms with whom he had lived and flown into battle. As far as Kitty knew, Kip had never discussed these losses with anyone. He had mourned but never fully grieved, and she knew that was a vital part of healing.

Kitty remembered how proud and happy Kip had been to bring Luc home to Virginia. She knew he loved the boy . . . perhaps had not realized how much until he faced the possibility of losing him.

Kip seems so terribly alone, Kitty thought. His own father was thousands of miles away, in Scotland. He no longer had Luc's mother to help him through this crisis, to help bear the heavy burden. Compassion wrenched Kitty's heart, and she prayed, *Dear Heavenly Father, be Kip's Father, give him courage to endure whatever he has to endure. Comfort him. . . .* However inadequate her prayer, she kept on praying as she went about skillfully performing her nursing duties.

Kip felt a rising tide of panic, reminiscent of the first time he had spotted a German plane speeding toward him, its mounted machine guns trained on him. He had been afraid he might die that day, and all the things he loved about life had come rushing through his mind in a torrent. On the brink of losing them, he had all at once appreciated the things once taken for granted.

He gazed at Luc, his tangles of dark hair fanned out against the pillow, the closed eyelids flickering, the movements of his little hands painfully spastic, the small mouth partly open, emitting low moans every so often.

Oh, God, please don't let him die! Kip begged from the depths of his soul. *I don't deserve any favors, I know that . . . but if You let Luc live, I promise to be a better father . . . a better man! I haven't been what I should be, but oh my God, please listen. Don't take Luc away from me. . . .*

Kip wasn't sure it was a prayer. Certainly it wasn't a *proper* prayer. But it was sincere. He had never meant anything more in his life. Luc was everything to him, and if Luc died, nothing else mattered.

The hours dragged. Mattie came to tell him of urgent phone calls from the campaign office, but her messages barely penetrated Kip's consciousness.

"Mr. Woodridge has phoned, I doan know how many times, Mr. Kip. He say it's mighty important you return his call, sir." She placed a cup of coffee on the table beside Luc's bed. She hesitated, then tried again. "Mr. Montrose, he say people are waitin' for you down at headquarters. . . ."

With great effort Kip turned to her, staring blankly, almost as if he didn't recognize her.

"Kip, what Mattie is trying to tell you is that you're scheduled at several events. . . . The campaign . . ." Kitty said.

Suddenly it registered. Kip blinked, then said harshly, "To blazes with the campaign! What could I possibly care about that, now? Tell Woodridge he can go . . ." He halted abruptly, shuddering. "Sorry, Mattie, Kitty." Then he reached for the coffee, downed it in two gulps, and stood up. "Yes, of course. I'll have to do something about it." With that, he walked out of the room.

The two women looked at each other. In a few minutes they heard Kip's voice raised on the phone in the hall.

When he came back into Luc's bedroom, he slumped down again in his chair. He glanced over at Kitty. "It's finished. I've withdrawn from the race. I can't think of anything but Luc."

chapter
27

AFTER THE PHONE CALL, Scott Cameron left his office and drove home, deep in thought. This was a shocking turn of events, and he had no idea how it would play out. Automatically he winced. Had he become so callous as to be more concerned about an election than a little boy's serious illness? No, he assured himself, not really. But it was, after all, a political reality. If Kip Montrose dropped out of the race, what did that mean for Frank Maynard? The campaign was too important not only to Frank, but to the whole district, not to consider all the ramifications of this unexpected circumstance.

Reaching Cameron Hall, he pulled to a stop at the side of the house. Instead of going inside immediately, he sat there, brow furrowed, elbow on the steering wheel, propping up his chin. There were two possibilities. Either one carried risks. The outcome of either, uncertain. He'd have to call an emergency meeting of Frank's committee, discuss what course of action they should take, decide how to handle the few remaining weeks of the campaign.

As he got out of the car, he saw Jillian coming up from the gazebo at the far end of the lawn. He stood watching her approach, the late afternoon sun sending dancing lights through her rich brown hair. As if suddenly aware of being observed, she turned and saw him.

"Hello," he greeted her, waving his hand and quickening his pace.

"You look awfully serious," she commented.

"It shows, huh? Well, something has come up, and I'm not sure just how it will all work out."

She was all concern. "What is it, Scott? Bad news?"

"Yes, rather. You've heard about the little Montrose boy, haven't you?"

"Of course. Kitty's over there nursing him. He isn't worse, is he?"

"No, at least I don't think so. But I do know that Kip has withdrawn from the race."

Jillian stared at him. "No!" she gasped. "What does this mean for Frank?"

"I'm not sure of anything except that Kip's name will still be on the ballot. The folks who don't know he's dropped out or don't hear before Election Day, may vote for him anyway, so it wouldn't benefit Frank." Scott ducked his head. "That sounds heartless, I know . . . thinking in terms of your candidate's best interest when his opponent is faced with a possible tragedy. But we have to be realistic. Kip's withdrawal does pose an unexpected problem."

"What can you do?"

"First, I need to run my ideas by someone . . . just to hear myself so I can decide whether or not they would fly. Would you be willing to listen?" At Jillian's eager nod, he tucked her arm in his and they fell into step on one of the garden paths leading from the house. "One way is to be sure that everyone who planned to vote for Kip *knows* he's no longer running, and hope they'll switch their vote to Frank. . . ." He paused.

"There's another alternative . . . to have a last-minute candidate . . . launch a write-in campaign for someone else to split the vote. I think Frank's backers will remain steady, and he may also reap the harvest of voters who don't want to cast their vote for someone they don't know. In politics, they call that a 'dark horse' candidate."

"But who could you get to run at this late date?"

"*Me!*"

"But how would that possibly help Frank? What if people think you would be a better candidate?"

"I doubt that would happen," he said. "As a newspaper editor, one collects a lot of enemies." They moved on down the path, and Scott continued. "I'll have to give it some more thought, of course, and put it before Frank's committee. Maybe it's a dumb idea." He shrugged sheepishly.

"And if it isn't . . . and you decide to do it . . . and win?"

"That's such an outside chance that there's hardly any use thinking about it. . . . But if I *did*, well how would you feel . . ."

"Me?" she gasped. "I'm an English citizen, don't forget. I can't vote in an American election. Besides, I know nothing about politics!"

Just then Lynette came running out onto the terrace, waving her arm and calling, "Uncle Scott, there's a phone call for you! It's Frank. Says it's important."

"Coming!" Scott called back. "Guess I'd better take this. Frank's probably just been informed," he said to Jillian. "Thanks for listening. It's good to bounce an idea off someone who can be objective."

He turned quickly and took the terrace steps two at a time, leaving Jillian to gaze after him. *But you're wrong, Scott,* she thought. *I'm not objective. I'm the most interested person you could possibly have found to talk to. I love you! And whatever happens to you is important to me. I think you'd make a wonderful senator . . . better than Frank, better than anybody! I've lost you anyway, but if that happened, if even by an outside chance you won . . . you'd be out of my life forever!*

The depression she'd been fighting off ever since their interrupted conversation in the library the week before, descended upon her full force. Slowly she walked up to the house, passing through the hall, where she could hear Scott talking on the phone, and up the stairs to her room.

Jillian had thought that coming to America would be some kind of turning point for her, but she had not counted on its breaking her heart.

From the *Mayfield Messenger,* May 20, 1926:

KENDALL "KIP" MONTROSE
WITHDRAWS FROM SENATE RACE

In a statement issued from his downtown campaign headquarters, Kendall "Kip" Montrose announced he would no longer be a candidate for the office vacated by the early retirement of Senator Wilcox. Citing "compelling personal considerations" as the reason for his decision, Montrose left the hotly contested race only a few weeks before the election.

This announcement came as a surprise to most political pundits who had predicted him to be the likely winner of the race. His decision raised speculation as to what those reasons might be. Some have suggested that it might be the threat of an undisclosed scandal that could have proved embarrassing to the candidate. This was vehemently denied by his supporters and campaign workers as "scurrilous rumors." Sources close to Montrose feel that it is more probable that the recent serious illness of his six-year-old son, Lucien, has been the motive for his withdrawal. In the last few weeks, Montrose has scarcely left the child's bedside, canceling many scheduled events. In the interim, the gap between him and the other leading candidate, Frank Maynard, has narrowed considerably.

Both candidates, who are strongly divided on issues, have campaigned hard for the senate seat. It is believed that Montrose's decision will assure Maynard of an easy victory over the two other men vying for the senate position.

Kip Montrose is well-known locally as a veteran, having served as an aviator with the Lafayette Escadrille, the American volunteer arm of the French Flying Corps during the recent Great War. A daring ace, decorated by the French government, Montrose is credited with downing more than fifteen German planes.

Asked to comment on Montrose's withdrawal, Maynard, a local lawyer and also a member of one of Mayfield's oldest and most prominent families, said, "I have great regard for Kip Montrose. He was a vigorous campaigner and a formidable opponent. I am sorry he has felt compelled to withdraw from the race, and I wish him well."

* * *

On election night, Cameron Hall was humming with excitement. Tension mixed with anticipation tingled in the very air, no one daring to voice either their hopes or their fears about the eventual outcome of the race. Some time tonight—no one was sure just when—the last vote would be cast and counted, and all their work in Frank Maynard's behalf would either pay off, or would have been an exercise in futility. But either way, they would know before the night was out.

Scott and Frank would remain at campaign headquarters until all the returns were in. Then they would bring the final count to Cameron Hall, where preparations were underway for a victory party. No one even whispered the word *defeat*.

Early in the evening the ladies began getting dressed. In their room, Lynette confided to Bryanne that she was planning to wear her emerald-and-pearl engagement ring in public for the first time. Win or lose, she and Frank would be married at the end of the summer.

"Since you'll be my maid of honor, Brynnie, we must pick out your dress soon, and a Gainsborough hat, I think, with a sweeping brim."

At first, Bryanne had dreaded the thought of her sister's being swept up into the political and social circles she would enter as Frank's wife, afraid she might lose the sister she had only lately come to know. But as time passed, she had found a firm niche for herself in Lynette's heart and knew that they would never lose each other.

About seven o'clock, when the polling places in the district officially closed, guests began to arrive at Cameron Hall. The atmosphere was a strange mix of optimism, apprehension, doubt, and confidence. People conversed in animated groups, their mood festive. The halls, both parlors, the music room, and the library were already filled with supporters, ready and eagerly waiting to celebrate their candidate's victorious race.

Blythe had hired a band, and music swelled above the buzz of conversation and laughter. Some of the couples were already dancing. Garnet, always in her glory on these occasions, drifted through the rooms as if this were still her home, and she the hostess.

Bryanne helped Grandmother Blythe set out the refreshments— platters of fresh fruit, cheeses, an assortment of sliced cold ham and turkey, pitchers of iced tea, urns of coffee on the buffet in the dining room. Huge vases of fresh flowers from the garden adorned every table. Everything was in readiness for the announcement of the winning candidate.

The evening wore on, too slowly for the waiting crowd. Some impatient ones decided to leave, drive into town, and check at campaign headquarters to see how the votes were coming in, then report back. Others were just enjoying this excuse for a party.

After a while, Bryanne slipped away from the lighted rooms, the sound of laughter, the clink of glasses, and went upstairs to freshen up. She was giddy with excitement and needed a moment to catch her breath.

Pausing in her room before the long mirror, she checked her dress. She was wearing the white muslin that Jillian had assured her was so becoming and had put up her hair for the first time tonight. She was feeling very grown-up and pretty . . . as Sean had often hinted. Then she whirled around and into the hall and ran back down the first flight of stairs.

Just as she reached the landing, she heard her name spoken in that slight Irish accent that she recognized at once. "Are you comin' or goin'?" he asked with a trace of amusement in his voice.

"Coming!" she called out gaily and sped down the rest of the stairs.

"I thought we might have a dance before the evenin' is completely over," Sean said, holding out his hand to her.

It was close to midnight when Scott and Frank finally arrived. A cheer went up that set the prisms in the chandelier dancing. Both men looked flushed and a little disheveled. Frank's gaze searched the room for Lynette, who was standing a little apart from the crowd. Scott was looking for Jillian and found her, her hands pressed together over her pounding heart.

"Well?" shouted someone in the room. "Don't keep us in suspense any longer. Who's our new state senator?"

Part V
Summer 1926

chapter
28

WITH THE ELECTION OVER and Blythe and Lynette off to New York to shop for Lynette's trousseau, Cameron Hall was strangely quiet. After being the hub of the political campaign, a peaceful calm had descended over the house and gardens. Except in Jillian's heart. There a stormy conflict still raged.

Should she submit her resignation to Mrs. Devlin now instead of waiting until she was given an official notice? Maybe she should leave. It was becoming more and more difficult to be around Scott, and she was somewhat relieved when he went off with Frank on a fishing trip to North Carolina right after the election. Both men, exhausted from the frantic pace of the campaign, needed to get away. Although Jillian missed him dreadfully, it was even more painful when he was near, yet so far out of reach.

Garnet was back and forth between Avalon and Cameron Hall, fretting over the kind of wedding that Lynette and Frank had chosen. She complained constantly to Jillian about it. "What better place than *here* at Cameron Hall? Why, *Vagabond* magazine featured the house in their 'Most Beautiful Southern Homes' issue. And the grounds and gardens, especially by the end of summer, will be spectacular, ideal for a large reception." She paused, then declared emphatically, "No matter what Lynette *thinks* she wants, a *small* wedding is out of the question. Why, our families have lived here for generations, and we'd offend so many of our friends if we left them off the guest list."

Jillian listened politely, making no comment. What could she possibly contribute to such a discussion? After all, she wasn't part of the family . . . and soon would be completely out of their lives for good.

It was clear that Bryanne no longer needed her. The girl, infatuated with young Sean McShane, was living in a world of her own. One Jillian was not about to intrude, nor give away their secret. First love was too precious, too fragile to risk the possibility of others knowing, possibly objecting.

On a day when Bryanne had disappeared to go riding with Sean, and Mrs. Devlin was in Mayfield visiting old friends, Jillian had the place entirely to herself. Taking a book out to the gazebo, she sat down and let her mind wander. She had no idea how long she had been sitting there when she was startled to hear Scott's voice.

"Penny for those thoughts."

She jumped. "Scott! What are you doing back so soon?"

"We came back a day earlier than planned. My lovelorn companion was restless, wanted to get back to his fiancée, only to find she's off to New York. May I join you?" he asked, putting one foot on the steps to the gazebo.

"Of course!" she replied, feeling both elated and dismayed. All these weeks she had been avoiding being alone with Scott. Now there was no way she could escape without appearing rude or foolish.

"I feel a little at loose ends," he admitted sheepishly. "I've been so caught up in the treadmill. Now that it's over. . . ."

"Did you enjoy your vacation, the fishing?"

"Maybe this will surprise you. But even while we were in the mountains, I'd wake up some nights in a cold sweat. Know why? Because I'd dream I had actually been elected and now had to do something about all the things I'd pointed out were wrong with our state government!" He chuckled, then turned to regard her long and steadily. "Want to know the other part of the nightmare? It was . . ." He halted, weighing his words—"that if I had won the election, I might have lost *you*. That is . . . I wasn't sure how you would have felt about being a senator's wife."

"What?" She looked at him startled. "What on earth are you saying?"

"Remember the day we were in the library together and were interrupted by Aunt Garnet's tantrum? I was about to tell you then. Of course, right after that I got caught up in Frank's campaign strategy. And when they agreed to put my name on the ballot as a ploy, and the momentum began to build . . . well, I didn't dare say anything until we knew the outcome of the election."

Jillian stared at him incredulously, hardly able to believe what she was hearing.

"I'd like to finish that conversation we started that day in the library. We were talking about the possibility of Bryanne's going away to school in the fall. I intended to ask if you had any plans of your own when that happens. Then I was going to suggest one of my own for your consideration."

Jillian held her breath. "And what was that?"

"First, I want to know if you have been happy here in Virginia."

"Yes, very happy." Her voice was little more than a whisper.

"Then would you consider staying on at Cameron Hall . . . as my wife?"

Wordlessly Jillian stared at him. Hope quickened her heart, brightened her eyes. Was it possible that her dream was about to come true at last?

Scott frowned. "Have I presumed too much? Perhaps there's someone else, someone in England."

Jillian shook her head. "No, Scott, there's no one. . . ."

"So . . . what is the answer?"

"Yes, Scott. The answer is *yes!* I love you. I just never dared to think . . ."

What she was about to say was lost. He drew her gently into his arms and kissed her, a slow, infinitely sweet kiss. When they drew apart, Jill's eyes were shining, bright with tears.

He kissed her again, and her mouth was warm and yielding under his. Feeling the security of his embrace, Jillian sent up a small prayer of thanks. It was the beginning, not the end, of her great adventure in America!

When at last they heard that the tide had turned and that Luc was on the way to a full recovery, there was rejoicing throughout the Cameron household. They had all become fond of the child in the time he had been here in Virginia, at Montclair.

Relieved that the crisis was over, Blythe went into action. She packed a basket with not only all sorts of delicacies to tempt the sick child's appetite but other foods that Mattie, still busy with nursing chores, might not have had time to prepare. Kitty had told her mother that she felt she could now safely leave her patient and asked if Scott could bring over her car and a change of clothes.

"Will you follow me over in my car?" he asked Jillian. "I may be a little while. If I can see Kip, I'd like to mend a few fences."

"Of course." Jillian was delighted. It would give her an opportunity to see the house she had heard so much about.

A smiling Mattie opened the door for them and went at once to tell Kip he had callers. In the circular hallway, Jillian's attention was captured by the paintings hanging on the wall alongside the main staircase.

"Those are the mistresses of Montclair," Scott explained. "All the Brides of Montclair . . . from the first to the most recent—Phoebe McPherson—Kip's Scottish stepmother."

Jillian moved closer to get a better look. At the bottom of each frame was a narrow engraved brass plaque identifying the bride. She was especially taken with the portrait of a beautiful young woman with tumbled black curls and an English-rose complexion. She was wearing a gown in the fashion of the 1700s—crimson velvet, its low, square neckline ruffled in gilt lace. When she read the name under the portrait, "Noramary Marsh Montrose," Jill gave a little gasp and was about to ask Scott about it when Kip came bounding down the stairs.

Now that Luc was out of danger, Kip was euphoric and greeted his old friend as if there had never been a rift or any animosity between them. He and Scott launched into an animated conversation about local events, and there was no chance for Jillian to interrupt to ask her nagging question.

Could this exquisite creature possibly be the ancestress her Uncle Greg had told her about? The little girl who had been sent to the colonies? Had she later married a Montrose and become the first bride of Montclair?

Jillian was bursting with curiosity, but this was obviously not the time to ask Kip about it. With a small bubble of inner happiness, she kept quiet, knowing that there would be a time later when she and Scott were married and living here in Mayfield. Then she would find out everything she wanted to know about this extraordinary link between herself and Noramary Marsh!

Jillian had wanted to be married in the small, gray stone church in Mayfield because it reminded her of the one in Kentburne village. But June was one of the busiest months for weddings, and the church had been completely booked for weeks. Because Scott felt he couldn't take any more time off from the newspaper and didn't want to wait until the church was available later in the fall, they set July fourth as the date of their wedding.

However, the day before the wedding, Jillian asked Scott to accompany her to the little church. There beside the man she loved, she knelt at the altar rail to ask God's special blessing on their life together. At first, wishing only to comply with her request, Scott himself was surprisingly touched by a feeling of deep peace, a confirmation that he and Jillian were indeed entering into a "marriage made in heaven."

The next afternoon, at Cameron Hall they met in front of the great fireplace to exchange their vows before a small gathering of family and friends. The hearth had been decorated with ferns, masses of peonies, and burning tapers in tall candelabra for the ceremony. Everyone, especially Bryanne, thought the bride was the picture of grace and refined elegance in a cream-colored linen suit, lace-collared crepe de chine blouse, amethyst-and-pearl jewelry.

Moved by the beautiful vows—"for better or worse, in sickness or in health, for richer or poorer"—Bryanne winked back tears. Of course, she knew, Jillian was marrying for *richer*. The Marsh family had lost everything at the end of the Great War, Jillian had been poverty-stricken, forced to work for a living. At last she was coming into the life she was born to, the one she deserved. Bryanne could picture Jillian after she moved in here as Scott's wife. She would give dinner parties and move with grace and charm under her new husband's adoring gaze.

Bryanne's own gaze traveled through the small group gathered in the drawing room until it rested on Sean's blond head, then back to see Jillian just turning from the improvised altar—the new Mrs. Scott Cameron. She looked so serene, with a smile that seemed to be savoring a lovely secret. The secret, Bryanne guessed, was one she was just beginning to understand. To love and be loved by another. What greater happiness could anyone know?

chapter
29

"Now that Mattie's sister-in-law, Vonnie, is coming to help out so Mattie can spend more time nursing Luc, you won't be needing me anymore," Kitty told Kip.

Kip put his hand on her arm. "I'll always need you, Kitty. I can't tell you what your being here with me during all this has meant to me. I couldn't have gotten through it without you."

She patted his hand, then gathered up her things and headed for the door. "I'm glad I could be here. But there were moments, I can tell you now, when I was really scared," she admitted. "Thank God, Luc's come through."

"I intend to . . . thank God, that is," Kip said seriously. "But Doctor Madison says you're the one to thank for the fact that he has no lingering problems." He gazed at her fondly. "You're a splendid nurse."

"Just take care of him." Kitty walked out onto the porch and headed for her little car.

Kip followed. "Kitty, what can I do to repay you?" he asked as she slid under the wheel.

"I don't expect any repayment, Kip. I'm just grateful it has all worked out so well."

"Kitty, I . . ." Kip started to say something, then thought better of it. "Just thanks, then, from the bottom of my heart. I'll call you in a day or two. You must come over. Luc will miss you."

"I shall, soon." She smiled and turned the key in the ignition. "'Bye, Kip," and she was off.

Kip stood watching the little roadster turn the bend in the driveway and disappear in a cloud of dust. A wild idea began to form in his mind.

192

Was it out of the question? He'd have to wait, find the right time, then see what Kitty's reaction would be. Thoughtfully, he rubbed his chin, feeling the stubble. He kept forgetting to shave. He smiled to himself. It had seemed so unimportant over the past few weeks.

Kip looked up at the scaffolding newly erected on the side of the house. Even in shirtsleeves, he was already feeling the heat of the midday sun. Did he really want to get on that ladder and start painting the siding?

He had spent most of last week laboriously scraping and sanding in preparation for the big job. It was one of the major decisions he had made upon Luc's recovery—to stop procrastinating and begin the renovation of Montclair in earnest. Viewing the mansion as a legacy to his son, Kip had a new sense of family pride, a new dedication to preserving Luc's heritage.

He smiled to himself. Of course, all these resolutions had been made in the unseasonably rainy last week of May. Now the Virginia summer was in full swing. Kip wiped his forehead with the back of one arm and scowled. The prospect of spending the afternoon wielding a paintbrush with the hot sun beating on his head was an unpleasant one.

"Hello there, Kip!" called a voice from behind him, and he turned to see Gareth coming up the drive from the woods.

"Well, hello yourself!" Kip greeted him cheerfully, glad to see his young cousin as well as having an excuse to delay his task longer. "What brings you over here on this warm day? Not that I'm not happy to see you. What's the latest news of the family?"

"Actually, that's what I've come about," Gareth said, stopping in a patch of shade provided by the huge oak in front of the house.

"Nothing wrong, I hope."

"No, it's about Lynette. You know she's getting married—to Frank Maynard. . . ." Gareth paused, feeling a little embarrassed. He wasn't sure how Kip felt about his former political opponent.

"Sure, yes, I know. Frank's a fine fellow. I've no hard feelings. What about them?"

"Well, Lynette has her heart set on being married in the little chapel in the woods . . . you know, the Avril Dumont Montrose chapel?"

Kip looked doubtful. "Well, I don't know, Gareth. It's been boarded up for I don't know how many years. No telling what kind of condition it's in."

"I was just over there, checking the place out, and it's built pretty solidly. I don't think it would take much to get it fixed up so it could be used . . . that is, if you'd give me permission. I'd like to tackle the job . . . a wedding present for my sister," he explained. "I'm pretty good with my hands." He shuffled his feet in embarrassment, suddenly aware that he might be perceived as bragging.

Kip glanced at him with new respect. "I guess I didn't know that, Gareth. Well, sure, it's fine with me if you want to take it on. Maybe I'll even help."

Gareth's eyes lighted up. "That would be great, Kip. With two of us working, it shouldn't take long at all! And since the wedding isn't until September, we've got plenty of time."

The painting could wait. Kip had years to work on Montclair. But getting the little chapel in the woods ready for a wedding couldn't.

Kip whistled as he hammered. He was working alone today, since Gareth had to drive his Grandmother Devlin to town to do some shopping. Now, as Kip positioned a nail in a warped window frame and drove it home in a few well-placed strokes, he felt inordinately happy. He was getting pretty good at this. It had been therapeutic, helping Gareth ready the little chapel for his sister's wedding.

Unconsciously, he was whistling Lohengrin's "Wedding March" as he pounded in the final nail and started down the ladder. Just as he reached the ground, he heard tires on the pine-needled drive in front and turned to see Kitty pull up in her small green car.

"It's looking wonderful, Kip!" she called to him. "I've been wanting to see what you two were up to." She got out and walked over to join him.

"Come see the inside." Kip slid his hammer back into his tool belt and preceded her up the chapel steps, then opened the door for her.

"Oh, it's lovely," she said in a hushed voice. "I can see why Lynette wanted to be married here. It's perfect for a small wedding."

Kip beamed. "So you think we did a passable job?"

"More than passable, I'd say. I'm really surprised. I wouldn't have thought you'd enjoy doing this kind of work." There was a flicker of interest in her eyes.

"I've changed, Kitty," he said seriously. "About a lot of things."

She gave him a long steady look. "Yes, I believe you have, Kip."

"I'm glad you believe me, Kitty. That's important to me."

Ignoring his insinuation, she glanced around. "Lynette is going to be so pleased. And, of course, Frank, too." She paused, then asked, "Any regrets?"

"About Frank? About the election?" Kip shook his head. "No, not one. Frank's a fine man. He'll make a good senator . . . and a good husband. . . ." He hesitated, then went on, "But other regrets? Plenty of them. Let's sit down, Kitty. There's something I want to say to you."

Somewhat warily, Kitty followed Kip to one of the back pews where they sat down. He took one of her hands in his.

"Kitty, I didn't dare speak to you about this when it first occurred to me. It seemed too soon . . . after Luc's illness, I mean. I didn't want you to think I had any ulterior motives." He halted, stroking the soft skin on the back of her hand. "Luc's being so sick helped me to see things differently. It was like what they say about a drowning person. My whole life flashed before my eyes when I thought Luc was slipping away . . . that I might lose him." He looked up, his eyes clear and shining. "You asked about regrets, Kitty. I regret that I've treated you so shabbily in the past."

"You were young, Kip. We were both young."

"But that's no excuse. Even though it's late, I want to say I'm sorry about that, Kitty . . . and to tell you . . . that I love you." His fingers tightened on her hand. "Do you think there's any way we could . . . that there would be a chance . . ."

Kitty drew in her breath. These were the words she'd longed to hear ten years ago. But she was no longer an infatuated, starry-eyed girl but a woman who had gained a hard-won independence.

Uncomfortable with her silence, Kip asked, "Unless it's too late. *Is* it too late, Kitty?"

She nodded slowly. "Yes, Kip, I'm afraid it is," she said gently. "Nothing stays the same, you know, no matter how much we may want it to. Everything changes. We're different people now."

"But, Kitty . . ."

"No, Kip," she said firmly, cutting him off. "You mustn't mistake gratitude for love."

"It's not just gratitude, Kitty. I do love you. . . ."

"Of course you do, Kip. And I love you. But it's a different kind of love, and it's no substitute for the kind marriage requires. After all, we've both had that . . . and it would be wrong for us to settle for less." She paused again. "I planned to tell you when I rode over this afternoon that I'm leaving for New York tomorrow. The publishers of Richard's first book of poems are interested in putting out a second collection. And since there are still dozens of unpublished ones . . . well, they've asked me to help select the ones to put in the volume. So, it's a new beginning for me, Kip." He walked her out to the car. "Wish me luck."

"I do—the best, Kitty." Leaning down, he kissed her lightly.

"There will be a new beginning for you, too, dear Kip," she told him.

"I hope so," he said.

"I pray so." She smiled. "Bless you, Kip."

"You, too, Kitty. God bless."

From the *Mayfield Messenger,* September 1926:

In a private ceremony attended only by family members and a few intimate friends, Miss Lynette Montrose became the bride of Senator Frank Maynard.

The noon wedding was held in the historic chapel on the grounds of the bride's ancestral home, Montclair. The small, white frame building was built on the property in 1830 to accommodate the many traveling preachers who were guests of Mr. and Mrs. Graham (neé Avril Dumont) Montrose during their lifetime.

The chancel area was flanked with masses of lavender-and-white gladioli in white wicker baskets. The bride entered the sanctuary on the arm of her father, the celebrated artist, Geoffrey Montrose.

Her bridal gown was ivory taffeta, the French illusion veil held by a pearl bandeau bangled at the front with a teardrop pendant to be detached and worn later as a lavalier. The neckline of her dress framed a strand of pearls, a gift of the bridegroom. Her bouquet was a borealis arrangement of stephanotis and small white carnations, centered with a purple-throated white orchid resting on a pearl-edged white Bible.

The bride was preceded down the short center aisle by her maid of honor, her sister, Bryanne Montrose, wearing a periwinkle blue French voile dress, sashed in darker blue satin, and a picture hat of braided straw.

The bride's uncle, Scott Cameron, stood with the senator as the bridegroom's best man.

Following the ceremony, a reception was held at the home of the bride's fraternal grandmother, Mrs. Blythe Cameron, at the family home, Cameron Hall, attended by friends and many of Mr. Maynard's political associates and constituents. An honored guest was Mrs. Jeremy Devlin, the bride's maternal grandmother, the former Garnet Cameron of Mayfield, now of England.

Following the wedding, the couple left for a wedding trip to White Sulphur Springs and will be at home next fall in the capital city when the senator assumes his seat in the state legislature.

Part VI

Paris
1928

chapter

30

IN THE SPRING of 1928 Kip received an invitation to the dedication of a Memorial in Versailles in honor of the American volunteer aviators who had served with the French during the war. Since Luc was now fully recovered from the serious illness that had nearly taken his life, he decided to take the boy with him to France. Etienette's parents had written several times saying how much they longed to see Luc, and he would leave the boy to stay with them while he attended the ceremony.

The Boulangers wrote back immediately saying how delighted they were at the prospect and how welcome they both would be in their home.

The Atlantic crossing was smooth, the weather pleasant. The ship, filled with American tourists now flocking in droves to peacetime Europe, offered an active social life. Given Kip's looks and personality, he was often the object of some of the lady travelers' interest and was issued many invitations to the many parties and other shipboard events. But Kip spent most of his time with his little boy. Luc's illness had forged a deep bond between father and son and Kip had determined to never again let any self interest take precedence over that relationship.

After docking at Calais, they took the train to the village where Luc's mother had been born and where her parents still lived. Much of the countryside they passed through was familiar to Kip, for he had flown over it. It was hard for him to believe that nearly ten years had gone by since those days when he had been a young, reckless pilot.

It all started coming back to him, the daily recognizance flights into battle zones. He could almost feel the tightening in his stomach, the dryness in his throat as he mounted into the sky, hear the throb of the engine, the hammering of his heart, the roaring in his ears. He reexperienced the tenseness in his neck as he kept moving his head from side to side, always alert, watchful, on the lookout for enemy planes with the Maltese crosses on their wings, zooming out of nowhere, feel his fingers move from the throttle to the machine gun—*rat-ta-tutttt*—the rush of elation when he made a hit followed by the sickening sensation, the sour taste of nausea as the other plane spiraled slowly down in flames and black smoke—even as he thought, *that could have been* me *falling to a fiery death.*

Shuddering, Kip dragged himself back to the moment. That had been war. Now it was over. Please God, there would never again be that kind of horror. Still shaken, Kip looked over at Luc. The little boy was kneeling on the seat, his face pressed against the window, enjoying the picturesque countryside through which they were passing. It all looked so peaceful. The world, too, seemed peaceful enough now. An uneasy peace, perhaps, but—Kip repeated his heartfelt prayer that his son would never have to experience the horrors of war.

Etienette's village still bore some of the scars of the war. Small towns had not the money nor the resources that the larger cities had. Many of the young men had not returned from the war or were disabled, and rebuilding had gone slowly, her father explained. All that was left of the church where Kip and she had been married was rubble, the result of bombardment. The old priest who had married them was dead, and a younger man came only twice a month to hold services in the school. That was the first thing to be rebuilt, Mr. Boulanger, the schoolmaster, was proud to say and showed Kip the new classrooms with justifiable satisfaction.

Their house had sustained minor damage in some of the German strafing raids, but these had been repaired. The Boulangers welcomed Kip and Luc with tears and kisses, exclaiming over how much *le petit* had grown and how much he looked like Etienette. Mr. Boulanger wanted to show Kip their large garden in back, and Luc helped his grandmother select vegetables for the salad she would serve with a delicious French meal.

If there was time before dinner, Kip said, he would like to see Etienette's grave. Sensitive enough to realize that he would rather go alone, Mr. Boulanger walked with him to the gate of their low stone fence and pointed the way down the road beyond the remains of the church.

202

The cemetery had been kept trimmed and planted, the neat white crosses gleaming in the bright sunshine. Kip found Etienette's grave right away. The stone was glistening, newly scrubbed, adorned with fresh flowers. Seeing her name engraved on its surface brought a lump to Kip's throat. It was hard to connect the pretty, laughing girl he had known and loved with the formal epitaph: *Etienette Montrose, née Boulanger, Vingt Ans*. Only twenty years old when she died; he, only a few years older. He could hardly remember being that young.

"Rest in peace, sweet Etienette," he whispered. "I am trying to be a good father to our son. I promised you I would. I've failed miserably often in the past. But—I renew that promise now and with God's help, I'll keep it."

After leaving Luc with the Boulangers, Kip traveled to Versailles to attend the ceremonies at the War Memorial. It was a much more emotional experience than he had anticipated. Since the nightmare of Luc's illness, Kip had discovered that his emotions were much nearer the surface than before. At the dedication of the magnificent stained glass window designed by an anonymous artist picturing an American eagle escorting planes over the Atlantic, a beautiful poem written by an English poet, Richard LaGallienne, and inscribed on the tomb was read. Listening to the words—"France of many lovers, none more than these, hath brought you love of an intenser flame. Their golden youth they gave, and here are laid. Deep in the arms of France for whom they died. . . ." Kip was profoundly moved.

He did not linger long after the ceremonies concluded. He needed an antidote for the painful memories evoked, so he took the next train up to Paris. He would see the sights, perhaps take in some of the tourist attractions, go the Louvre, visit the cathedrals, things he had no time nor inclination to do when he was on leave during the war.

It was not the Paris he remembered. That one had first been seen through the eyes of a young man on the brink of adventure. A few months later as a swaggering, newly certified aviator proudly wearing the uniform of the French Flying Corps, he and some of his buddies had come on leave to "do the town." There had been an unspoken rule among them to live life to the fullest, however long that would be. Then he had met Etienette and fallen headlong in love. After that, everything changed for Kip. In that magical spring there must have been other starry-eyed young lovers strolling along the sidewalks, sipping coffee at a little café in those same afternoons; but too absorbed in each other, they had been unaware of them.

He and Etienette had only had a few weekends, the brief ceremony in her little village church, two days more, then he had gone back into combat and she to report to duty as an ambulance driver. They had hoped for a lifetime together. What they got was the equivalent of a month of days strung out a few at a time. Then it was all over. Her death soon after Luc's birth, coming as it had only a few weeks after the Armistice, had been a bitter blow.

Now, in Paris again after all these years, Kip felt at loose ends. For two days he wandered around the city alone, systematically checking off some of the things he felt he should see, revisiting some of the places he vaguely remembered. The third morning, feeling desperately lonely, he took out the address Kitty had given him and made a phone call.

Kip took a taxi from the hotel, handing the driver the slip of paper upon which he had written the address that Cara had given him over the phone. His French being rusty, he was not sure that his pronunciation would land him in the right street. While the man studied it, frowning, Kip wondered if maybe his phonetic spelling was as confusing to the driver as his verbal directions might have been. At last, the man nodded in understanding and exclaimed, *Ah, oui. Alors, allons nous.*

It was a wild ride, careening around corners, alternating jerking spurts of speed with hair-raising jolting stops. Finally, with a slam of the brakes, they came to a screeching halt in front of a formidable gray structure behind black wrought-iron gates. "Voilà!" the driver announced triumphantly.

Kip got out of the cab, handing the driver a crumpled franc. With a wave the cab departed. He surveyed the austere building dubiously. It looked more like a convent for cloistered nuns than a home for children. Then he saw a tarnished brass plaque on one of the stone pillars, which read *Maison pour Les Enfants de la Guerre.* He pulled the leather thong at one side, and the bell it activated resounded into the chill morning air. He pushed the gate, and it creaked open. Entering the cobbled inner court, he approached a massive oak door. He turned the door handle and walked inside. Almost at once he felt a change in atmosphere. From somewhere deep within the building he heard children's voices and laughter. Fainter still, a piano playing a sprightly tune and the marching sound of small feet.

He stood in the tiled vestibule uncertainly for a minute. Then a door opened to his left and a pretty, young woman stuck her head out. "Bon jour, monsieur."

"Madame Brandt?"

"Ah, oui! Un moment," she nodded, smiling, and disappeared again.

He looked around curiously. From the look of it, this must have been some wealthy family's town house, turned over to some organization for the care of orphaned and abandoned children, the saddest consequences of war. This could have been Lucien's fate, too.

Suddenly a familiar voice spoke, and he spun around. Cara!

He couldn't speak at first. It seemed so strange to see her—here in this place and because it had been so long. His first thought was how much she had changed. Even in the figure-concealing blue smock, he could tell she was thinner than he remembered. Her cheekbones were visible and as she came toward him, smiling, he saw there were lines around her mouth.

"Kip, how wonderful to see you. Sorry to keep you waiting." She held out both hands.

"And *you!*" Kip took her hands, squeezing them tightly. The first shock began to wear off. Thankfully he noticed that her smile was the same and her eyes were shining as if she were truly glad to see him.

"I can hardly believe you're here," she said, lifting her face for his kiss. "Why didn't you let me know sooner that you planned to be in Paris?"

"It was a spur-of-the-moment decision. Couldn't we go somewhere so we can talk, try to catch up? May I take you out to lunch?"

"I'd love to, but I can't. I'm on duty today. But I have half an hour until I have to report to the dining room. We can go out to the garden and talk until I have to go. It's sheltered and we can sit on the bench over there in that small patch of sunshine." She laughed, and Kip was pleased to hear the old lilt of gaiety in her voice.

Kip made quick work of telling her about his trip to Versailles and of leaving Luc with his grandparents for a visit.

"Oh, I'd love to see him. He's all recovered then?"

"Yes, thank God. There seem to be no lingering effects. Thanks to Kitty's skill and her knowing what to do right away. It was she who suspected that it might be infantile paralysis even before the doctor could get there and make the diagnosis. I owe her a lot."

"Yes, we all were so relieved and grateful that he came through. How lucky that Kitty was there when you needed her."

"Dr. Madison said Kitty's a born nurse."

"She certainly knew her vocation, didn't she? Even when everyone tried to talk her out of it." Cara shook her head sighing, "Sometimes we don't even seem like twins. Kitty never seemed to make the kind of mistakes I did."

"Mistakes? What mistakes?" Kip looked puzzled. "Surely you don't mean your marriage to Owen?"

"Oh, no!" Her protest was emphatic. "*That* was the best thing I ever did." She paused, gave a rueful half-smile, "It may have been *Owen's* mistake, although he didn't live long enough to find out."

"I doubt if he ever thought it was a mistake. He loved you very much. I'm sure you made him happy. You two were meant for each other. I think I knew that, even that summer at Cape Cod; I was just too angry to admit it."

"What a long time ago that all seems."

They were both quiet for a moment as if remembering. After a while Kip asked, "So what are your plans now, Cara? Are you going to stay here?" He gestured to the house surrounding them in the enclosed garden.

"Not much longer. The staff is now almost all French, and they are doing a magnificent job. Those of us, English and American, who came at first are being replaced, and that's how it should be. Actually . . ." Here she hesitated as if undecided as to whether to tell him something. ". . . actually, I'm waiting for some red tape to clear, perhaps having to sign some more papers to . . ." She turned to him with shining eyes. "Kip, there's a little girl, Nicole, brought here when she was only a few months old. I've taken care of her from the very beginning. She was very tiny, very frail. No one even thought she would live, but little by little, she gained and began to struggle to live. It was as if she felt it might be worthwhile after all." Cara smiled. "Anyway, I became very fond of her, and she grew very attached to me." She paused, then announced, "The fact is, I'm trying to adopt her."

Kip looked startled. "You are?"

"Yes. Owen and I wanted to have a houseful of children. Some of our own and adopt more; we talked about it . . . a lot. . . ." Cara's voice trailed off reminiscently but not sadly, "So now that I'm alone and I've found Nicole. . . . Well that's it. I have to wait until everything clears."

"So when is this going to happen?"

"I'm not sure. It's going rather slowly. At first, the French government was desperate to have these little war waifs taken care of, taken off their hands actually, to be fed and housed. They allowed adoptions quite freely. But now I think they're beginning to worry about losing a whole other generation or—" she smiled again, this time the dimple at the corner of her mouth showed, "—maybe a few potential Pasteurs and Molières and Renoirs, perhaps even Sara Bernhardts! . . . might grow up in America, or Heaven forbid, England or Australia for *them* to claim."

They laughed heartily, recalling the strong Gallic competitive spirit. Even being Allies during the war had not eliminated old hostilities between the ancient rivals.

"Would you like to meet Nicole?" Cara asked.

"Yes, of course."

"Oh good!" Cara jumped up. "Wait here and I'll run up to the nursery and bring her down."

"And I'll take a picture to show your family when I go home." He tapped the camera on the strap slung over his shoulder.

"Wonderful. I'll be back in a jiffy!" she said as she hurried off.

Left alone, Kip tried to put this new bit of information about Cara into perspective.

His thoughts went whirling down through the years. Images of Cara, mischievous, adventurous, the instigator of so many of their childhood games, always teasing, challenging, irritating, frustrating, and irresistible. She had always been full of surprises, but this was something that he would never have imagined Cara's doing. Adopting a child? A French war orphan! Who would have thought it? It seemed out of character. And yet, somehow it *was* characteristic. She had always been impulsive, generous to a fault. But taking on this kind of responsibility? It didn't seem like the Cara he had known all his life, the one he thought he knew. . . .

"Here we are, Kip."

She was back, pulling him out of the past into the present.

"This is Nicole." Cara's voice had taken on a whole new softness.

Kip turned to see her standing at the entrance to the garden. She was holding the hand of a little girl about five or six with a halo of dark curls framing a rosy-cheeked, olive-skinned face. Large dark eyes gazed at Kip with a mixture of curiosity and shyness.

"Say 'bon jour' to Kip, Nicole," Cara urged.

"Bon jour, Keep," lisped the child.

"Let's get a snapshot," he said, wanting to capture this enchanting picture immediately. "Stay right where you are. Perfect."

He took two just to be sure. That was something he'd learned from Crystal, he thought with a touch of irony. Sometimes the quick, uncontrived shots could be the best.

Nicole tugged at Cara's hand, pointing it to the fountain in the center of the garden. Cara released her, and Nicole ran over to it. As she leaned peering into the water, both hands on the edge of the pool, the white eyelet ruffle of her petticoat showed under the uniform pinafore.

"Isn't she precious?" whispered Cara, sounding every bit the proud mother.

"Yes, indeed," Kip agreed, amused to see the same look on *her* face that he was sure was on *his* when watching Luc at play.

They heard a bell ring. Cara sighed and got to her feet.

"We'll have to go in now, Kip."

"So soon? We've hardly had a chance to talk." He was disappointed. "What about tomorrow?"

"Tomorrow I have an appointment at the office where my adoption petition is filed. I go to check on it every week, just in case they've misplaced it or something. I could meet you afterward."

"All right. Where? What time?"

"Let's see. Why not the Luxembourg Gardens. Say, noon?"

"Great," he agreed.

Cara called Nicole, took her by the hand, and they all walked to the front door to see Kip out.

"Tomorrow, then," Kip said, all at once filled with an excited happiness.

"Au revoir, Kip," Cara said, and as he turned to leave, he heard a small piping voice echo. "Au revoir, Keep."

The next day as Kip walked through the gates of the Luxembourg Gardens, he felt a sense of déjà vu. There was something very familiar about it, a faint smell of hyacinths in the air, the damp smell of earth in the rows of flowerbeds. Had he come here before with Etienette? He couldn't remember. In his old memories of Paris the sky had always been a cloudless blue. It could just as well have been the same overcast *gris de perle* it was today. Anyway, it wasn't important. What did matter was that he was looking forward very much to *this day,* of spending it with Cara.

He saw her before she saw him. She was standing watching the children lined up to have a pony ride. He called her name. She turned around and waved, smiling, as he started toward her thinking how smart and rather French she looked in a blue knitted suit with a silk scarf at her throat and wearing a velvet tam at a rakish angle.

"You look happy," he said.

"I had a successful morning." She tapped her handbag. "Papers all completed. Just one more hurdle to clear and Nicole will be officially mine. I was just thinking while I was waiting for you how much fun Daddy would have had picking out a pony for her, teaching her to ride."

Kip drew her hand through his arm and patted it sympathetically. They walked on for a few moments, not saying anything. They found a bench and sat down. She turned to him and smiled, "Doesn't it seem strange? You, me, here in Paris?"

"Yes, in a way, but somehow natural, too."

"Tell me about the Dedication," she prompted. "Did you see lots of old friends?"

Kip raised an eyebrow. "Cara, *flyers* don't have many *old* friends."

"Oh, I'm sorry, that was a thoughtless thing to say. I didn't think—"

"Never mind." He shrugged. "It was such an unreal time. We were all so young, invincible; it always happened to the other guy. You know what I mean? Suddenly it dawned on you that those other guys were all gone . . . and that your number might come up next. After a while you stopped making *close* friends, made it easier when they went . . ." Kip gave himself a little shake, "Didn't mean to get morbid. It's just that being there at the Dedication brought back a lot of memories."

They lapsed into silence for a few minutes. Kip stared beyond the formal flowerbeds out to some unknown horizon. Cara allowed him his silent tribute to his departed comrades. Then he glanced over at her, grabbed her hand, and stood up.

"I'm cold, aren't you? That sun gives no warmth at all. Let's go somewhere, get some coffee or chocolate."

They left the gardens and walked along the street, looking for a restaurant. At a flower stall at the corner he bought her a bunch of dewy violets, and she pinned them on her shoulder. They came upon a sidewalk café with none of its tables occupied, so they sat down, not seeming to think it strange that they were the only ones seated outside. A waiter finally came to take their order for café-au-lait, came back a few minutes later, then disappeared again.

Unmindful of the wind that flapped the awnings above the windows, they began to talk. Words tumbled pell-mell, interrupting each other as one topic led to another and then another. They laughed and teased and reminisced about old times, hometown news, childhood remembrances, people they knew, events they had shared. Their conversation was intense, a mixture of the accumulation of nearly seven years of living an ocean apart, on different continents, in different worlds.

All at once Kip thought of the time capsule they had placed in the hidden room at Montclair. While playing "Sardines" with the other children one rainy afternoon, he and Cara had found it by accident. On the wainscoting of the old nursery, somehow one of them had touched a concealed spring that slid back revealing a hidden room with a staircase that led down and out through the garden to the river at the end of Montrose property. They had been ten and eleven years old at the time and had told no one else about their discovery. Later they had found out that it had once been used as an escape route from Indian attack when that part of Virginia was still largely unsettled. Possibly it had been a secret "safe holding place" for slaves seeking freedom by the Underground Railroad. It had been Cara's idea to make up a time capsule and place it there to be opened when they were twenty-one.

In all that happened in recent years Kip had forgotten about it. Remembering it now, Kip wondered if Cara did. When he reminded her of it, she declared, "Of course. We were to have opened it on New Year's 1913, weren't we?"

"Amazing! Wouldn't it be fun to open it now and see what we thought were important documents in the year 1900?"

Kip's eyes searched hers for some response. A wistful expression crossed her face. Softly he asked, "Don't you ever get homesick?"

Suddenly Cara was assailed by a dozen mind pictures—the apple orchards, trees covered with pink blossoms, green fields dotted with the white sheep that pastured them in the spring, the lambs frisking on the hillside, the scent of autumn, and the exhilaration of racing on horseback along the paths in the Virginia woods . . .

Kip laid his hand upon hers where it rested on the table.

"Come home with me, Cara. That's where you belong. Where we *both* belong. Together."

Cara's eyebrows drew into a frown above doubtful eyes. "Why do you think it would be any better for us now than it would have been ten years ago?"

"Because we're different. Everything's different. We've both grown up; what we've been through, the good, the not-so-good, the terrible things that have happened to both of us, have all been meant for something."

A slow smile touched Cara's mouth. One of Owen's favorite quotes. "All things work together for good for those who love the Lord and are called to His purpose." Was that Scripture verse saying something to her now?

Cara was cautious. She did not want to be swept away by Kip's compelling charm, his ability to persuade. As she hesitated, Cara regarded him. Kip's smile was just as disarming as it had ever been. But there was more. There was character in the once-handsome, boyish contours of his face, tiny squint lines around his eyes and at the sides of his mouth that only pain and suffering could have etched. There were love and tenderness in eyes that had once demanded and mocked.

Kip was suddenly filled with impatience, excitement. He wanted Cara to feel and know that was true as well. "Don't you see things have come full circle? We've proved that we can face problems, disappointments, losses and not only survive but grow from them. We're ready now to deal with the past, cope with the future. Don't you see how much better it would be together? You, me, Luc, Nicole. We'll be a family, a *real* family."

He gently placed his hand alongside her cheek. "Darling Cara, please say yes. Come home with me. I've always loved you. It's been there all along. Something's been terribly missing in my life. *You.* Come home with me to Montclair."

Cara felt a rising hope, the stirring of happiness. Maybe Kip was right. It seemed that they were back to the beginning of their relationship but with new insight, wisdom, faith. Something warm and sweet and infinitely comfortable spread all through her.

"Oh, Kip, I'd almost forgotten how much a part of me you are." She leaned forward and kissed him. "Yes, let's go home."

Collect the Entire Saga!

The Brides of Montclair Series is one of the most dramatic and extensive family epics ever written, containing twelve volumes that tell the story of a single Virginia family from before the Revolutionary War to the decade of the 1920s. The series has garnered rave reviews, and individual titles have even been honored with awards. Don't wait. Get the complete set now.

1. *Valiant Bride*
2. *Ransomed Bride*
3. *Fortune's Bride*
4. *Folly's Bride*
5. *Yankee Bride/Rebel Bride: Montclair Divided*
6. *Gallant Bride*
7. *Shadow Bride*
8. *Destiny's Bride*
9. *Jubilee Bride*
10. *Mirror Bride*
11. *Hero's Bride*
12. *Senator's Bride*